ORDE

Ordeal at Lichfield

Anthony Clarke

CORONET BOOKS
Hodder and Stoughton

First published in 1998 by Hodder & Stoughton
A division of Hodder Headline PLC
A Coronet paperback original

ISBN 0 340 71254 6

Typeset by Hewer Text Ltd, Edinburgh
Printed and bound in Great Britain
by Mackays & Chatham PLC

Hodder and Stoughton
A division of Hodder Headline PLC
338 Euston Road
London NW1 3BH

For my mother

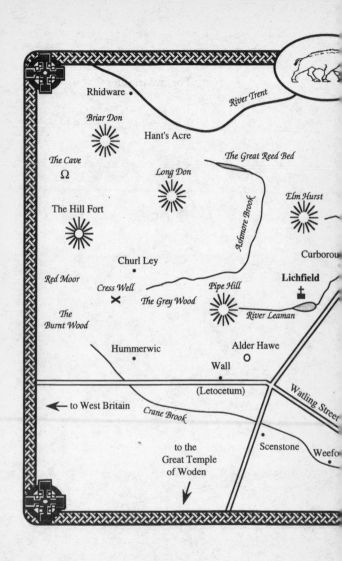

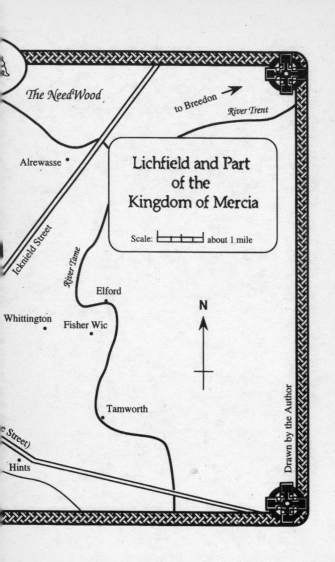

The NeedWood

to Breedon →

River Trent

Alrewasse •

Icknield Street

River Tame

Lichfield and Part
of the
Kingdom of Mercia

Scale: about 1 mile

Elford •

N

Whittington •   Fisher Wic •

Drawn by the Author

Tamworth •

e Street)

Hints •

Chapter 1

'Tomorrow they take me to Lichfield. If they say "guilty" I shall be hanged or sent into slavery. If they say "innocent" I shall be free but maimed for life. So much for Anglo-Saxon justice, eh? And I speak as an Anglo-Saxon.'

The two men turned their faces to me but said nothing.

I slumped against the wall. My shoulder rubbed on the figures of a man and a bull cut into the stone. You could feel their balls. Balls and bulls – symbols of energy and new life. But I had no energy and my life was ebbing away.

I lifted my arm and I heard my own distant voice. 'My hand is going rotten, I know it. Here, see for yourselves.'

My companions appeared not to understand, but they quickly drew back at the stench.

'Do . . . you . . . understand . . . what I say?' I asked.

They were restless and lifted their heads like hounds listening for the huntsman's horn. I tried again, this time in what little Welsh I had.

'Going we are to Lichfield. Tomorrow.'

They regarded me in silence. The pale light from the moon shone down through the grid and made strange patterns on their faces. Much like the way they used to paint themselves, I mused. They turned to each other and began talking rapidly. In that silvery stream I caught a little fish of a name.

'Owini? Do you know him?' I asked.

'Owini? Oh, yes, he is known to us,' they hissed. 'He is a

son-of-a-Saxon-whore and will die with a dagger in his heart.'

I understood few of the Welsh words but I got the gist. I raised my hand and said, 'Owini did this.' On impulse I said it in Latin.

They looked at me more closely. One spoke, also in Latin. 'You are one of Chad's creatures.'

It was not a question, more an attempt to unmask me. But I, too, could be cunning. I framed my reply with care. 'Ah, yes. Bishop Chad of blessed memory.'

They nodded at my answer. Then with swift silent movement they were one on each side of me. They spoke in turn, almost singing, close to my ears.

'Spawn of Rome.'

'Bearer of untruths.'

'Violator of the true religion.'

They had the talk-craeft but I knew that trick. I had seen it done on feast days in Tamworth when the Mercian folk were merry with ale. A comfortable farmer with a fat purse would be singled out. Each rascal would speak in turn, weaving magic with silvery tongues. The bemused man's head would spin and he would beg to be let go. Later he would find his purse was empty. But I was no rich farmer and I had no fat purse; instead, I had a fat hand. That was a good joke and it made me laugh aloud.

'You betrayed us with promises.'

'You let us be enslaved and punished.'

My head was turning this way and that. I felt dizzy.

'You crushed us with the evil stones of your Church.'

'You corrupted the beliefs of our people.'

The Welshmen were weaving a spell around me. I had to turn it back upon them.

'If what you say is true, why am I down here and not warm in my own bed?' I said.

It was a feeble attempt and deserved to fail. They came closer. Their lips brushed my ears. The smell of wood smoke and cattle dung filled my nostrils.

'You are here because you have been sent to spy on us,' breathed one, as tenderly as a lover.

'But we found you out, and now you've got to pay the price. Let us make an end of it for you. Nice and easy. You'd like that, wouldn't you?' whispered the other, as if asking to possess me.

As the bindweed bends the young sapling, so their skilful words were bending my mind: 'an end of it . . . nice and easy'.

I found myself desperately wanting to agree with them, but my inner voice warned me that I was becoming spellbound.

We were close together in the straw. They pressed up against me from shoulder to ankle. I was holding my bad hand up. My other hand was pinned between me and my would-be possessor. I expected to be stabbed at any moment. I wrenched my good hand free and tried to sit up.

They were so quick, I didn't see them move.

The chain that joined the unfriendly Welshmen by their necks was now also around my own neck. They lowered me lovingly back to my resting place on the floor. Of course they had no knives. We none of us had weapons of any sort. Not down here in this pit.

They slowly tightened the chain.

'As a man is drawn to truth, comes he to me, Finn,' said one.

'As a man is drawn to eternal life, comes he to me, Ardal,' said the other.

'I have done you no wrong,' I croaked.

They looked like ghosts in the moonlight with their white skin and pale eyes. Ghosts that were intent on crushing my neck.

Anger drove the clouds from my head and I punched the one called Ardal with my good hand. He gasped and rolled away.

'Why don't you ask her?' I said rapidly to Finn. 'She will tell you the truth.'

I nodded towards the sleeping Leofgifu in the deep shadows over against the far wall.

They had taken no notice of her before. Ardal now stretched out a foot but could not reach. Watching me closely, they took the chain from around my neck and Ardal gave the sleeping form a kick in its broadest region. She came awake in an instant and cried out. We hissed at her to keep quiet but it was too late. The light of a flaring torch appeared at the grid overhead.

'What goes on here?' came a rough Mercian voice. 'Molesting the women prisoners is not allowed.' Then he guffawed. 'That's my job.'

I thought that his laughter might be a good sign, so on the principle of befriending one's gaoler, I raised myself up and called to him.

'We are thirsty, good sir. May we have something to drink?'

'Thirsty, eh? Right you are, your holiness. Here, a blessing from heaven for a renegade priest.'

A stream of piss came down on my upturned face.

'Now shut your gobs,' he said, 'or I'll make it worse for you tomorrow.'

The burning torch went away and plunged us into

gloom. Leofgifu sat down by me and gently began to wipe my face.

'May Woden rot that wretched man's feet to stumps,' I cursed.

'There, there, never mind,' she said. 'All in your lovely golden hair, as well. And on this silly shaven patch in the middle of your head.'

'Thank you,' I said, forcing myself to calm down. 'But must you use such a stinking rag on my face?'

'It is but the hem of your own robe.' She sadly smiled. 'We have no other.'

A rustle and a movement in the straw instantly brought my mind back to the two murderous spell-weavers. Their demeanour had changed, though, as if they had realised their mistake about me.

They came over and sat down at a respectful distance.

'Hens will brood on stones and fish will swim into pools that dry in the summer,' said Finn, then paused. 'The moth will fly into the flame of the lamp, taking it for the sun,' he added.

The two men had judged me to be a spy, but now their pride could not allow them direct admission of so gross an error.

'Come, let us be brothers in adversity,' I said.

Smiling ruefully, they patted my knees and shoulder.

My head was burning with pestilence from my hand but I saluted our new-found friendship by speaking with them, again in their own tongue.

'I expect you find Mercia somewhat different to West Britain?'

A silence ensued.

'Forgive us, Brother Edwin,' Ardal replied in Latin, 'but we are Irish and find your Welsh dialect somewhat . . . elusive.'

Then they went and sat a little distance away from us.

Leofgifu was restless at not being able to understand. 'What are you two going on about?' she demanded, pulling me towards her. 'He said your name, didn't he? How did he know it?'

'Yes. And he also called me "Brother", even though the gaoler called me a priest. That's more than coincidence,' I murmured.

'By the look of them I'd say they were Irish,' she whispered.

This vexed me. I had misread these men and their tongue, yet she had straightway seen them for what they were.

'That is plain for all to see!' I said. 'But it puzzles me why these Irish men should be here, in Mercia. Now, you rest while I think upon this.'

'All right, Edwin. But there's no need to snap at me,' she said and fell silent.

I tried to take thought but my head felt as if it were bursting and my body felt light as though the swans were already lifting me up to heaven. My spirit would not be much longer on this earth.

Leofgifu's voice came as if from afar. 'Edwin. Do you think they are two of the Irishmen brought over by Bishop Chad to ornament his holy books?'

'I think not. They all went back shortly after he died.'

'People say that Owini enslaved some but King Wulfhere found out and now he is angry.'

'And how would you know what the king does and doesn't know?'

'I heard it while you were undergoing ordeal of iron.'

At her mention of the word 'ordeal' my hand started throbbing again. The stench was worsening and my eyes felt as if they had hot needles behind them.

'That is correct, Leofgifu, Owini did enslave us,' Finn's voice broke in. 'But, Edwin, we have heard talk of your bravery at the threefold ordeal. Tell us what that means.'

My head was spinning. A moment ago they were sitting apart from us, now they were close again. Before they were speaking in Latin, now they were speaking in Englisc . . . and what's more they knew Leofgifu's name.

I answered slowly, 'It means I carried in my hand an iron weight of thrice the usual one pound over the full span of nine feet.'

'And this iron. It was glowing red-hot?'

I nodded. They made small noises of sympathy and shook their heads.

'May we ask again. Why more than the usual weight?'

'It was threefold because King Wulfhere wanted to punish me severely for not doing his bidding.'

'In the name of Woden,' broke in Leofgifu, glaring at them, 'can't you see that he is unwell? He is feverish and might even die if his fate wills it. So leave him alone.'

Her flaxen hair in its thick plait hung down her back and glimmered with a faint halo in the moonlight. How I loved her!

'All these questions,' I protested. 'But what of yourselves?'

'We are from the monastery on Inishboffin. You may know it? Our abbot learned that Chad was bringing in outsiders to do work and since we had the skill of book ornamenting, we were sent here to do Chad's bidding. When he died, we . . . we had to stay. And shortly thereafter Owini enslaved us, forcing us to labour on his new church.'

Deep in the back of my befuddled mind a memory stirred. There had been talk among the Britons about these events.

I used one of Chad's tricks. 'And?'

'And what?' said Finn.

'There is more, is there not?'

'We tried to escape but we were captured and put in here. We do not know what will happen next.'

'You said, "when Chad died we had to stay." Why did you say that?'

Ardal jerked his head up and looked anxiously at Finn, who in turn looked directly into my eyes.

'I take a risk telling you,' he said slowly, 'but we are brothers in adversity, are we not?'

'By my life and that of my beloved Leofgifu, we shall reveal nothing to any other man.'

Finn looked at me, then decided. 'Very well. We were sent to save Chad from the domination of the Church of Rome. He was to be restored in the true British Church. The British people, united under one Church and one leader, would rise up and throw the Saxons back into the sea from whence they had come.'

I stared at him in disbelief. Did they really think the aged Bishop Chad could have led them? Could they see that tired old man going into battle on his equally tired old mare? They seemed not to realise what they would have faced. Did they think that King Wulfhere would be their only opponent? Here in Mercia people were thinly spread, but to the east the Anglo-Saxons were thicker than fleas on a dog. The East Anglians and the Jutes of Kent had armies of warriors clad in link-mail. In Kent all the thegns rode horses and carried swords!

Their quest would have been hopeless and their actions would have brought about their own destruction.

The damp chill of the pit seeping into our bones was like that of the grave awaiting the Britons and their children.

Finn and Ardal waited for my response.

'Naturally, you had to give up the plan when Chad died?' I said.

Leofgifu's arm crept around my waist and she laid her head on my shoulder. I should have realised that she was warning me.

With glittering eyes, Finn leaned forward and put his hand on my knee. His whole being was dominated by his cause.

'True, it was great loss. But Chad's death brought about a change in the plan, that's all. We have an army a-gathering, Edwin. We have brave Welshmen, and strong Britons and even men from Wessex to support us. Our objective is simple: we are going to take Lichfield back from the Mercians. We want to take it by surprise, to avoid the spilling of innocent blood, but we shall fight if necessary. God must be on our side, Edwin, because when we win, our plan is to restore the land to its rightful owners.'

Then his voice softened. 'Earlier you spoke of justice but now your face shows something else – revenge, perhaps? Is there a wrong you will put right, Edwin? And is there something in your soul that cries out for justice?'

He was silent for a moment, his eyes searching mine, then he whispered, 'You can do nothing on your own, Edwin. But together we can put things right. What do you say? Will you join us?'

He'd looked into my innermost heart and had seen a fire there, burning more hotly than even the poison in my hand.

I felt naked before him, with no secrets and nothing to hide. A thrill went through my body as I responded. 'Yes, I will join you.'

The tension went out of them. They smiled and nodded their heads. Finn patted my knee again, and then he indicated that we should all rest. I was glad, for I felt quite dizzy after the intensity of the moment.

I turned to Leofgifu and cuddled up to her, but she stiffened.

'Why Lichfield?' she said, in a quiet but tight voice. 'It's just a small settlement. Why not Tamworth?'

'You may not understand,' I said, 'but Lichfield, being at the very heart of the country, is a powerful symbol to the Britons. Also it is the source of their spiritual strength.'

'Perhaps it is,' she said, 'but when the Welshmen raided us before, Wulfhere punished them for it. Just as you will be punished!'

'Just let him try. Anyway, this isn't going to be just a few Welshmen. The army will be from all the Celtic people, together with their allies from Wessex. And it won't be a raid, it is much more important than that.'

'But Irishmen and Welshmen fighting together, alongside Britons? My grandmother says they've never been one with themselves, not even before the coming of our people.'

'Hush, now,' I said, soothingly. 'They really are one people, just as . . . well, just as Saxons and Angles are.'

'Great God, Edwin, you are such a fool!' she said.

I was pleased that she had taken up the point of Lichfield and not Finn's astute comment about the revenge in my heart. I wasn't ready to tell her about it just yet, but she was upset and needed reassurance. I gave her a little kiss and tasted salt on her face.

'Don't worry,' I whispered in her ear, 'it was a show of support. How can anybody do anything down here? Take comfort, my little cabbage, nothing can happen to us, I promise.'

Chapter 2

Something was tugging at my robe. I half opened my eyes.
Daemons with black bodies were sliding down a shaft of light.
Others were prancing and capering about me. Several of the
fiends were plucking at my clothing and pawing my face.
Above me hung a myriad of glittering tiny jewels. I opened
my eyes further, just in time to see Leofgifu being borne aloft
to some terrible torture. I tried to shout her name and started
to get up but two of the daemons seized hold of me.

'Come, Edwin,' said one. 'It is time.'

'Get thee behind me,' I cried, but a leathery hand clamped
across my mouth.

'Be quiet or we'll all be dead. Come on, we'll help you.'
His accent was guttural but his voice was human.

Then I saw the grid was gone from over the pit and a
notched tree-trunk stood down into it. In a moment I too was
borne aloft. Not by daemons but by men with soot-blackened
bodies.

They put me upon my feet. I shivered in the dark from the
clean chill coming down from the stars overhead. I inhaled
deeply to rid my lungs of the stench of the pit.

'Are you ready?' whispered a voice. It was Finn. He still
had the iron collar around his neck. The broken chain was
wound around his arm.

We set off with him close by my side lest I should stumble
and fall.

'Leofgifu is in front,' he murmured close to my ear. 'We have to get past Letocetum now so be very quiet. We will rest when it is safe.'

I started off well. We came down the slope from the pit and carefully skirted the shabby huts and the silent stone ruins huge against the night sky.

Finn had used the old name. I said it to myself like a child saying a rhyme – 'Le . . . to . . . ce . . . tum' – and the sound made me giggle. He took hold of my good arm with a tight grip. It hurt but I gained comfort from it.

We came out on to the weed-grown Street and made our way to the west. The blackness of the thick woods on either side contrasted with the lighter sky on the horizon. We stumbled as we caught our feet on the loose blocks of the road.

With a sudden squealing, two wild pigs burst across directly in front of us. Too close for one of the warriors, who fell down the agger.

Other shadows that I could not name also crossed the road – shapes that I would not want to name. We were taking great risks going about at night.

Then I saw a large wolf. It took its time crossing and stopped close by the edge of the road. It watched us go by but none of our group remarked upon it.

'Here is Crane Brook. Go right,' Finn ordered. We swung off the Street and went up a gentle slope. The thick floor of last leaf fall silenced our movements. Now we were climbing steeply. We came out on to a track. Finn called out, 'Radmoor Brook. Rest here.'

The hillside jutted into the sky, hanging over us. Finn brought water and splashed it on my face. It gave the night breeze a keener edge and I shivered.

'I'll have to rest again soon,' I told him.

'Not long now, then we'll be safe.'

'But there's nobody here, surely?'

'Two days ago outlaws killed a pedlar for his bracelets and necklaces. Not far from here. Come on, get up.'

He pulled me to my feet and we set off again.

'Halt,' came a voice out of the darkness. 'Identify yourselves.'

'Finn, Ardal and party.'

Muted cheers broke out beyond. We went in through a narrow gateway with steep banks on either side. Two warriors led me through the darkness to a tent. They told me to sit by it, and moments later Finn came up with a drinking horn.

'Drink and then rest,' he directed. 'It will ease your pain. Tomorrow, depending on how it is with you, there will be a council.'

I emptied the horn, knelt down and made my way into the utter darkness of the tent. There was another person there. I tried to stretch out without touching him. At first I could only smell the leather of the tent. After a moment, though, I became aware of the smell of the other person's hair. The smell was familiar and very dear to me.

'Leofgifu,' I said quietly. 'Is it you?'

'Oh, Edwin,' she said and turned to face me. We kissed.

'You are crying.'

'Yes. I fear that you will come to harm.'

'Oh, no, you silly goose. Finn will protect me. Has he not already saved us both? We will talk of this tomorrow.'

We were still for a while and drowsiness began to steal over me.

'Edwin, do you remember the first time we met?'

'Yes. Down at Weeford. Why?'

'You were working with the Britons there and at Hints, healing them and teaching, weren't you. They loved you, you know.'

'For the leechcraeft, mainly.'

'Don't be cynical. I remember you saw me making sacrifice at Weeford temple and later you said that it must have been the power of my pagan ways, but you had only one thought in your mind thereafter. Do you remember?'

'Yes, but why are talking about it now? We must rest.'

'Yes, Edwin. As you wish.' But she was so close that her sweet breath went into my mouth. My body responded to hers as it always did. She slid my robe up as I felt for the fastenings of her tunic. They were already undone. Forgetting the pain in my hand I yielded to her inner warmth.

A warrior was jabbing me with the butt of his spear.

'It is time,' he grunted.

Leofgifu was gone. I crawled out of my tent and stood up, blinking in the early spring sun.

Around me were many other tents. They looked like the brown hillocks pushed up from the meadow by Brother Mouldywarp.

I felt well. My head was clear and my hand pained me only a little. I was grateful to Finn for the potion he had given me. The active ingredient could well have been meadowsweet, and I wondered who it might be who had such powerful leechcraeft.

The spearman escorted me to the latrine pit. There I took the opportunity to look about me and saw that I was in a hill-fort. The palisade with its freshly sharpened stakes was manned by armed look-outs.

In the centre of the fort was a large gathering of warriors. The spearman prodded me towards them but what I saw when I came close brought me to a halt.

Their appearance was startling. They seemed to be Britons but I had never before seen so many looking so well fed and proud.

Chad had told us that the Britons hereabout were of the once great Cornovii tribe. The monks had laughed, saying they could see no connection between that famed tribe, held to be the equal of the Ancient Roman army in warfare, and the wretched Britons who now slept among the pigs and stole their food.

However, some of the elderly Britons at Hints had themselves told me, in great sadness, that Cornovii was indeed their tribe. Only they knew that; the younger Britons cared nothing for their own origins.

Could these fine-looking men, perhaps living deep in the Cannock Forest for generations, be part of this same tribe now come to claim what was rightfully theirs?

I approached them.

Out of their quiet talking came the names 'Chad' and 'Owini' and other identifiable words. In my confused state yesterday I had been unable to differentiate between the various Celtic tongues but today was different; with a rush of emotion I realised that they were Welsh. How differently they carried themselves from the Saxon-dominated Britons.

I kept my silence this time for I was sorely embarrassed at yesterday's mistake and would not make it again.

A tall red-haired man came into the centre of the circle. His dun-coloured tunic was gathered at the waist by a twisted leather belt from which hung an ornate dagger. As he turned I saw it was Finn.

'Edwin,' he called. 'Come over here. Sit at the front.'

I took a place among the warriors.

'Guard him well,' Finn ordered, then in a softer voice he spoke to me.

'I hope that the outcome of this will be . . .' He hesitated, as if trying to find the right form of words. 'I hope that it will be such that you and I can become good friends. Whatever happens, though, don't worry about Leofgifu. We've talked to her and she's—'

He broke off as an older man with greying hair and a short beard came into the circle of men. The gold torque round his neck and his dark robe edged with silver showed him to be a chieftain or leader. With him was his champion, a huge man who wore armbands and carried an unsheathed sword.

Finn went to the older man. They discussed something and he asked me a question. I did not understand so I shook my head.

Finn came over to me. 'Prince Madoc has agreed for me to be your interpreter. You must give an account of who you are and how you came to be here,' he said.

I felt like saying, 'Because I was dragged here by a madman in the middle of the night; but I desisted. Finn had been kind to me but although not chained or bound I was undoubtedly a captive and my wit would be out of place.

Madoc's muscular champion caught my eye and he grinned as he turned his gleaming blade to and fro, making it flash in the sun.

A spasm of fear gripped my bowels. It was clear that I was to be put to the question. If they decided that I was Owini's spy then the cruel bite of that blood-hungry edge would spare me all future earthly pain.

Madoc sat on a folding stool and clapped his hands for silence then he indicated that I should speak.

'I am called Edwin,' I began. 'My father was Angle and my mother was a Briton.'

Is this what the man called Madoc wanted to hear? He made no sign, so I continued.

'At the age of twelve I was put to Lastingham.'

Some men frowned at that, so I explained, 'A monastery in the north. It was founded by Chad's brother, and the British tradition is observed there, even now.'

Finn smiled and looked pleased but Madoc just nodded.

'Two years after I entered Lastingham, Chad become the abbot. I worked in the herb gardens and didn't see him often, but people said he was a kindly man. He was only there for two years then went to York.

'In one sad year many of my brother monks died of the plague but I was spared. Later, in my twentieth year, the King of Northumberland fell ill. On his deathbed he made a gift to his Mercian pledge-brother, King Wulfhere.

'He sent vestments and altarpieces for the Mercian churches. He also sent me as a gift, saying that since I had been spared the plague I was clearly favoured by God and would bring grace to Wulfhere's kingdom.'

I paused. Finn rapidly interpreted and many of the warriors nodded at his words; it was also a Celtic custom to make such gifts.

'Wulfhere placed me with Chad and in this way I came to Lichfield.'

I stopped and looked enquiringly at Madoc. He signalled for me to continue.

'I was at Lichfield for only a few months when Chad sent me to study at Breedon Minster. There, after much thought and prayer, I vowed to go against Chad and his instruction, but he died while I was still at Breedon.'

Madoc lifted his hand.

'You vowed to go against Chad?' he said slowly, in Englisc.

'Yes. He said we were to baptise or attend only to Angles and Saxons, whether pagan or Christian. But there are many Britons who need our ministry. I gave it.'

My reply caused nods of approval.

'After Chad died, I stayed on at Breedon. I'd heard that Owini without Chad controlling him was like a bull without a nose-ring. After more than a year the new bishop, Wynfrid, recalled me. A new ruling from Rome had been made: all monks must live and work in their own diocese. I saw it straightway as yet another attack on the British Church.'

At this, Madoc looked sharply at Finn, who nodded in confirmation.

'I came back but I wouldn't go to Lichfield church. Instead I went to Hints where I lived and did my ministry among the Britons. Owini found out about my work and my vow against the ruling. His men came and took me to the church of John the Blessed at Wall where he accused me of apostasy and witchcraeft. He said that I had gone to the top of Brock Hurst . . .'

Some men near me frowned.

'. . . a hill near Hints . . . and there I had danced naked in the dawn in the company of others, chanting pagan spells.'

'Dancing naked in the dawn?'

'I was just with a . . . a friend, that was all.'

I tried hard not to look round for Leofgifu. Some of the warriors smirked.

'The accusation of apostasy is serious?' queried Madoc.

'Yes. And renouncing one's religion is bad enough, but

being found guilty of that and of witchcraft as well carries the greatest punishment. I have no defence against the charge.'

'No defence?'

'Not for me. If I took my oath that I was innocent, and twelve or more oath-helpers swore the same, then the charge would fall. But Owini knows that I have no kindred to take oath for me.'

'What of the other monks at Lichfield?'

'I couldn't be certain of them. They hardly knew me.'

'I hear the Saxons are fond of money . . . ?'

'Yes. An accused person can pay wergild and that is the end of it. The wergild for this crime is very high, though, and Owini knows that I have no money.'

'He sounds a cruel man, but is he clever?'

'A monk or a priest who cannot pay wergild for a religious offence is to be brought before the king himself for judgement. Owini is clever enough to know that.'

Talking broke out and I felt the Welshmen were sympathetic to me.

Madoc continued his questioning: 'The king can accept a plea and be merciful, can he not? After all, you are a monk and therefore protected.'

'He can dismiss witchcraft but not apostasy. Not only that, I learned that it was Wulfhere himself who had instructed Chad to attend only to Angles and Saxons. Without realising it, I had gone against the king. For that reason I had to undergo the threefold ordeal.'

Madoc looked at me closely. 'Tell me, what will be the outcome of this ordeal?'

I hesitated. I didn't want to bring into the open the very thing I was hiding from myself. Reluctantly, I spoke. 'To my knowledge, no one has survived the threefold ordeal before.

But even if I don't die from it, Wulfhere will either have me hanged or sent into slavery for life.'

Madoc nodded. 'It seems that this Owini has cunningly worked for what he wants,' he said, 'and has trampled on justice to get it. He will be punished when we take Lichfield.'

He talked to his men and Owini's name was mentioned a few times. They listened intently and many were nodding agreement. Then he stopped talking and folded his arms. At that, the warriors fell silent. Madoc sat pensively for a moment then called Finn over. I couldn't hear what was being said but suddenly I sensed that things were not going so well for me.

Finn took a pace back and Madoc, unfolding his arms, stood up. He spoke briefly but this time faces turned towards me. Many of the warriors were shaking their heads. He asked them a question and they shouted their reply as with a single voice. There was menace in the sound.

Without intending it my eyes sought Madoc's champion, the keeper of the door to the Otherworld. He licked his thumb and ran it lightly down the edge of his keen blade.

Finn came over to me. He looked anxious. 'Be brave, Edwin. We – I mean they – have decided that you are not Owini's spy.'

'It doesn't seem to please them, though.'

'Please don't joke at this time, Edwin. There is a suspicion that you are . . . how can I interpret it . . . they feel that in spite of your ordeal you are still loyal to Wulfhere.'

'But look at my hand! And I was in that stinking pit, and poor Leofgifu!'

Finn put his hands on my shoulders. 'Calm yourself,' he said. 'Remember, I have seen what is in your heart. Tell them about it. They, too, will see it is the truth.'

I stood and looked at the blurred faces of Madoc and the warriors and the champion with his eager sword.

May Woden take them, I thought angrily. I'm afraid to die and they know it. I'm forced to tell these painted barbarians what's in my heart of hearts.

'He's afraid,' shouted one warrior, in Englisc.

'He's got tears in his eyes, like a woman,' shouted another.

'Then let me use him like a woman . . . but before you cut his head off, please,' called yet another, this time from behind me. Laughter swelled up all around.

I dropped to one knee and, under the pretext of saying a prayer, managed to wipe my face.

The pounding in my head eased and I stood up slowly, looking about me. The warriors were silent and still – respectful, almost. Finn made a little smile and nodded encouragingly. He would interpret what I was to say. He would have to because hardly anybody there spoke Englisc! My mind swam as I realised that there had been no jeering, no laughter. I had simply heard what I feared most.

'All that I have told you is true,' I began, 'but if you fear that I would betray you then I must say more.'

I darted a look at the champion but he simply gazed back with dark unblinking eyes.

'Finn has it aright,' I continued. 'There is something in my heart and I will speak of it. I have carried it for many years. I have told no other man and I know you will respect my secret once you know what it is.'

As Finn's voice echoed mine, the faces around me changed and became attentive.

I had never spoken of my secret burden and I was finding it difficult to frame the words, but gradually they took shape.

'I have told you how I was sent as a gift to King Wulfhere.

That act was also a gift from God to me, for it gave me one of the greatest opportunities that a man could ever have in his lifetime. It opened the door for me to avenge the death of my father!'

A great murmuring broke out among the warriors. Finn and Madoc exchanged glances, and I saw Leofgifu staring at me in astonishment.

Madoc indicated that I should continue.

'I was about five winters old when Wulfhere's father, King Penda, came to ravish and conquer my home country of Northumberland. He came with a mighty host but although greatly outnumbered, brave King Oswiu killed Penda and put the army to flight.'

I paused, then decided not mention Catgabail the Welsh king who, with his army, deserted Penda during the night before the battle. I was trying to persuade these warriors to accept me, not to antagonise them.

'People still speak of the Battle of Winwaed,' I went on. 'Some boast, but others speak of betrayal and there is one act of treachery which must not go unpunished. My father stood shoulder to shoulder with King Oswiu during the battle. He fought with bravery and killed many Mercians – too many to count, some say. But when the fighting was done he became once more the kind and forgiving man that he was.

'Most of the enemy were killed by the blade, but others ran away and many drowned in the water or in the mud of the river. A fitting death for traitors.'

The warriors nodded their heads in agreement, for in the old days a warrior who fled a battle would be tied hand and foot then his people would stamp him into muddy ground, there to perish with dishonour.

I was at the bitter part of my story and I could feel the tears starting to my eyes.

'My father heard one Mercian drowning in the mud shouting for help. Instead of killing him, my father pulled him out of the mud then slipped and fell himself. The Mercian snatched my father's scramasax and ran him through. The wretch then ran off, away from the field of battle.'

I paused again, this time overcome by grief. As I struggled to gain control of my voice I could hear the warriors growling in anger at the double treachery of the Mercian. I cleared my throat then continued.

'Later, when I was old enough to take the vow, my uncle swore me to avenge my father's death.

'All the time I was at Lastingham I fretted at the thought that I would not be able to come south to find and kill that man.

'Then a miracle! God sent me to wicked King Wulfhere, to Tamworth, to the very heart of the Mercian enemy where the slayer of my father yet skulks in the darkness of his foul deed.'

I stood with my head bowed but I could feel the sympathetic gaze of every man there upon me.

In the silence Madoc's voice was gentle. 'We accept your story and declare that your heart is true and your cause is just. I should like to ask you just one more question. How do you know that the man whom you seek is still alive?'

'When I first came to Lichfield I started to ask people,' I said, 'but Owini came to hear of it and became suspicious, so I had to stop. It was the Britons who found him for me. He is a churl and he lives not far from Lichfield. I don't know his real name, for even the Mercians only know him by his nickname.'

'And what might that be?' queried Madoc.

'Shitlegs!'

Finn dutifully interpreted and the solemnity of the proceedings was broken by great howls of laughter from the warriors. I had to smile myself at their glee, for these fighting men knew only too well the sight and smell of a broken man fleeing in terror from battle, his legs streaked with brown.

When they had calmed down Madoc stood and made a short speech, Finn interpreting it for my sake.

'I, Prince Madoc of the kingdom of Powys, remind you that when the soldiers of Ancient Rome came they drove many of the people into the cruel hills to the west. There in spite of adversity they grew in strength under the banner of the Red Dragon. When the Roman invaders left, the people prepared to return to claim their own. But the once strong Britons had become Romano-Britons and were thus unable to resist the Saxon invaders.'

The warriors muttered to each other and shook their heads.

'Now it is the Church from Rome that is harming us,' Madoc continued, 'but the Welsh people had long discovered the true Church. The Welsh nation sprang from the soil and flourished. Now it is even stronger and will take back what rightfully belongs to it.'

The warriors banged their spears on their shields in agreement.

Madoc raised his arms for silence then resumed his speech. 'The people of Wales wish to embrace all the races who at present live in this land. Angles and Saxons who worship in the true Church are welcome to stay. Angles and Saxons who worship the gods of nature may continue along their own path, safe from oppression.

'All foreigners must, however, recognise that this land belongs to the British, and that they have the right to it.

'Finally, the King of Powys himself extends the hand of protection to all those who fight with him to right the ancient wrong.'

Finn fixed me with his eyes. 'You, Edwin, are especially welcome.' Then he added in a quiet voice, 'But you must put aside the Church of Rome, for it is a false Church.'

I felt that the last words were his and not Madoc's. I looked at the prince, who seemed to be waiting for an answer.

Finn's voice rang out. 'What say you?'

The warriors stiffened and all turned to look at me. Some took hold of their sword handles.

I looked Finn in the eye and cried, 'I, Edwin the Northumbrian, accept with thanks and pledge my loyalty. I will serve you.'

The warriors relaxed, some smiling.

Prince Madoc nodded graciously. 'Welcome, Edwin and Leofgifu, Angle and Saxon,' he said, speaking carefully in Englisc. 'You, Edwin, have committed no real crime, but you must learn to accept authority. Your youth, your good work and your faith have saved you for now. In the meantime you must have your hand attended to. You will need all of your strength to support us in our struggle.'

A great sense of relief swept over me as I realised that this ordeal, at least, was over.

The Welshmen started talking excitedly as their thoughts turned to what lay ahead.

Then, with a wild cry, Finn suddenly leaped into the centre of the circle. He held aloft an ancient-looking staff.

I was taken aback by such a rapid change in his mood.

He danced round in the circle stamping his feet and stabbing at the sky with the staff. In a loud voice he began uttering a rhythmic pounding chant.

The warriors sprang to their feet, gathering up their weapons. They joined in the chanting and stamping, beating in time on their little round shields. They struck heroic postures and shouted war cries then burst into gleeful laughter. As their muscles writhed and bunched, the beautiful and intricate tattoos on their limbs and bodies moved and took on a life of their own, making the warriors look even more ferocious.

The sudden noise and furious activity shook me back into reality. These men were looking forward to the joys of fighting, and unless a kindly fate intervened I too would be among them when it happened.

Leofgifu carefully skirted the whirling warriors and came to my side.

'He said we will be safe here. Please, come and rest,' she whispered.

Turning, I caught my hand on the rim of a shield. Blinding pain brought vomit into my mouth and I fell to my knees. In the onrush of darkness I heard Leofgifu call my name and then I heard no more.

Chapter 3

I sat before our tent and studied the fort. As I did so the maggot of doubt stirred again within my stomach and began to gnaw at my courage.

The palisade was not as strong as it had seemed yesterday and the number of warriors was not as great as I had thought. It was clear that the fort could not withstand an onslaught from a determined foe.

I saw Finn standing by a section of the earthworks. He beckoned, so I rose and went over to him.

'How goes it?' he asked.

'I am better after resting, but my hand pains me. What is happening? You are busy and I have not seen your brother in the fort. Is he gone?'

'Don't worry. Ardal set off yesterday to Wessex to seek spiritual strength and, God will it, help of a more secular nature. He will return soon, perhaps tomorrow.' He paused. 'We would like you to tell us about Chad this evening.'

'What is there to tell?'

'What manner of man he was. Not hearsay, though, but as you yourself saw him.'

'I'll do my best,' I said, but in truth I felt there was little I would want to say that they would want to hear.

Finn smiled. 'That's good. By the way, would you like to meet a fellow holy man?'

'What, here in the fort?'

'Certainly. Wait here and I'll invite him across. Perhaps he'll be able to help you.'

He went away and I rested on the short-cropped grass.

A fellow holy man, he'd said, pointedly not saying 'monk' or 'priest', so he didn't mean anybody from Lichfield, Breedon or Repton. And he certainly didn't mean the pagan High Priestess from Lichfield whom Chad had met and talked with several times.

'Misguided but honourable' was how he had described her. He told us King Wulfhere had expelled her from the Great Temple at Wodensbury and then, in a gesture that puzzled some, had made her a member of his own royal household. I saw it as a cunning move by Wulfhere, however, for he had placed her in the one position where she was safest from attack by the Church of Rome.

I started to wonder if I could meet her. It might be possible to persuade her to teach me some of her leechcraeft; as a pagan Saxon priestess she would know some powerful medicine. Then it came to me that if she fled to Wulfhere's household when we took Lichfield a meeting would be very difficult if not impossible.

As these thoughts were going through my head I became aware of a strong dog-like smell. I sniffed at the air, then a faint sound made me turn.

A great wolf stood barely an arm's length away. Its baleful yellow eyes stared at me. They held me in their thrall – I was unable to call out or move.

The shaggy grey head slowly lifted up to the sky and I found myself looking into a pair of human eyes. They were as black and fathomless as the tarns of Northumberland. The grimy face was swarthy and seamed.

In as steady a voice as I could muster I said, 'You must be the holy man of whom Finn spoke.'

As he studied my face I had a feeling that we had been near each other recently, and now fate had brought us together.

'I see some strength here,' he said, more to himself. 'Some self-control. But it needs training.'

He edged closer.

'I am Oak-man,' he offered, by way of explanation.

'Oak-man?'

'You say "Oak-man" in that way because you are looking outwards,' he observed. 'Now try looking within.'

'Is this a riddle?'

'Perhaps. Try looking inwards.'

He relapsed into silence and stared into the distance.

Leofgifu came over and sat with us.

'This is Oak-man,' I explained. 'He says I must look within to understand this . . .'

Unhesitatingly she said, 'Look at him. What do you see?'

'A man. A wolf. A tree?'

'No, he is not a tree, but he has the spirit of a tree. The oak. Now do you see?'

Dimly I began to understand. 'The oak is the most ancient and wisest of the trees. So he is a wise man of the most ancient of the . . . faiths?'

'Yes. My grandmother says it was the first faith in the land,' she explained.

'But it was all destroyed in the early days,' I said to the motionless figure.

'Wishful thinking on the part of your Church.'

'Not my Church but that of Rome.'

Oak-man looked at me hard before he spoke. 'Your

tongue says one thing, but your hair says another. Perhaps your heart says yet another?'

'Woden take me!' I cursed to myself, for I had forgotten that my hair was cut in the Roman tonsure.

Finn came back to us. He put his hand on my shoulder and kept it there while he spoke to Oak-man. 'How goes the healing?' he asked. 'Fast, I hope, for we may soon need Brother Edwin.'

Finn's gesture and calm voice gave me confidence anew.

'You are to heal me?' I asked Oak-man.

Without answering he unwrapped my hand and slowly turned it over, talking to himself. 'Pink is good. Yellow is liquid and will out. Dark green, not good.'

The smell from my hand penetrated that of wolf.

I looked away when he started to pull at the strips of skin and I began to feel faint when he set to picking off the darker bits of my flesh with his blackened nails.

'Good, good,' he grunted. 'Now wash it,' he commanded Leofgifu and she gently bathed my hand with water from a little pot.

I looked at her face, severe with concentration. She was a pagan, the same as Oak-man crouched at my side, yet they were both ministering to my hurt with care and devotion. The powerful leaders of the Church of Rome, such as Augustine, were surely wrong in their condemnation of people such as these. True, Oak-man spoke in riddles, but then so did Chad and nearly all of the other elders of both the Churches.

The picking and bathing ceased. Oak-man unrolled a small bundle by his side and from it produced a short stick wound with a grey substance. He took some and gently wound my hand with it. It was softer than anything I had ever felt. Softer, even, than the piece of silk that my mother once had in her special box.

'What is this wondrous stuff?' I asked.

He was too absorbed to reply but Leofgifu answered. 'Cobweb from the great barn.'

Oak-man carefully put the stick back into his bundle. 'I hope it will be enough, but very soon I will need all of this and more besides,' he said gravely, nodding his head to where the warriors were gathered about.

'What does it do?' I asked.

'Nature undoes what man and nature do,' he replied and rolled up his bundle.

'It heals cuts and burns,' Leofgifu explained as she wrapped my hand with the cleaner strips of cloth over the cobweb.

'Is it good against the shot of elves?' I teased her.

'Edwin,' she snapped, 'sometimes you make me very cross.'

'I am sorry,' I apologised. 'It's just something our priests say to the old women.'

'Your religion is trying to destroy ours. One way they do it is to belittle all that is good about our ways. Some of your learned men write special books which they say contain our healing-craeft. But they make up the things in those books, things that are not true. Even things that are dangerous and hurt people.'

Oak-man chuckled.

'Why do you laugh?' she demanded.

'Some of the things we do are indeed dangerous and hurt people.'

'Yes, of course, when necessary. But most of that craeft is known only to you. I am talking about the white craeft.'

Oak-man turned to me. 'Can you take shapes?' he said.

'No, I cannot.'

'I can,' he said. 'Wolf, deer, buzzard . . . and can you raise people from the dead?'

'No. God alone can do that,' I protested.

'There are three things that God alone can do: endure the eternities of infinity; participate in all things that are, without changing; renew everything without annihilating it,' he said. 'All other things man, with the help of God, can do. With his help I may have to raise Finn soon. Perhaps tomorrow.'

He suddenly busied himself with his bundles as if he had revealed something that only he knew was going to happen.

'Finn freed me and saved my life,' I said, 'but I know nothing about him save he acts like a warrior and talks like a learned man.'

'That is often the case in Ireland. It was once the same in this country but now things are changing,' said Oak-man. 'Finn is a scholar and a monk and holds an important position in his monastery. He is destined for greatness, but if he falls then so will much else besides. For those reasons I must be ready to raise him.'

'If it is his fate to fall, then surely he will fall, won't he?' I said, but Oak-man would not answer.

He made to pick up his bundles but paused. 'I hear you are to tell of Chad after sundown,' he said. 'That interests me for I understand that our beliefs would have been happy companions.'

'Your beliefs and his . . . ?' I echoed, scarcely able to hide the incredulity in my voice.

His eyes of fathomless black seemed to engulf me. 'Yes. A man comes to God by his own works,' he said. 'Chad was building a great cathedral was he not? Now, Edwin, go and rest. Let the healing-craeft do its work.' He took his bundles and turned to go, then added, 'And make sure you rest all five of your limbs.'

Leofgifu looked puzzled, then she blushed as she realised what he meant.

Chapter 4

I crawled out from my tent and stood up in the red light of the sunset. I felt strong and renewed and ready to tell my tale. For this I gave thanks in my heart to Oak-man. It was he who had made the potion that Finn gave me and his work on my hand had made it well-nigh pain-free.

The warriors had gathered together in a circle around a fire, some sitting, others lazing on one elbow. Madoc was seated on his stool and Finn stood ready to interpret.

'Hear me, listen. I will tell you of Chad and of some of the things I remember,' I began.

Someone passed me a horn of ale and I drank deeply.

'When I first came before Chad I saw he was old and clearly ill. His face was lined and he walked badly. His hands shook although his eyes missed nothing.

'He drove us with his tongue by praise or rebuke or threats of hell.

'One day he sent me to the pagan temple at Wall. My task was to destroy the idol that was there. When I had done that, Chad would consecrate the building for use as a church.'

I held aloft my near-useless hand so that it was visible to my audience.

'See this. I myself was nearly destroyed in the very place where I had earlier gone with intent to destroy. Fate surely moves in a mysterious way.'

The warriors murmured in agreement. I was taking them with me.

'The idol was a life-sized figure of a woman,' I continued. 'She wore a thin robe in the ancient style and a thegn's cap. Although I knew she was made of baked clay and painted, at the same time she was a living being, a goddess. When I came back to Lichfield, Chad sent for me.'

'The idol. Was it destroyed?' said Chad.

'Oh, yes,' I replied, perhaps a little too eagerly. 'Yes, yes, she's gone.'

A lie. I'd not been able to bring myself to destroy the mother goddess. I'd buried it late at night in a secret place.

He regarded me with a level gaze. 'Hmm,' he said, his face without expression. 'You may go.'

I felt chill for it was as if the Pope had pronounced a sentence of excommunication on me.

One warrior said something. Finn said, 'He wants to know what "excommunication" means.'

I felt a twinge of apprehension at the question, for I had made a slip of the tongue.

'It's when God turns his face away from a person.'

'And the Pope can make this happen?'

'Yes,' I said.

'How can another man come between you and God? You are responsible for yourself to him, are you not?' the warrior persisted.

Finn stepped in and saved me from the questioning. I was glad because it was something I couldn't resolve for myself, let alone for anyone else.

'It's a good question,' he said, 'but let's hear about Chad

before the spirit moves Edwin and he rushes back to his tent with his . . . friend.'

The warriors laughed at my apparent discomfort but I smiled gratefully at Finn.

More ale was offered and I took it gladly.

'Hear me, listen. I shall tell you another thing,' I declaimed. The warriors fell silent.

'One day, Chad was recounting his vision of the new cathedral,' I began . . .

'It shall be made with brick from the city of giants at Wall and the best stones from Scenstone,' Chad said.

'Are we to build it, Bishop? We are good builders in timber, but as for stone . . .' asked one of the brothers.

'We shall bring the stonemasons from across the sea,' replied Chad. 'I fear that they are not to be trusted, for they swear oath to a secret guild. We shall make use of them, none the less.'

A small gasp of annoyance escaped from Brother Owini's lips but Chad either didn't hear or chose to ignore it and continued.

'We must give the best to God but sometimes our own best is not good enough. We shall get master-craftsmen from many lands. We shall have Irish scribes to help in the new scriptorum, for example.'

'A new scriptorum, Bishop?' asked Trumhere the scribe.

'Yes. It is in my mind. But when depends upon how much land King Wulfhere gives us. You will be responsible for it of course.'

'Thank you, Bishop.' He beamed.

'That reminds me. Wynfrid, I want you to go on being my

deacon. It will mean more work now that more money is coming to us. What say you?'

'I shall serve wherever I am wanted.'

'I am grateful to you. Now, to the next item. Lichfield is established as a bishopric so we cannot all stay as monks. There is need for a new priest. Not all of us are quite ready. I propose that Edwin put his mind to the path of higher service. What say you, Edwin?'

A shadow of jealousy passed over Owini's face. Chad may have noticed but he said nothing.

'I am grateful and humbled by your consideration but I cannot,' I replied.

Silence.

'Tell me, why not?' Chad asked quietly.

'I am unable to be quiet about things I know to be true.'

'Yes? Go on.'

'We seem not to care for the first people of this land. Not only are the Britons neglected but the Church of Rome prefers to suppress the beliefs of the British Church. Every day we are torn in the struggle between the Churches.'

'The struggle?'

'Yes. Between the power of Rome and the simple faith of the British Church.'

'The argument over Easter has been resolved.'

'It's more than that. The British Church should have primacy. It not only works with other religions but respects them as well; the people respect it in return.'

Owini broke in. His face was red. 'As well you might know, you . . . you . . . lover of pagans!'

The brothers round the table drew back with a hiss of breath but I was glad Owini had said that. It would force Chad to say what he really thought.

He sat unmoving for a while before he spoke. 'Yes. It is true. We, I mean the British Church, were first to bring God's truth to these islands and we worked with all. But it was in error on a number of doctrinal positions. The Church of Rome can be tolerant but it is insistent on clarity of thought.' He paused for a moment then said more briskly, 'Edwin, I shall send you to Breedon. Spend some time there. Study. Meditate. Then come back and respond to my suggestion. I am certain that you will make a fine priest. That is all. Now it is time for prayer.'

'But what about me? I'll do it,' burst out Owini. He spoke to Chad but he was glaring at me, his eyes bulging with anger and jealousy.

'We all have our strengths and weaknesses, Brother Owini. You have a good spirit and your back is stronger than that of any three men put together. However, your gifts are not with words or the complexities of the world. I know that you have difficulty with reading the scriptures. Not that you aren't open to the Holy Spirit of course, as we all are. No, Owini, be my servant and be my builder and together we shall raise a cathedral such as this present generation of men has never seen before.'

Darkness had fallen over the hill-fort. The warriors were silent as I concluded my brief account by saying, 'That's how it was with Chad. On one hand, Owini had been mollified because he thought he had been given promises of great building. On the other my anger had been blunted by being sent away to study and to pray – and, of course, to come round to his way of thinking.'

A drinking horn was pushed into my hand. I was thirsty after telling my tale, so I upended its point to the stars.

By now many of the warriors were sprawled out, their glazed eyes set in puffy red faces caused by the good ale that had been going the rounds. Fighting men they might be but they couldn't take much drink.

Then I had the good idea to reduce Chad in their eyes a little, so I called for silence. Some of the ale ran over my chin as I spoke.

'It wasn't fair, you know. It upset me, being sent away from the brothers and my friend and that, it upset them as well . . . but all Chod could do . . . I mean Chad, sorry . . . all he could do to ease the pain was to tell us a riddle.'

I looked at Finn. He seemed to be smiling at something as he interpreted. The men brightened up. Some of them called out, and the ale was passed to me again. I took my time with the drinking, trying to get the words right in my mind. I shut my eyes, the better to think, but fatigue made me sway so I opened them again.

'They want to hear the riddle, Edwin,' Finn said. It was unnecessary of him to say that, I thought.

'All right! I'm just going to tell it,' I replied with some dignity, and took up the posture of the story-teller.

'Now hearken! Hear the riddle.'

I am the strangest of beings. I satisfy women – in every household – yet no one one suffers because of me, except whoever slays me.

They watch me grow tall, upright in a bed.

Sometimes, according to her need, a beautiful girl will bravely take me in her hand and sees that I'm hairy underneath.

She holds tight my reddish skin, pulls off my head then slips me into her pantry.

Straightway that girl with the shining hair who has hidden me away remembers our meeting as her eyes grow moist.

What am I?

The fearsome warriors sat with bated breath and wide eyes while Finn turned the riddle into their own tongue. As the final challenge was uttered they turned to each other and began to discuss the problem.

Gestures were made which indicted most clearly what the answer might have been.

Argument grew. Men would utter a response only to have it immediately dismissed as being too obvious by their neighbours.

The debate grew loud and shouting started.

Finn called to me, 'You'd best stand up, Edwin, and tell us the answer.'

A couple of warriors helped me to my feet. Madoc's eye was upon me and the assembly fell silent.

'The answer is,' I said slowly, spinning out the moment, 'an onion!'

They shrieked and rolled about choking. They pointed at each other then held their sides in pain of laughter.

I was so happy as I stood among these fine men. I had a sense of power at my mastery of the riddle but I was also one of their number. Here was comradeship, here was what the warrior in the hall of his lord had, and what I was denied. I had no lord to give me iron rings for my finger or to praise me. I felt sad at the great unjustness of everything and fat tears rolled down my cheeks.

I raised both arms to the great sky above, home of Woden and of Christ, they who would help me.

The sound of Finn clearing his throat brought my attention back to this gathering of heroes.

'Edwin! Prince Madoc will address you.'

'We thank you for telling us about Chad,' began the fine chieftain. 'But you may count yourself lucky, Edwin, that he had the wit to send you to Breedon before you gave yourself away and were arrested for being a spy. Had that happened you could never succeed in your mission of revenge.'

Woden take me, I thought. I had been careful not to reveal those parts of Chad's words that I wanted left unsaid, but, like many of his race, Madoc was able to see through the curtains that men hang around their speech.

I was unsure whether he was praising Chad or belittling me, so to be on the safe side I maintained a dignified silence and smiled benignly upon this grey-beard, the leader of men.

'I see from your face that you feel I am scorning you,' he went on, 'but this is not so. My thoughts are turned to Chad. Clearly, he was among the wisest of men, and it is my sorrow that I shall never meet him – in this life, at least. However, Edwin, I am fortunate in that you are here. You sat at his feet and learned from him. Through the disciple I shall know the master.'

He placed one hand on my shoulder and raised his other hand to the heavens. In ringing tones he declared, 'I, Madoc, Prince of Powys, do vow before all here that Edwin the Angle shall be at my side when we march into Lichfield.'

A roar of approval followed his speech and then, as if on a signal, the warriors scrambled to their feet. Madoc left the circle and the men began to drift away to their tents.

I sat down again and thought over the day's events. My hand was giving almost no pain, and telling about Chad had eased my soul a little. All in all I was at peace.

Unbidden, Madoc's sharp words came back to me. Of course I had realised Chad's intention when he ordered me to Breedon, but in spite of that I had hardened my heart and defied him. Not just in the matter of ministering to the Britons, or in being a priest, but particularly in the blood feud. Chad had wanted me to abandon my 'wicked mission of revenge' as he called it.

Tiredness stole over me and I sought out the latrine pit before going to my tent.

In the dark I stumbled over a warrior who, even in his sleep, reached out and took hold of his sword. I moved hastily away.

My thoughts turned to Chad and his reproof about my vengeful purpose. He had said I had only to look in the Bible to find the basis of his challenge to the ancient custom. 'Forgive those who smite thee,' he said. 'It could not be plainer, could it!'

I was teasing these words around when I came across the dark hole in the ground that was the latrine pit. The events of the day had made me weary; I might have swayed a little as I pulled up the hem and loose folds of my robe and put them out of the way over my left arm but my mind was crystal clear.

I recalled how I had made the point that I had no authority to abandon my vow to avenge my father, but Chad had claimed that, on the contrary, it was I who had no right, no authority, to take vengeance. 'Then who, exactly, has the right?' I had asked and his answer had ended the discussion.

As I stood at the edge of the pit in the darkness his final words came back to me. I said them aloud. Their sound and their meaning pleased me, so I gave voice to them again, this time shouting my loudest.

'Vengeance is mine, saith the Lord!' I cried and the effort made my water spray into the night sky.

To my horror, answering voices came back. Not from the sky but from the ground at my feet. What I had taken to be the latrine pit was the black scar of a camp-fire. Men were stirring all around me and they would be mightily angry when they discovered how wet they were.

I crept stealthily away and made my way back to our tent.

The night was warm and the riddle came to mind again. I repeated it to myself and thoughts of Leofgifu began to rise up.

As I entered our tent I called softly, 'Hello, little cabbage. Are you there?' but there was no reply. I slipped my shoes off and loosened my belt to be ready for her return. I hoped that my resolve would stay firm as I settled down to wait for her.

Chapter 5

The morning light hurt my eyes and my head ached. Leofgifu hadn't come back to the tent and I felt bad-tempered.

I saw that many of the warriors had also become moody. It was the third day in the hill-fort and quarrels were breaking out among them. I remembered that Finn had said they were waiting for Oak-man to declare the most propitious moment. The waiting was affecting them badly.

I found Oak-man and sat with him. He was silent for a while then gestured with his chin. 'Regard the warriors yonder. What do you see?'

A group of Welshmen were practising swordplay in pairs. Their swords were long with sharp edges made for cutting and slashing.

The men had three main movements. They chopped from the wrist, from the elbow, and from the shoulder, making great sweeps using the whole arm. Many of the latter were done horizontally at neck height.

As I watched, one man caught his heel against a loose rock and fell backwards. As he fell his sword hit the sharp edge of another rock. Straight away the two men stopped their practice and stood together, one holding up the sword. They were sighting along the blade. Even from where I sat I could see that the edge was curled from the impact.

The owner of the sword found two suitable rocks. He swiftly and expertly straightened out the damaged edge using one as an anvil and the other as a hammer. He seemed unworried at the ease with which the edge had buckled.

I knew little of these matters but I had seen enough of Mercian arms training to know that the Saxon blade would not have buckled so easily.

'Although their swords are beautifully made with handles like little human figures, the blades seem to bend easily,' I said to Oak-man.

'Those swords come alive in battle. They have a will of their own, and fly to where the foe has a weak spot. It is the nature of iron.' He added, 'Iron has been the downfall of my race and will be of these people as well, for it is a metal of the Otherworld.'

I was curious as to the land of his origin so I said as meaningfully as I could, 'I am Northumbrian born,' but he did not respond.

'Now I will make them invincible,' he said. 'Soon they must resist the Saxon spear.'

'Have they link-mail or leather tunics?' I asked, for I could only see swords and small round shields.

'They are called Welsh although once their people were all Britons. They are of the true race of Celts. They will be fighting for their land, their freedom, for their souls. What is to come will be no mere cattle raid.'

He saw my puzzlement at his oblique reply.

'They will fight naked,' he explained. 'Their faith and my craeft will protect them. Now I must go.'

Later I saw him with the warriors. They were performing great feats of jumping and slashing with the swords. He was jumping with them, chanting to the sun god and urging them on with shrill cries.

First here and then there a fighting man would mime

chopping off a head, which he would pick up by the hair and hold aloft for all to see.

They were working themselves up into a frenzy.

One man made a different move against his imaginary opponent. He chopped and slashed below waist height. Then he put down his sword.

The other warriors fell to their knees in silent anticipation.

Slowly the victor knelt down, picked up some dreadful bloody thing and stood up, stretching both arms to the sky. He offered the mess in his gore-stained hands to the sky god and then, unmistakably, wolfed down the severed genitals of his enemy.

He was transformed. Now he was a warrior full seven feet tall. He gave a fearsome throat-swelling roar, showing his wide-open mouth and teeth red with blood. The other warriors broke from their trance-like state. They leaped up with such a great shout that my heart jumped in terror in my ribs.

Oak-man had it aright – these warriors were truly invincible. Now I understood why these Welshmen of the British Church had Oak-man with them. His religion was much more ancient than theirs, and they respected that, but more important to them was his command of great powers. I felt ashamed that I could not do magic like that.

Around noon I sat to eat with Finn and a group of warriors. The barley bread we were chewing was stale and the watered-down ale was flat. Propitious moment or not, I realised that the food was running out. Soon we would be forced to march on Lichfield or else disperse.

I needed to be with the army when I sought Shitlegs. For all his cowardice he bore a scramasax and would find me easy meat if I were on my own when we came face to face. I was thinking about what I should do if our army had to break up when one of the Welshmen spoke to me. I had no need of Finn to interpret.

'Tell us what you understand of this Owini.'

The others nodded in agreement.

'He is East Anglian,' I said. 'He was once chief thegn to a great queen and steward of her household. He told us that he had decided to renounce the world, and so gave away all his possessions out of devotion to the faith. He knows little of humility, though, for he never forgets that he was once a thegn, and tries to give us direction.'

The warriors around nodded in sympathy; they too resented being given direction.

'Bishop Chad told us that Owini had come to him at Lastingham monastery wearing but a robe and carrying an axe and a trowel. It is said that in the times when he could study no more he would perform great feats of manual labour, for he has immense strength.'

The warriors seemed interested in my words, and talked among themselves for a moment or two.

'They are discussing who will be given the first chance to fight him when we march into Lichfield, but there is some doubt about killing him because he is a holy man,' said Finn, smiling at me. 'Perhaps you could tell us something about him which will make our decision easier?'

I could indeed.

'Owini followed Chad around like a dog,' I said. 'Chad would summon him by clapping his hands. Something the rest of us would never accept. One of the brothers – our brewmaster, I remember – once told Owini to his face that he was a cringing cur. Owini said that he would never forget the insult, and would have his revenge. That seemed strange coming from one who professed so great a love of God.

'One day, Owini came across the same brother and his helper, a nun, coupling on the straw of the brew-house. He started lashing at them with a stave, calling them fornicators and adulterers.

'The other monks rushed in and hurled themselves upon Owini but it took all of their joint strength to overpower him.

'Chad had to be told. I and one other went to tell him. He was most dismayed and demanded to hear all there was to be told.

'Owini was unrepentant. He ranted about how the blessed Augustine of Hippo had said that sin is transmitted through carnal knowledge of women.

' "Women are filthy and the source of all sin," he shouted. "Those of you who lie with women are corrupted and in mortal danger. It must be stopped – now!" '

At this point in my tale the warriors began an animated conversation among themselves. Finn placed his hand on my knee, so I waited until they were ready for me to continue. Finn himself joined in from time to time. Finally he turned to me.

'I'm sorry,' he said, 'but we are all very surprised by Owini's interpretation of that matter.'

I looked at these painted men with their matted hair and oiled bodies. 'It is a fine point of doctrine,' I said.

'Their knowledge of scripture often exceeds my own,' said Finn, 'and in matters of doctrine they are sometimes my master.'

He put his arm around my shoulder. 'Don't be downcast,' he said. 'It is a matter of fact, and was not intended to be a rebuke.'

He kept his arm around my shoulder as I resumed my tale of Owini and his claim about the transmission of sin.

Owini turned to Chad and said, 'Is that not the ruling, O Bishop?'

Chad looked at Trumhere, our tutor in the scriptures. 'What do the scriptures tell us?'

Trumhere referred us to the warnings about adultery and the commandments. 'But note,' he said, looking hard at Owini. 'Our Lord loved and blessed all women, including the woman taken in adultery.'

Owini glared at us all. Then he spoke, hatred contorting his face. 'It will soon be the case that monks and priests shall not know women, and shall not marry.' Then he added, triumphantly, 'It is a ruling from Rome. The Pope, who is descended from Peter, has the authority.'

'How do you know that?' someone asked.

'I knew many important and wise people in East Angle land. Better people than you here . . . well, most of you, anyway,' he sneered.

We were all much dismayed. These were not our beliefs and many of the brothers went with women. The rage vented upon the love-making pair was daemonic in nature, and was completely at odds with our views of love and care for each other.

We turned to Chad. 'Tell us, O Bishop, what is the truth of this matter.'

'I agree with Trumhere in his reading of the scripture, but Owini is right.' Chad sighed. 'There is talk of celibacy but it is only talk for the moment. We may expect to hear from Rome soon. Augustine of Hippo has not been refuted in this matter.'

The ill-treated brother protested vehemently. 'I am not a

fornicator,' he cried. 'The woman is not an adulteress. We have known only each other. We love each other.' His face showed his anguish. 'What happened here, what has been said, places a great decision before us.'

Chad was silent for a moment, then he smiled a little. 'Do not be down-hearted, brothers. The love of our Lord enables us to overcome all earthly desires and longings.'

He went out of the room, leaving us sorely grieved.

I had wanted to ask Chad why Owini was not to be punished for his act of violence and non-brotherly love, but it was too late.

Those of us who had come to the Lord from the British tradition were extremely distressed by all that had happened. My heart began to harden against Owini and Chad.

That evening there was much discussion about the incident. It was pointed out that the tradition of descent of priesthood from father to son would, at a stroke, be nullified for ever.

'Who, then, would decide upon the succession of priests in our Church?' asked one monk.

'That is an easy riddle,' answered another monk. 'It would be Rome.'

We felt very downcast as the truth of that observation made its mark.

A few days later the slighted couple left the community. They put themselves at great risk, for they were no longer protected by the Church and could be regarded as outlaws, to be killed on sight.

Some of the brothers seemed more concerned about the loss of our ale though, and indeed several of us became ill through drinking the foul water from the lake.

*   *   *

I looked at the faces of the warriors and felt that I had done enough.

'Such is Brother Owini,' I concluded.

The warriors sat in grim silence. At length, up rose the man who had asked me to tell them about Owini. He held his sword aloft. 'I swear by the sword of the Blessed Michael that I will take Owini and with this blade I shall slice off his balls,' he vowed, and a general growl of assent followed this promise.

'And I swear that I will be by your side when you take your revenge in Lichfield,' Finn said softly in my ear.

Later on I was asked to go to Madoc. Finn was with him.

'Although I have been here in Mercia for three years you will appreciate that I haven't travelled much,' Finn said, with some irony, 'so I shall have to ask you about the settlements to the east and north of Lichfield with names such as Whittington.'

I nodded.

'What we want to know is, do these names have a military significance?' he asked.

'Whitting means the followers or people of Whitta,' I replied, eager to share my knowledge. 'They are numerous and rich enough to have a ton . . . a settlement. The leaders in this district are Whitta, Esine and Wicga. They are all thegns and command men in time of war. There's another man called Pacca, a Norseman, but I don't know much about him. All these men have a settlement.'

'How many warriors?' said Finn.

He was unnecessarily terse, I thought.

'Whitta could call upon nearly fifty men. Together, the

four thegns can provide near one hundred men, most with their own weapons.'

'What else?'

'There are the halls, which are much like the large houses where the Britons used to live. Each has about twenty men, women and children living there so that would be, say, five warriors from each hall. There's Eden hall and Duna's hall. That's about ten men. I wouldn't expect much from Croka's hall. Ah, yes, there are people at Cat Holme but it is said they have the sickness and none will approach them.'

'And the king. What of the mighty Wulfhere?' broke in Madoc.

'King Wulfhere has about fifteen men with him most of the time, but I don't know if he is here or not. When I was cast into the pit he was at Tamworth. Now he could be at Repton or further north. Anglo-Saxon kings never settle in one place.'

I could see that Madoc was becoming impatient so I finished by saying, 'Of warriors, then, the number would be about one hundred and twenty.'

My mouth had said the words unfeelingly but my stomach went chill with fear of facing such an army.

Madoc turned to Finn and raised his eyebrows in question. Finn slowly nodded as if seeing the balance in our favour.

Madoc turned to me and, smiling, said, 'Sometimes, Edwin, it is useful to be bookish.'

In the late afternoon there was a buzz of excitement and the warriors started off towards the gateway. I joined them and was in time to see the gates opened.

In came a band of armed men. At their head was Ardal,

leading a fine horse. The Welshmen cheered and stabbed at the sky with their swords and spears.

Our number had grown even more and so our chances had improved greatly. I blessed the name of Fortuna, goddess of luck.

The excitement died down somewhat when the new arrivals had been inspected more closely. Ardal had done his best. There were eight West Saxons, five Britons and four large tough-looking men whom I later discovered to be Frisian mercenaries.

The Britons were runaway slaves. They made up for their lack of weapons with an unyielding hatred of the Mercians. Two of them were too crippled to fight but were willing to serve. The Frisians, easily as large as Madoc's champion, were very well armed with weapons that were greased and razor-sharp. The West Saxons said they were outlaws, but I saw that they had not been kissed by the branding iron, neither had their ears been cropped. They did have good weapons, though, and seemed keen to fight.

The horse turned out to be lame.

One Welshman waxed indignant, saying that Ardal should return the animal and get his money back.

Ardal politely responded, 'It is unfortunate that the beast is lame. Perhaps I should ask the unlucky owner if he would be so kind as to let me steal a better one?'

The laughter that followed made up a little for the general disappointment that Madoc would not be riding on a horse when he led us into Lichfield.

That evening Oak-man made a pronouncement: the time was auspicious.

Madoc and Finn swiftly finalised their plans. Our force

consisted of Madoc, Finn's brother Ardal, fifty Welsh warriors, seven West Saxons, three Britons, and four Frisians. A good force of fighting men.

The two unfit Britons and the oldest of the West Saxons formed the baggage train. They would carry extra spears and replacement shields.

If we had the bad luck to come up against any Mercians in number then Finn, Oak-man and myself would invoke the gods of protection in battle. Also with us there the spirit of any warrior who fell, depending on his beliefs, would be more speedily taken to heaven, to the Otherworld, or to the Hall of Warriors.

How could we not succeed?

When I was back in my tent and on my own again, though, a sense of unease returned.

Two matters disturbed me. One concerned the West Saxons, a people I had never met before. On the times when our paths crossed in the fort they seemed to take on a haughty manner, as if I were of inferior rank. Perhaps they took me for a Mercian. In speech they clipped their words, yet somehow contrived to slur them as well, making them difficult to understand. In truth, I felt them to be untrustworthy.

The other matter was far more weighty. I was getting closer to Lichfield and my father's murderer, yet my spirit was feeling heavier and heavier. Leofgifu seemed to have deserted me as well.

Was my fate warning me that I had taken the wrong road?

I could slip away in the night and go back to Wall. There I could tell a tale of kidnapping and escape and make something of my loyalty to Wulfhere. Then I remembered what our spies had told us; Wulfhere had not been seen out of Tamworth recently. He seemed to be spending all his time in the

Great Hall. People said he had received wounds in a recent battle: perhaps he was resting while they healed.

As I mulled these thoughts over, one of the Welshmen in a nearby tent started talking. I couldn't understand the words but I listened to the rhythm and the tone, and then it came to me – he was praying.

I sensed others were listening, and when he finished a number of voices softly echoed the Amen.

A great wave of certainty swept over me. How could we not succeed?

Chapter 6

The dawn light came and drove away the grey ghosts of the dead that had been prowling round our tents.

We none of us had slept well, I supposed, but now this great day had come our spirits soared.

We set off in good humour and made our way down the southern long ridge that was the approach to the hill-fort. After a few hundred paces we turned to the east, towards Lichfield.

The Welshmen were not naked but wore breeches loose to the knee then tied tight below the knee with criss-cross thongs down to the ankle. Wise Madoc had said that they were to enter Lichfield as home-comers, not as naked warriors intent on destruction.

We came into a valley that took us eastwards, a valley that was so tight we had to string out.

First in were the Welsh, led by Prince Madoc and his champion. Then came the smaller group of Britons and the Frisian mercenaries. This group was headed by Finn who now wore his monk's robe. He carried the ancient staff I had seen earlier. Finally came the West Saxons, led by Ardal. The baggage train followed.

This was a change to the earlier plan, but Madoc had altered it because during the night one of the West Saxons had slipped away. Finn surmised that he had simply lost his courage but Oak-man saw it as a bad omen, saying that the man might be going to alert the Mercians.

As part of Madoc's new plan, Ardal's group halted before coming into the valley. If trouble broke out, they would be the reserve. They would only come on once the main force had cleared the valley.

I marched alongside Finn. Oak-man ran to and fro. He scanned the hilltops, then looked closely at the ground. He sniffed for tracks and scent marks, as if he were a dog. He was wearing his wolfskin and a leathern apron. His swarthy skin glistened with smeared oils and ointments. He ran on, picked up something, and came loping back.

'Look,' he said to us. 'What name do you give this?' He held out a handful of dark green leaves, wet from the water it grew in.

'It is called cress,' I said, 'and many people eat it for its special properties.'

'Cress! It is bad,' said Oak-man with vehemence and threw the leaves to the ground. The expression of contempt on his face indicated the extent of the gap between the beliefs of his religion and those of the pagan Saxons, for he surely knew that cress was one of the magic nine herbs given to man by Woden.

'This place is called Cress Well,' I said, in an attempt at reconciliation. 'They say the water is very good.'

Oak-man did not reply, but went ahead.

I picked up the cress and pushed it into my waist-purse.

The warriors were talking quietly and I saw apprehensive looks from time to time. People with fighting experience do not like being in narrow valleys.

Oak-man came back. 'There is trouble here,' he said to Finn. 'We should be careful.'

He turned to me and said, 'What is the name of this hill? It has a bad feel to it.'

'I know not, but some have seen night creatures dancing

there,' I told him. 'There is an ancient stone on the top they call Puck or Hob's stone.'

Oak-man became very agitated. He seized hold of Finn's arm. 'We must go back, now,' he said. 'There is badness here. Something terrible will happen. Turn the men around. We must flee.'

Finn slowed his pace then stopped. He held his arm up, and the warriors following him came to a halt.

'What is wrong?' called one.

'Why have we stopped?' called another.

Finn signalled for silence. 'What do you see?' he demanded of Oak-man.

'Daemons over our heads, bitterness at our feet, and the silence of the blackness,' he said urgently.

Finn stood and studied the hilltops to left and to right of us. He looked up the valley, then turned and looked back at the way we had come.

I felt that Oak-man was right, for the hills seemed un-naturally quiet and the sky was going darker.

Oak-man said, 'I will warn Ardal,' and he loped away.

'Very well,' Finn said, 'and I must tell Madoc.'

He called out to the warriors, 'Stay yourselves, but do not rest. Be on your guard. Wait for my order.' He set off in a run up the valley.

Scarcely had he passed the rearguard of the Welshmen when a cry went up from those at the front.

'The Mercians,' they shouted.

Ahead, a double line of heavily armed warriors blocked our way. They had appeared as if out of the ground. They stood in silent menace. The only moving figure was a thegn slowly riding his grey horse along the line. The thegn wore a dark blue cape over his link-mail shirt which glinted as he turned.

From his fine armour I knew he must be one of the king's companions.

A thin rain began. The warriors near me shivered – from cold or fear I knew not. The thegn gave an order and some of the Mercians levelled their spears. Others raised their war axes.

We all stood as if bewitched.

Madoc broke the spell. 'Turn back. Re-form at the rear,' he ordered. The warriors nearest him began to turn, as if to make their way back.

Had they all heeded his call things might have gone differently but the warriors at the front suddenly gave a great shout and rushed at the line of cruel spears.

I offered up a quick prayer to Tiw, that terrible god of battle.

The Welshmen chopped and hacked at the Mercians with ferocious energy. Heads went rolling, some with mouths open in frozen screams, others bearing foolish grins. Severed arms and hands flew into the air. Blood spurted, and men died in mid curse.

Such was the momentum of the assault that the Mercian line fell back, broken in one place.

Through the gap came the thegn, now dismounted. He straightway killed two men with his scramasax. Then he gave a fierce cry and forced his way towards Madoc, intending to slay our leader.

Seeing this, the Mercians reacted with vigour. Their heavy spears began to stab and stab and the little round Welsh shields splintered and shattered. Once the light shields were out of the way the heavy Mercian war axes began their dreadful work, work which made a sound as of the chopping of sodden wood.

Our men formed into a line to face the foe but the slope of the land on each side made them bunch together, hindering their sword arms.

The Mercians had recovered from our initial charge. They re-formed and, levelling their spears, raised their shields to form a long shield wall.

They started barking a war chant, 'Ut! Ut! Ut!' At each bark they came forward a short step, stamping on the ground.

A whirling mix of roaring Welshmen, Britons, and Frisians hurled themselves again and again upon the unyielding shield wall.

There was dreadful slaughter.

A horn sounded and down the slope of the hill from our right came more Mercians. We were being attacked on two sides. In moments, men were fighting everywhere along the length of the valley.

Rain ran into their eyes. Trampling feet mixed the blood with the water, making the grass treacherous underfoot.

Weapon-craeft became clumsy; long and tearing wounds were inflicted.

One warrior, only stunned, fell into the little pipe or stream and drowned.

I saw Finn praying loudly and exhorting the warriors to redouble their efforts. He chanted with them as they hacked and chopped. He shouted out warnings in their own tongue whenever anyone was about to be surrounded, and his ornate dagger found useful work in the kidneys of the foe.

The Mercians' anger grew at this and several times they made threatening gestures at him. He responded with threats of hell and excommunication, and feinted at them with his heavy staff. They were unwilling to attack a holy man, but their ire was rising.

He ran up the slope towards me a little and looked ahead to where our vanguard were fighting. I could see Madoc with his champion surrounded by fallen of both sides.

Near me four Mercians had seized one of the Frisians. They were dragging him away. He struggled violently but his feet could not gain purchase. He was facing us and roared something to his fellow Frisians.

They knew the Mercians would cruelly rip our plans from him. A Frisian seized a heavy Saxon javelin and hurled it with full force directly into his compatriot's chest.

The strike was true and the Mercians fell over the captured Frisian as his full weight pulled them down. One of the Mercians tugged his head up by the hair, while another seized the javelin shaft and worked it to and fro. There was no response. The fearful spike had done its work.

I raised my arms and called on Woden and Christ to take the fallen Frisian's soul.

'Victory or paradise,' I shouted.

The warriors fell to with renewed energy. Alas, it didn't last long, for they were tiring.

The axes of our own West Saxons were doing good work but I saw with horror that the Welshmen's swords were failing. Men were trying to fight with bent blades. Fatigue and slipperiness caused the men to miss their mark. When they hit the wings of a Saxon spear or the head of an axe, so damage was done to the sword.

A grim mood had seized our men. They kept a dreadful silence, broken only by the sound of their breath rasping through distended throats and wide-open mouths.

The baying of the black dogs with red eyes echoed along the valley. They had come for the souls of men. Amidst the carnage and the reek of blood I felt my hair stand on end.

Finn came running towards me. 'Edwin,' he called, 'tell Ardal to come in and cover our retreat. Go like the wind.'

I turned to run but my feet slipped on the bloodied grass and I fell heavily. Two Mercians ran at me. One held his spear poised, the other raised his scramasax. I half rolled to one side and stretched out my arm to fend off the hungry blade.

I was looking at the very face of death, but the blow never came. The grizzled Mercian standing over me stared down, unmoving. His gory scramasax hung motionless at the top of its swing and in his bloodshot eyes there was a look of sheer terror. Finn hurled himself at the frozen warrior, who went tumbling across the grass, to be skewered by three Welsh blades. The other Mercian launched his bloodhungry point, then fell, cleft in twain from head to waist.

Finn, standing across me, took the cruel spike in his chest.
He fell and did not move.

I knelt and cradled his head on my knees. 'Oh Finn, oh Finn,' was all I could say. His face was losing its colour. He was taking on a waxen appearance like that of a church candle.

He said in a small voice, 'Flee the battle, Edwin. All is lost here and it is no dishonour to go after I have departed the field.'

'I will never leave, Finn, for I love thee,' I whispered, choked with emotion.

At our side there appeared three figures in cloaks. From whence they had come I had no idea. One reached out and with a slim white hand pulled the hating steel from Finn's chest. He groaned.

The three figures raised him up, two at his head, and one at his feet. I could not see their faces but from their hands I knew them to be female. Seemingly with no effort at all they bore him away up the slope. They moved ever faster.

I called out, 'Finn, take me with you.'

I could scarcely hear his reply. 'You cannot come with me. You must stay here and be faithful to the truth. You will be with me when the time is right.'

'Wait, I am coming with you,' I cried.

One hooded figure said softly, 'You may not, for we are going to the Otherworld.'

They seemed to melt into the hillside and vanished from my sight.

I stood, looking after them. My mind was a whirl of emotions; part of me was numb at the shock of seeing Finn killed, but I also felt comforted by the realisation that it was the mother goddesses who had come for him. Their appearance at the scene of a battle meant that a birth would surely follow – perhaps in this case Finn would return from the Otherworld.

Then I remembered the order that Finn had given me. I ran along the slope, round to where Ardal and the reinforcements should have been waiting.

Fear seized my heart at what I beheld. Four of our West Saxons lay butchered upon the rough grass. The others and the baggage train were fleeing up the narrow rake towards the thick woodland.

Of Oak-man there was no sign.

Towards me came a formation of Mercians. They carried spears, shields, and long scramasaxes. Some wore link-mail shirts.

I ran back, ready to warn our weary men in the valley, for the new attackers were not churls. They were well-trained Mercian soldiers, most likely from Tamworth fort.

They were being led by a large square man wearing a crimson cape, sitting comfortably on a black stallion. The handle of his scramasax glinted with gold and a fine halo of light shone around his burnished helmet, wet from the rain.

He checked his horse and turned in his saddle to look up at me, for my running had drawn his attention. I could see his blue eyes and the confident jut of his broad jaw.

He unsheathed his scramasax and spurred his horse as if to come after me. Fear robbed me of movement and my knees began to buckle.

The knight took another look at me as if to impress my face upon his memory, then turned and galloped after his men.

He caught up with them and gave an order. The fresh Mercian troops swiftly formed a ring around the exhausted combatants. On another order the treacherous Mercians keeping our men bottled up in that valley of blood drew back behind the ring of iron.

The knight spoke loudly to his men. 'Brave Mercians, companions to the great king. Here you see traitors, outlaws and deserters. They must be destroyed. Here stand Welshmen, wild descendants of the pagans once entrusted with the land that is now ours.

'They were neglectful stewards, and God drove them out. They will not work the land. They will not care for its bounty but they come stealthily to take everything from you and your king.'

I stood unable to move, fixed by a terrible fascination.

'The heavens above tremble at God's wrath,' the knight continued, 'just as the evildoers tremble before you. Send them to God that he may pass judgement.'

He gave another order and a wave of javelins hurled into our men.

I saw Madoc go down but his champion remained on his feet, side by side with the remaining Frisian and a handful of other warriors.

They stood exhausted but with scramasaxes defiantly at the ready. The last of these brave men who had set out with such high hopes this morning were now doomed.

All around them lay our bloodied dead, their sightless eyes staring unblinking up into the sky. Welshmen, on the ancestral lands they had come to reclaim. Enslaved Britons, freed at last. Outlawed Saxons, now beyond the laws of man.

The knight dismounted. 'Forward,' he ordered, raising the terrible blade aloft.

The last of my friends went to meet their fate.

From just behind me, Finn whispered in my ear, 'Flee, Edwin, flee. The knight in the crimson cape is turning his thoughts to you.'

My heart leaped at the sound of his voice. I whirled round but there was only bloodstained grass and the lonely trees.

No matter. With him to protect me I could yet survive.

I ran for my life.

Chapter 7

I knew I must not flee in the same direction as the West Saxons and our baggage train. They had gone into thick woods but beyond were marshes, a lake and the Street.

They had trapped themselves.

Mercians were relentless in the pursuit and these soldiers would hunt them down in revenge for their own dead. To the south lay Hummerwic. The people there might not hesitate to capture or kill a fleeing man, holy or not. Beyond the settlement spread the great clay valley where I could get bemired.

Instead, I ran northwards towards the River Trent. I tried to avoid going too near to Lichfield or the hill-fort we had but recently vacated. I was carrying Finn's staff. I could not remember picking it up but now, heavy though it was, I would not part with it.

The hillsides were streaming with water after the rain. Alder trees grew in the marshes that lay in every valley bottom, and the hilltops were thick with spiny gorse which tore at my clothes and flesh.

Images of the knight in the red cape filled my mind and drove me on. I ran, all the time listening for the sound of hooves or the squeal of war dogs.

All around was a maze of small hills. I rounded a slope and came upon a familiar-looking tree. Despair filled my heart for I had passed it but a few moments earlier.

Half running and half walking, I made for Rhidware.

Each step jarred my hand. To take the pain away I started to imagine the scene ahead of me. I would stand on the bank at Rhidware and call, 'God be with you.'

One or two of the Britons that dwelled thereabouts would hear my call and come through the rushes on the other side. They would see my robes and my staff.

'God be with you, too,' they would answer in their distinctive accent.

'Is it safe to cross?' I would say.

'Wait there, your holiness. We know where the bottom is sandy, the footing safe,' they would call and they would come out to carry me across. On the other side they would refuse payment from me; instead I would bless them and perhaps also bless a child or two.

'Have you any people with the river illness?' I would ask. There always was, among these dwellers by river and marsh.

They would take me into one of their small huts made of rush and reed. There, on a bed of rushes would be a sick person, trembling and feverish. After a moment or two of prayer, I would bless the poor person and the household.

And then, God grant it, I would be offered some food.

Or perhaps I would just cross the river and ask for food at the nearest door? There would be risk but they were unlikely to take captive a person in the robes of a monk.

Perhaps it would be safer to try and find something to eat along the river's edge, but what?

Even as that thought came to me my feet went into nothingness. The sky whirled and I fell headlong down a slope into water. The crashing sound of brittle reeds rent the silence. Water birds flew up with loud cries of alarm.

I cursed myself, for I knew of this great reed bed lying

between Rhidware and Lichfield. On my earlier travels through the area I had seen people cutting the reeds for roofing, yet I'd fallen into part of it.

I started to crawl out of the mud, which was belching bubbles of stinking vapour, when I heard voices.

I stopped struggling. My legs gradually sank down. Then most of my body went down. Slowly I came upright. The reed roots were entwined about my chest and right arm. I reached down with my feet, but I could not touch the bottom of the pool. I was slowly sinking into an abyss.

Chad had warned us of these pools. They were bottomless. The reeds formed mats that looked firm enough but underneath was a void. Cattle, horses, wild boar and even people had disappeared beneath the stinking layers.

The voices came closer. The mud was up to my neck and ears. I tilted my head back with my face to the sky.

'Come on out of it, Grendel, you monster,' laughed one.

Panic took me by the throat; I could feel the slime-fanged merebeast coming up to seize me. I wanted to cry out but the fear of capture froze my tongue.

'There you are, see? Nothing at all,' he continued.

'Don't joke about Grendel,' said the other. 'Look, we both heard something, right? It sounded like someone calling out, just before that noise in the reeds. The birds flew up from along here somewhere, and they don't usually scare that easily.'

This voice was quieter and more thoughtful than the first.

'Yeah, well, I'm a warrior, not a bleedin' bird-catcher like you,' said the first voice.

'I'm not a bird-catcher. I'm a farmer. I'm going back.'

'You know your problem, don't you?'

'What?'

'You ain't loyal to Aethelred.'

'Wulfhere is my king and I'm loyal to him right enough. But tell me this – how is it that his brother can call us out?'

'Look, Wulfhere is ill so he asked Aethelred to call the fyrd out. For practice, see? Aethelred's a real warrior, though. Anyone gets in his way and he chops 'em up.'

'And how would you know that, since they think you're only fit to guard this reed bed?'

'Look, I'm getting fed up with you. I was willing to go with Aethelred and the main party, but I couldn't because I'm in the church militia. Instead I was sent up here to head off any of the enemy who might flee this way,' said the militia man. 'That's tactics that is. Aethelred has lots of tricks like that, and that's why he wins all his battles. Anyway,' he continued, 'if you are such a brave warrior yourself, how is it that you were sent out here as well?'

'Same as you – to capture anybody who thinks to run this way. That includes any deserters who might want to flee to Needywood. It's already full of the king's enemies, outlaws and all sorts.'

'Deserters! What, from the enemy?'

'No, of course not. Deserters from your lot!' retorted the farmer.

The water was trickling into my ears but I wasn't sinking any more. Finn's staff, which I was clutching with my left arm, spread my weight across the reed mat. It was stopping me from sinking. Without it, I would have gone right under.

The two men fell to arguing.

'Don't you insult my mates like that or, by Great Woden, I'll cut your balls off,' protested the militia man.

'You? You could get your dick out quicker than your scramasax,' said the farmer in an agreeable voice which on an instant turned harsh as he suddenly snapped, 'Halt! Let go of the handle! Now, still want to knife me?'

'All right, all right, put up your spear. I was only joking.'

'Anyway, you're a pagan,' said the farmer, resuming his agreeable voice. 'How can you be in Wulfhere's household when he says we've all got to be Christians?'

'Oh, that? Take the spear away and I'll tell you,' the militia man said, then lowered his voice to a near whisper. 'I overheard Wulfhere tell Aethelred that the new Church was worth two legions of warriors to him, if not more, so I'm a Christian now, right?'

'Mixing with the king and his brother, eh? I see that I was wrong. You are more important at Tamworth than I thought.'

This farmer was certainly intelligent but he may have overdone the flattery this time. I was desperate to hear what he would say next. I leaned forward, and water ran into my mouth. I struggled not to cough. Luckily the militia man continued boasting. Now he was so close I could see his feet. I stared at his clay- and dung-stained shoes. At this dangerous time I found myself being fascinated by their shape. They were almost as broad as they were long. A man with feet like this could never sink into the marshes.

'Yes, well, when you're in the Great Hall,' he boasted, 'you get to hear what's going on. Wulfhere wants to be the High King of all the Saxons, Angles and Jutes. He's going to sort out Northumberland, do a quick clean-up of Wessex, and then he will be king of everything. Just think of that, all those people being loyal to my king. I might get a long scramasax, even a mail shirt out of it.'

'What about the Church of Rome?'

'Well, the priests go about frightening people with threats

of burning in hell, and telling them they've got to obey the king. That's because God has chosen Wulfhere to be the king, see? Then it's easier for Wulfhere to rule all the people, especially round here.'

'Why especially round here?'

'What, are you a foreigner or something? Didn't you know that the plague, Woden protect us, made all the clod-hoppers round here lose their faith? They all became pagans again, 'cos the Church couldn't protect them like the good old gods could. So they said they didn't owe any loyalty to Wulfhere's father, the old king, see?'

'We clod-hoppers pay for your upkeep, and a lot it costs as well,' said the farmer sniffily. 'Why don't you work for a living, like the rest of us?' Then he lowered his voice to a conspiratorial tone. 'Anyway, what did Aethelred say to that?'

'He was really angry. He's a true believer, we reckon. You know, prayers all day, and on top of some woman all night . . . Here, where are you off to?'

The farmer's voice came from some distance. 'I reckon that's enough fyrd practice for today. I'm going back to my cattle. You coming?'

'Wait for me, there's no way I'm going to be out in these fens after dark.'

His feet squelched off.

I waited till I thought it was safe, then eased myself out of the foul slime and on to the bank.

I was stiff and cold and feeling faint from hunger, but that was as nothing compared to what I felt about the fyrd. It was such unbelievable misfortune for us that Aethelred had chosen this day to take the men out. Fate had struck us the cruellest of cruel blows. I sat and bowed my head as black despair began to take over my heart.

Like a dog coming back to its own vomit my mind returned over and over again to the same questions. How could it be that the fyrd was called on the very day that the future of the Britons was about to be decided? Was it the fate of the Britons to be for ever servile? Were we being punished for trying to go against fate or was I being denied my revenge?

A groan sprang unbidden from my lips and the sudden sound of my own voice startled me into realisation of my situation.

As part of Aethelred's tactics there might have been an outpost of his men at the Rhidware ford as well. If there were, they would be coming along this path any minute now.

There was only one way for me to go.

I made towards where the sun was bending down to rest. I skirted the small cott on Long Don and made for Briar Don. I had to avoid the skyline, yet the never-ending valleys slowed me with their mire.

Each hill sucked my strength. The wind was getting fresher, and clouds moved swiftly across the greying sky.

I picked my way between a steep-sided valley thick with yellow flowering gorse on my right and an area of scrub on my left. Around me alders and ash were giving way to thinly spaced oak trees. Ahead, the ground rose steeply to the dark oaks of Cannock Forest.

In the lee of a small hummock I knelt, partly to rest and partly to pray. I needed strength, both physical and spiritual. As I rested I thought of what I should do.

I recalled that at one time Chad had taken us to mark the boundaries of the land all about Lichfield.

His dry voice came back to me. 'Edwin, take note. This hill is called Briar Don. The Britons cleared and planted it with the briar. We, like them, harvest the hips in leaf fall. The hips make a good remedy for the flux, which many of our people suffer from in the early spring. Observe the ridge of which the hill is part. It forms the boundary between the Tamsaetan people and the Wreocensaetan people. The Tamsaetan are amiable. They are content to work the land, and are loyal to their thegns and the king. They are easy to baptise, but they just as easily go back to their pagan ways. That is why we are building our church in their midst. The Wreocensaetan are spread out, but they are more warlike and in conflict with the Britons. Their land stretches far to the north and west. They will be harder to baptise.'

As Chad's words came to me I was surprised to feel no anger towards him. Perhaps I was too tired, but in any case now I knew where I had to make for.

There were dark forces at work in those never-ending trees but there would also be refuge in the no-man's land between one people and another. Forcing myself to my feet, I began scrambling up the slope.

As I entered the edge of the wood I looked back. There, below me, was a man on horseback. He appeared for a moment as he breasted a hilltop. Then he disappeared, only to come into view again but this time closer. The rider wore a crimson cape and his horse was black.

I turned and fled. Thin branches whipped at my face. I slipped on the wet forest floor. I heard the scrabbling of hooves on the slope at the edge of the forest.

The knight urged his mount on with hunting cries.

Finn's staff caught between my knees and I went sprawling. With a thump I fetched up against a huge log. I lay on the leafy floor bound and tangled with ivy stems and waited for the cruel scramasax's bite.

The knight charged on and the thin undergrowth closed behind him.

I leaped up and ran off to his left.

The horse crashed back through the undergrowth, out to the edge of the trees. It turned in my direction and made better speed. He was gaining on me.

If I went into the thicker forest I'd slow down. If I went towards the edge of the ridge I'd run into him.

Bursting through some bushes, I came out on to a narrow track. I turned into the forest and ran.

The thunder of hooves told me that he too had found the track.

I came to a fork. To the left, the track widened and became more grassy. To my right, the track narrowed, then bent. I ran to the right.

Around the bend, no more than twenty paces away, stood a huge grey wolf. 'Come, Edwin. Follow me,' it said.

There was cursing, crashing and muffled thuds behind me. The knight was pulling his horse round. I ran with the wolf. Further on, the wolf stopped. It ran on again as I came up to it. The sound of hooves was getting fainter. The horseman was falling behind.

I followed the wolf for how long I cannot say. I had lost my sense of direction and from time to time I fell. The light was almost gone. The track had petered out but I went on, spurred by occasional glimpses of the wolf.

I rounded a large oak and there he was, looking off to one side. He looked at me with yellow eyes then looked to one side again. I could scarcely see for the sweat in my eyes and the gloom but I could make out a rock face. Crouching, I forced my way up the slope to the rocks.

There, in front of me, was the mouth of a cave.

Chapter 8

Without thought of danger I squeezed into the darkness, pushing Finn's staff ahead of me. The low entrance passage was about five paces long. The cave then opened up and turned slightly to the right. Over against the right-hand side was a flat area of dry sand and there I sank down.

I placed the staff across the mouth of the chamber and wrapped myself in my mantle.

I tried to pray but I could not frame any words. My heart slowed down and began to miss beats. I felt cold, clammy and very drowsy.

A scratching sound woke me. It was very dark in the cave but I could see a severed hand and forearm as it pulled itself along the sandy floor with its fingers. It dragged itself past me and went on into the back of the cave.

I tried to stay awake but exhaustion overcame me.

I was awoken again, this time by a sad voice.

'Edwin. Edwin,' it called.

I opened my eyes. There, not more than an arm's length away, lay a head.

I recognised one of the Welshmen. He was facing me, but was looking slightly upwards.

'Edwin, oh Edwin,' he reproached me. 'You left us. They stripped our bodies. They took our torques and armbands.

They took our scramasaxes and spears. They left us for the crows and the buzzards to pick over.'

He repeated the last few words, and as he did so his right eye burst out of its socket and fell into his open mouth. Then the head faded away.

Desperate for sleep, I shut my eyes.

A thumping sound jerked them open again.

A West Saxon was standing against the back of the cave. In his right hand was a broken scramasax. He held his left arm up to ward off a blow. He tried to shrink back into the rock. Then came the swish of a war-axe and his legs, from the knees down, disappeared.

He fell. The raw stumps thudded into the ground, making the noise that woke me.

'Oh, God,' he screamed. 'I can't move. Avenge me, Edwin, avenge me or my ghost will wander for ever.'

I turned my head away and then looked back. He was standing there again, imploring me in despairing silence. The same thing happened. The same swish, the same thumping sound, the same screams.

Later I found myself sitting with my back against the cave wall. I had my knees up under my chin and I was hugging myself and weeping.

Repeatedly I had seen a Briton trying to use his fingers to keep his guts from spilling out from his sliced-open belly. Each time he had choked out, 'Help me, Edwin. Heal my wounds with herbs.'

I huddled in the dark of that ghost-ridden cave, fearful of the ghastly things in there with me, but unable to escape from them.

After agonisingly slow hours, daylight gradually filled the cave. My hunger, together with fear of the monsters in the gloom, overcame the fear of what might be outside and I felt compelled to emerge. Picking up my staff, I crawled painfully to meet the fate that awaited me, be it spear or scramasax.

It took me a long time to get into a position whereby I could see out. The morning breeze swayed the fresh-sprouting bushes and every movement made my heart pound.

A browsing deer raised its head, saw me and dashed away. The stillness of the forest gave me courage so I came out and stood up.

No arrow pierced me. No spear skewered me through.

I was standing on a small shelf about twenty paces long and five paces wide. Behind me a rock face went up nearly sheer. In front, the ground sloped down steeply. All around were the strong oaks.

To my left was a spring set back in a cleft in the rocks. Mosses and ferns grew in the cleft and water ran from the hole about a man's height from the ground. It fell into a shallow pool it had made, then ran away down the slope. The small pool was sandy, with water plants growing on its edge.

I fell to my knees and drank deeply. The pool became murky in an instant from the dried mud and blood on my hands and I resolved to wash when the day was warmer.

I made my way along the shelf and then slowly up through sparse shrubs and undergrowth. In a bare patch between the bluebells I found mushrooms, and, in a woodcock's late nest, two eggs. One smelled as though it might be edible.

I took my finds down to my shelf and there forced myself to eat. The egg almost made me retch but I remembered the cress in my waist-pouch and the dark green leaves took away the worst of the taste. The other egg smelled bad, but I kept it. It might serve as snare-bait for some animal or bird.

By midday the sun was shining on the shelf and my

shivering stopped. I put my heavy mantle and shoes aside and I washed myself, my robe and my under-linen in the pool. It was a stinking task because I had fouled myself; it had happened, I realised, at the end of the battle when the knight in the red cape had fixed me with his eye and made as if to charge at me. I spread the clothes and shoes out on the sunniest face of the rock and laid me down to rest on the short grass.

My body was bruised and my legs were cut and torn in many places but the sun warmed me and my pain and hunger were assuaged for a short time.

I dozed till the sun went behind a cloud.

I opened my eyes and was astounded to see Finn standing nearby. His head was tilted to one side a little and he was regarding me with such tenderness that tears came to my eyes. I quickly tried to stand up but I was overcome by weakness.

Raising myself up on one elbow, I called to him. 'Finn, is that really you? I implore you, come and sit by me. I cannot rise, for my legs are weak.'

He did not answer me nor make to move but simply stood in silence.

I called again. 'Finn, as you are my friend and my brother, come to me.'

Mute, he stood. His image began then to shimmer, as a reflection in the waters of a lake. I thought it was caused by my tears, and hurriedly brushed my eyes. I looked up, but he had gone.

'Finn, Finn, come back. In the name of God I beseech you, come back,' I pleaded.

I crawled over to where he had been and searched in the mean scrub and bushes bordering the shelf. As I went I called his name but my search was fruitless as I knew in my heart it would be. This was no comfort, and I crawled back to my resting place and wept.

God had been most cruel, showing me Finn in such a manner. I gained some joy from Finn's appearance, for he had not been condemnatory, but instead had looked upon me in a kindly and loving way. He had come back from the Otherworld to give me comfort. Perhaps he had forgiven me for failing him in the battle, and for my offences against Chad.

My hand began to hurt a little so I inspected it. To my astonishment I saw that although there were two raw patches on the palm and one on the thumb, the rest of the flesh was nearly healed. I could not touch my fingers to my thumb nor straighten them, though, and it still looked like a claw. No matter, I thought, my fate had guided me to Oak-man, and I gave thanks for his powerful leechcraeft.

Recollection of the day before came to me and I realised the wolf that had guided me must surely have been him. I wished strongly that he were with me again, for there was much I wanted to learn.

The sun went off the shelf and I knew that I must face night in the cave again. I had no choice for I could not walk far.

I put on my shoes and clothes, still damp, and taking my staff, crawled back into the darkness.

The cold in the cave was bearable.

My eyes swiftly became accustomed to the gloom and as I looked around something caught my eye.

A scream arose unbidden from my throat. There, on the floor of the cave, were bones. There were ribs and leg bones and a jaw. In terror I backed away and reared up. In so doing I cracked my head hard against the cruel rocks. The pain brought me to my senses.

I reached out and poked the nearest bones with my staff. They were real, not monstrous shadows.

My fears calming somewhat, I bethought me about these bones. Clearly, they were the remains of some animal's meal. I picked up the leg bones and looked at them. They were quite long and finely shaped – those of a deer.

The animal that had dragged this body into the cave would have been strong with powerful jaws. The cave entrance was too small for a grown bear, and a wild cat would not have splintered the bones so.

This was the work of a wolf.

There were fragments of meat still on the bones so, after a word of thanks to my absent host and guide, I gnawed on them until they were clean.

The light outside was almost gone. I placed the staff across the entrance to the chamber and covered myself with my mantle. It was stiff with blood and stank of slime from the marsh. It might create more monsters for me in the night, but I needed its warmth.

To keep my mind off the night-hags that were waiting for me, I forced myself to think of the Lichfield church as I had left it. I became a bird soaring far above men and their pain. I could see the church raised on the flat ground above the pool and marshes.

Beyond sparkled the great mere. I could see fish in the clear water. Below me was our little church, just a small hall with low stone walls and a tall timber roof. There was the open porch on the south side where the swifts flew in and out. I flew down and in through a gap in the eaves. It was cool inside and the light was soft.

I perched on a cross-timber. I could see the roof where it was supported by two curved arches, one across the nave and another across the chancel. I looked down on Owini's balding head and bull neck. He was calling the arches a 'bad influence'. I saw Chad. He reproved Owini, saying that they were the original Celtic arches of an earlier church and all forms of church were acceptable to God.

I flew out again and up into the sky which was full of birds. We sang our songs which grew louder and louder till the birdsong of this world awoke me.

Feeling better, I crawled to the opening with great caution.

Any person or beast without would surely have thought that a bear was coming out, for my stomach rumbled and roared so.

A hedgehog guided me to a morel mushroom and in a little clearing I came upon a few piss-the-beds. I picked some of the younger leaves and took them back to my shelf where I ate greedily.

Feeling stronger, I washed my mantle, discovering in its seams and folds shreds of human flesh that were not mine.

I spread my mantle on the rocks to dry and went back into the forest. I fashioned a cross from fallen sticks and, coming back, fixed it into the rocky wall above a smooth patch of grass. This would be my altar.

While searching for breakfast I had felt great pain in my feet. Now I saw that my shoes had dried in the night and had stiffened with a grip like that of Weyland the blacksmith's vice. I threw the shoes into the cave, ready to be greased with animal fat should the opportunity arise.

The exertion had tired me greatly and I knew that I would have to conserve my energy. I rested on my shelf and bethought me about how I should live.

I felt I could survive here if my fate intended it. While at Breedon I had lived in a smaller cave. There, in early times, the holy woman Modwen had spent much of her life before she died. I had been permitted to retreat to the cave named after her for solitary meditation.

In that cell I had begun for the first time to understand the oneness of God's work. The single thread of all his creation, from the lowliest worm to mankind, from the tiniest ant to the greatest oak, woven all together to make the whole. I learned the rudiments of harnessing the forces of this world with those of the next and those of the Otherworld. I also relearned the truths that my mother once taught me, but I had forgotten: that the spirits of the trees, the deer, the eagle, and the wild boar, all are but part of the spirit of our Lord, which is the spirit of the world itself.

Leofgifu came to mind. In her pagan beliefs she too was of one with the world and all that is in it. She, therefore, was also of the Lord.

My life's work became clear. I would live as a hermit till I had achieved wisdom.

These thoughts cheered me and I knelt to pray.

Then the hair on the back of my neck suddenly prickled.

The rite of prayer and the rhythm of the words were having their soothing effect, but part of me, that part we all share with the animals, had stayed alert.

It gave a warning: there had been a faint sound behind me and to my left.

I forced myself to stay still.

I would not yield to the nameless terrors from the battle, neither would I behave like a guilty fugitive who has been discovered by his pursuers. On my knees, head bowed, I strained to hear.

'Ho there, friend. I come in peace.'

The sudden voice made me jump. I spoke without looking

round. 'Get thee back to the Underworld, where the ghosts of dead men squeak and gibber like bats in the darkness.'

'Hold on, holy brother, don't condemn me before you know my purpose.'

I slowly stood and turned around. There on the edge of my shelf stood a Mercian with an axe.

Sharp fear tore at me but then abated when I saw that he was a woodsman and the axe was for cutting wood.

'Forgive me,' I apologised, 'but I have heard and seen many ghostly shadows of late. God has been putting me to the test.'

'Yes, well. But I am no shadow, begging your worship's pardon. I am a real man, seeking something or someone.'

'What do you seek?' I asked. 'Wisdom?'

'Ah, that would be fine,' he answered agreeably. 'For certainly I am dull of wit. No, I seek a young, yellow-haired priest, wearing a patterned mantle.'

'What would you want with such a one?' I asked, trying to still a sudden quavering in my voice.

' 'Tis not I who seek him, begging your worship's pardon. Now, I must go back and say what I have seen.'

He turned, and walked a few paces, then stopped.

'I am forgetting my obligation,' he said. 'Have you much food up here?'

'Very little. I do not need much, but some bread would be welcome.'

'Right. When I come back with the others,' he said cheerfully, 'I'll bring something for you.'

'Thank you. Farewell,' I said. Then I added hastily, 'And God bless you.'

As he slipped soundlessly away through the trees his words echoed in my ears. He was coming back 'with the others'.

I hadn't the strength to flee and I was not able to think of a plan. I could only kneel again and try to pray.

The silence of the wood was all-engulfing. Then I heard the woodsman's voice calling, 'This way, my lord.' He broke through the thin bushes and held the branches aside.

I walked stiffly to the edge of the shelf.

Looking up at me was the large man in the crimson cape, mounted on the black stallion.

Chapter 9

He sat as still as stone, regarding me intently.

'I salute thee,' croaked my dry mouth. I spoke in Latin, hoping to hide behind the formal language of the Church.

He dismounted in an easy movement and the woodsman, without bidding, ran to take the reins. The knight placed his hand on the handle of his scramasax and came swiftly up the slope towards me.

Involuntarily I backed towards my little altar.

He stopped and his gaze swept across the pool and the cave opening then came to rest on the cross. 'A hermit, eh?' he finally said, in Englisc. 'What is your name, and how came you here?'

I could do no other than to reply in the same tongue. 'My name is . . . Adhelm,' I said, giving the first name that came to mind, 'and I come from the monastery at Lastingham.'

'Yes, I'd know that accent to be Northumbrian a mile off, Adhelm,' he said nastily. 'But why come all this way to live in a cave?'

Before I could think of an answer he took a step nearer, his hand now clasping the handle of his scramasax. He smelled strongly of wood smoke. Perhaps he had just come from the Great Hall but his shoes and the stallion's legs were heavily muddied.

'How many are there here?' he imperiously demanded.

'I am a recluse . . .' I began, as loftily as I could.

Without looking round he shouted, 'Search the cave.'

The woodsman let the reins drop and ran up the slope. Unhesitatingly he fell to his knees and pushed his way into my cave. As the search proceeded the knight stood looking intently into my eyes. The woodsman emerged and reported, 'Nothing, my lord.'

'Nothing?' bellowed the knight. 'Nothing? No pots, no bedding? Was there a patterned mantle?'

The woodsman cringed before this onslaught. 'Begging your worship's pardon,' he stammered. 'There was a hermit's staff and a pair of very old shoes. Apart from that there was nothing. No, my lord. Certainly no other person and no patterned mantle.'

The knight seemed mollified by this. He turned, and while he had his back to me I quickly pulled my bandaged hand up into my sleeve. I knew I would not be able to withstand questioning about it – not from him, for sure. He walked to the edge of my shelf. There he sat down.

'Come,' he said with complete authority. 'Sit by me.'

He sat for a moment staring at his muddied shoes. On his face were little flecks of wood ash.

Then he said, as if to himself, 'I am looking for someone, but I think he is not here.'

I dared not say anything, for the relief in my voice would surely have alerted him.

'Northumberland, eh? Perhaps your father is known to me?' he asked.

'Alas, he is long since dead.'

'I see. Any uncles?'

'One, but he and my mother were slain by Picts.'

'Hmm . . . You say you were at Lastingham. Now you are here. Why are you not at Lichfield church?'

This was a question I was prepared for. 'I undertook to walk from Lastingham to Lichfield for a penance. On the way a raven told me that I was not ready for forgiveness. I am to stay near the church that is being raised. When the time is right I will be received with joy.'

'A raven told you this? What shall you do till you are received?'

'The blessed Cuthbert said that a man must work,' I said, and I pointed at the woodsman, 'or be a warrior,' and I indicated the knight's scramasax, 'or he shall pray. That is what I shall do. God grant me patience in this.'

The knight nodded. He sighed, then spoke in tones of one about to confess to an evil deed. 'Hear me. I am Aethelred, brother of King Wulfhere. He is ailing and I must do his duty for him. I am proud to do this for so great a king, descendant of Woden.'

He paused and looked up at the sky.

'I, like you, am striving to be accepted by God,' he continued. 'I would follow the Christian precepts, but many of the king's closest and most loyal companions take issue with the words of Christ.' He lapsed into silence.

After a moment I prompted him, for if ever this man were to become king, God forbid it, I must know more about him. 'Is there one precept in particular they do not accept?' I said. 'Sometimes there is explanation of them to be found in the actions of our Lord where there are no words in the scripture.'

He shook his head. 'Our Lord matched his words with his deeds,' he said with reverence. 'I will quote him. "Forgive thy enemies," and "If thy enemy smite thee, then turn the other cheek." He said these things, and he also did these things. He forgave the most terrible wrongs.'

'And the problem for the companions of the king, your brother?'

On an instant, Aethelred twisted towards me and seized my robe at the throat. 'Revenge!' he shouted. 'Revenge is all they want!'

His spittle sprayed my face as he shook me back and forth to emphasise his words. 'We are attacked, and we defeat our foes. The enemy's companions and kinsfolk then want revenge. They come by night. They come by day. They come one by one, the assassin's knife in their bosom. They come in force, wanting to avenge the death of kinsfolk who died two or even three generations ago.'

The shock that his words and action wrought turned my limbs to water. My neck was unable to hold my head steady and it flopped as he shook me.

All was lost! Aethelred knew of my mission to avenge my father!

Pain twisted and churned in my bowels like the agony that would be mine when he drove his glittering blade into me.

I wrestled with the pain. I tried to hold my head steady, and I tried to force my mind to listen to his words, to listen for the slightest hint of mercy or forgiveness in his voice.

He released me and I nearly fell backwards. My chin slumped upon my chest.

'I see you are moved,' he was saying. 'Yet there is more. I have just fought a battle with an army of Welshmen who were seeking to overthrow Wulfhere.'

My senses were returning to me but my right leg sought to betray me as it trembled and twitched of its own accord. Luckily, Aethelred took no notice of its moving, wrapped up as he was in his own troubles.

'It was three generations ago that our people drove their

forebears off this land,' he said, 'and still their descendants come back and still they want revenge. I had to kill them all, lest some escaped, but their kinsfolk will find out what took place and then they will want revenge. What is worse, they even had West Saxons with them. Our own people, Adhelm! They were claiming revenge for the chastisement that Wulfhere had been obliged to bring to Wessex.'

My heart swelled with rage at the hypocrisy of this monster who sat next to me, shaking his head in mock disbelief. 'West Saxons' and 'our own people', he'd said, in the same breath. The brutality and the butchery of the Mercian raids into Wessex were talked of in every cott and every farmhouse across the two kingdoms.

'They also claimed revenge for the death of their king, although that was not brought about by my brother,' the monster added in a peevish voice.

I dared not think how he had found that out – perhaps he had taken somebody alive. Then I suddenly remembered that, at some time before we had set off from the hill-fort, a West Saxon had slipped away.

Praying that Aethelred had not discovered my quest for vengeance, I drew his thoughts back to his near confession. 'So there is conflict between the Christian precept and the ways of our people?' I croaked.

'Conflict? Ah, yes. It is like this: I want to forgive our enemies, as Christ said we must. But the king's companions and royal thegns say that I am like a traitor because I do not want revenge. They say that I am not a true warrior and that I will bring about the downfall of the Mercian kingdom. If I do not take revenge upon the deaths of our people, they say, then I must pay the biggest wergild of all.'

'You mean they would . . . take your life as forfeit? How can they, for you are a prince of the royal household.'

'I am but one of the king's brothers. There are sisters, too. Either could be queen. But what is my life, if the Mercian people are at risk?'

We sat in silence. I fervently wished that he was not telling me these things. For all his talk of Christian precepts and his real grief, there was fresh blood on the blade of his scramasax.

'My brother believes his fate will bring him to be the High King in this land,' he continued, now quiet. 'There will be much blood spilled over it. There will be many lamenting widows and starving children. Then he must either kill all of those who would take revenge for this, or make peace with them. But he was wounded last year fighting Ecgfrith to bring Northumberland back into our Mercian kingdom.'

He looked at me and in a sharp voice said, 'Are you known to King Ecgfrith? Luck was on his side at that battle but it won't be, the next time we meet.'

Before I could reply he turned his head and stared at his feet again.

'I fear for my brother's safety as I fear for his health. I love him but his ambition sits like a fever on his brow. Whether he lives or whether he dies, I, Aethelred, will be forced to take part in this great undertaking. I beseech you, Adhelm, help me.'

As he finished speaking his head sank upon his chest and he seemed to shrink with the very weight of his burden.

The thought came to my mind that if I could say something pleasing to him, then perhaps I might be able to come out of hiding. I could even seek his patronage, despite his hypocrisy and swings of mood, if he ever became king.

I spoke gently to him. 'We should pray for guidance. But

from whom? Will you choose, Prince Aethelred? Should we seek help from Tiw, mighty in battle, or from Christ, the forgiver?'

A groan escaped his lips as he said, 'You have seen into my heart. I am trying to ride two horses at once.'

We sat in silence.

Then he spoke again but this time in a much stronger voice. 'How wise you are, Adhelm, for now I realise that I cannot fight my battle with the daemon of revenge until God helps me to choose between the new gods of Rome and the old gods of our people. I will ask him to help me.'

He seemed reluctant to leave. He took off his helmet and raked at his scalp with his fingers. He stretched out his legs and turned his toes in.

His helmet with a boar's head on the crown was tarnished and scratched. His shirt of mail was pulling apart in places and was patchy with dark stains. The crimson cape that had caused me such fear was muddied and torn.

His gold-adorned scramasax, his mail shirt and the fine gold and garnet clasp that held his cape around his shoulders indicated his wealth and high rank, yet at this time he seemed like any other man.

I took a chance and asked, 'You say you were looking for someone. May one ask as to the nature of this person?'

Aethelred looked up at the sky and the branches of the oaks where the fresh green leaves were beginning to appear.

'At the battle there was a young, yellow-haired monk wearing a patterned mantle. Monks who support an enemy can cause great trouble, for they can turn the tide of battle with their prayers. I would have liked to question him but he ran off. I bethought me that he was here but it seems he has fled far away. But let me ask you a question instead.'

He looked at me with a smile about his lips. 'This is my question,' he said. 'We – that is Wulfhere and myself, our families and most of the people – would be baptised and embrace the Lord through Christ, yet many of our people still worship trees. Pagan Mercians, Adhelm! What think you to that?'

He seemed to be at ease with himself now but I felt most uncomfortable. All the while I had a feeling that he was testing me. Were I to speak falsely he would become wrathful and wreak some awful thing upon me.

'To worship trees is wrong,' I replied, as evenly as I could, 'but to revere them is understandable and acceptable. Trees are our life here on earth. They are our brothers.'

His blue eyes were regarding me with a look as cold as winter ice.

I continued, even as my mouth was drying, 'We should remember that our Lord owed his early sustenance to the wood of the tree, for Joseph was a carpenter. We must also remember that Christ left this earthly life held aloft in the embrace of the tree of glory. Not only can we all witness the giving of his life so that we may live, but his fate as the god who bled also reminds us of our bond with trees. Reverence for trees is reverence for the spirit and for life.'

Aethelred nodded slowly then said, 'Another question. What do you think of the story of Noah? His boat was made of wood, was it not?'

'Yes, indeed, and that story, too, shows us how we are beholden to trees and what they give us, for without timber from the trees the boat would not have been built and mankind would have perished.'

'If the story is true, then where are all the beasts that were in the boat?' he demanded. 'There are many snakes hereabout, yet a man from Ireland told me there are none in that land. There is a great dragon in the north lands, yet there are no dragons here in Mercia. Why is that?'

'It is a true story, but it has hidden meaning.'

'Hidden meaning, eh?' he said quietly, closing his eyes and leaning back on one elbow. 'Tell me of it.'

'Almighty God first made the world, the wide fields, surrounded by the seas. Then he made the sun and the moon. Then he covered the earth with trees, and then he made all things that move,' I said.

'Yes, yes, I know well that poem,' he said, 'but where is the hidden meaning?'

Where indeed? Against my will I turned my head and looked at his face. The fear-making blue eyes were still closed. I had sought to tell him the Northumbrian story of the Creation but seemingly it was as well known in Mercia as it was at home.

In desperation I started to make a tale. 'The trees were made first before all other things on the face of the earth so that . . . so that . . .'

My voice was beginning to fade, and I took refuge in a cough. Aethelred fidgeted and rearranged his scramasax to make himself comfortable.

I gave thanks to God for his helping hand.

'Of all the things on earth, God first made trees so that warriors could have lime wood for their shields, ash for their spears, oak for their fine halls, and sweet apple for their fires,' I babbled. 'The warriors grew strong and were at first able to protect their lands and their families against the giants, the elves and monsters. But the people fell into wicked ways and became unable to defend themselves. Then God forgave them and sent a great flood to drown the giants. Because

95

we had wood we could build a boat and so we were saved. The hidden meaning is that we should respect trees. That is perhaps why they are venerated and even worshipped.'

He frowned, and I added hastily, 'Though mistakenly, of course. But if we do not venerate trees, then the flood will return and we shall all perish.'

'And the snakes and the dragon?'

'In Ireland they follow the Lord, so he took away the loathsome snake. But in the lands of perpetual snow they are yet wicked, and so they are beset with dragons.'

'Hmm,' he said, and sat up. 'Back there in the depths of the forest,' he said, jabbing a thumb over his shoulder, 'they do more than just worship trees,' and as if he had reminded himself of something, pulled on his helmet. He stood up.

'Here, woodsman. You have done well,' he called out. He unfastened the purse at his belt and took out a silver coin which he tossed to him. 'You may tell your thegn that I am well pleased with you.'

He turned to me and I scrambled to my feet.

'Your grasp of the scriptures is impressive,' he said, 'but I prefer the Noah story as told by one of your brother monks. He says it is the story of our own people. Great floods came to the Angles and Saxons in their old land. It drowned all the wicked giants, but God told our forefathers to build boats and into them went the people together with their animals and their women. Then God showed them the way to this land. To this land, you see?'

I nodded vigorously.

'We are God's chosen people,' he went on, stabbing his chest with his finger as he spoke. 'It is God's will that the Mercians shall be rulers of all.' A fervent look came into his eyes and he continued in an excited voice. 'God gave us ascendancy over the Britons, the Welsh, the Picts – all the lower people,' he said. 'That is the meaning of the story. We must worship him, not trees or animals.'

His voice became more prosaic. 'Yes,' he said. 'You will try your knowledge against this monk who often comes to the Great Hall. His name is Owini. Not only does he tell me stories that I like, he is a stickler for correct procedure.

'No doubt he will tell us that according to the synod of Hertford, monks cannot wander from place to place without permission from their bishop. No doubt you will show us why you can.'

He laughed at his own witticism and I forced a grin of appreciation.

'Your arguments must surely entertain and instruct King Wulfhere and myself,' he went on. 'Especially me, for I know little of the Church people in this diocese. My interest is in the church of Peter at Peterborough and the cathedral abuilding there. However, you shall stay here till we send for you. It will give you a chance to practise your arguments before you pit yourself against Brother Owini, eh? But I warn you, if you lose the argument I will put you on bridge-building duties, old though you may be.

'Now, I give you thanks for the guidance you have given me. God bless us both. Farewell.'

Without waiting for any reply he went down the slope to his stallion. The woodsman ran down and made a back for him. Numbly I watched him take up the reins. He seized the fine red leather saddle and, stepping on the woodsman's back, swung himself up on to the huge black horse.

As he turned its head away he raised one arm in salute.

Chapter 10

I sank to the ground, bereft of strength.

The woodsman came back to me. 'Begging your worship's pardon,' he said. 'He is a powerful man, is he not?'

'Yes,' I barely managed to say, 'and he is agreeably pious.' Then my voice strengthened and I said, 'But what has he been doing that he is so muddied and covered with wood smuts?'

'He was in a battle with some invaders. He slew most of them but some escaped into a wood just away from here, down near Hummerwic. The forest there is so thick that he could not get his men safely into it. I heard that among the foe were West Saxons. Whoever they were, they fought back bravely.'

He continued to speak, but in a curiously flat voice as if talking of something that was of no concern to him. 'That seemed to make him very wrathful, so he fired the wood. It's still aflame but they'll all be burned to death by now.'

I could scarcely believe what he was saying.

'Did no one escape?' I said.

'We of the fyrd wanted to let them out and make slaves of them but Aethelred said they must all die.'

'You wanted to let them out? You mean . . . ?'

'Yes,' he said, 'they were screaming and trying get out but Aethelred forced his spearmen to drive them back.'

Grief overwhelmed me and I sat with head bowed.

'Shall we pray to the Lord Jesus to forgive Aethelred?' I began, but the woodsman cut me short.

'There can be no forgiveness for him, not for that foul deed. And what's more, many people depended on that woodland for their livelihood; there will be starvation among his own people now. Double death must have its own reward,' he said, with a flash of anger in his light eyes, 'but you can pray to your Jesus if you want. I have my own beliefs.'

He paused while he contained his emotion, then he said, 'But thank you for trying. I respect that in a man. Here . . .' He opened a pouch at his waist and brought out some bread and a small bag of wet cheese. He cut the hard bread into chunks with a sharp knife and handed me the food. 'Take this. It's not much, but later on I'll bring you more.'

I thanked him then asked, 'When you were first here, you said that you would come back with others. Instead you came back with Aethelred. What was the reason for that?'

'The reason? When I saw that . . . that grim deed with the fire, I said to my thegn that I would no longer do such devilish work. It is the duty of the fyrd to defend the land, not to do these things.'

My respect for this man increased. Not only was he outraged at the cruel slaughter but he was also prepared to go against his thegn. He ran the risk of getting a scramasax between the ribs for rebellion. The risk was much higher when the king and his companions were about, for thegns who failed to keep order were themselves swiftly punished.

'My thegn told me to search for the yellow-haired monk because I knew the woods better than any. He sent two soldiers with me – they were searching further down. In the meantime, someone told Aethelred about my disobedience and he came after me, to cut me in twain. It was lucky for me that I came across you. Before he could do me harm I told him of my discovery of an old hermit in a cave. Thank the gods, he straightway lost interest in me.'

I was aghast at this tale. The man Aethelred was surely a monster. I looked at the woodsman but he seemed unconcerned about the recent threat to his life.

'But will you ever be safe again with him? He will know you again, surely?'

'Well, it may be, but it was not my fate to be slain this day. You remarked the coin he gave me? It is his way. He does a terrible thing, then he is bitterly remorseful and gives his possessions to those he has offended. If they still live, that is.'

Our eyes met and in our despair and disbelief we laughed together.

'Now,' he said firmly, 'I must go. My name is Wihtred and, as I said, I shall return, for I feel a bond between us, even though you are a monk.'

'I shall welcome you. God be with you,' I said, not fully understanding his last remark.

Wihtred turned and walked off through the bluebells covering the woodland floor.

He didn't look back and I was glad, for I did not want him to see that my earlier fears had returned. While we were talking the spirits of the slain had been held at bay but I sensed that now he was gone they would be coming at me again. I sat with my back against the rock face and waited.

A severed head rolled slowly by, the eyes fixed upon mine. I could see the yellow teeth in its mouth. The head fell out of sight over the edge of my shelf. A noise to my left made me turn. Dodging between the trees came a headless man clutching a scramasax in his only hand. He moved swiftly and as he came closer I lost sight of him. I jumped up, ready to flee. For long moments I stood but he did not reappear.

I sat me down again and looked to left and to right, in case the grotesque figure caught me unawares.

I must have dozed, for I awoke with a start. The sun was losing its power and I needed to eat. I gave thanks to Wihtred for the bread and the wet cheese. I found it very rich after my earlier fare but I knew it would sustain me till the next day.

As I ate, my eye fell upon the woodsman's knife. He had left it propped against the rock face by the pool when he had cut my bread. I thought I should return it but I had no notion whatever as to the direction I should take. Besides, I was too weak to go far. He would return.

I thought back on what I had heard. Both Aethelred and Wihtred seemed certain that I was not the man they sought. My mantle, soaked with fresh blood, had caused it to be taken for a patterned one. I gave thanks to God that I had washed it. I sucked the juices from the cheese cloth and licked the breadcrumbs from my robe. Then it was time to drink. I went to my little pool and knelt to take a handful of water.

Staring out at me from the water was a demented-looking old man with bloodshot eyes and a mop of pure white hair. I whirled around, ready to face yet another daemon. There was no one there.

I looked back into the pool. There he was again. I reached up and touched my face and the aged loon did the same.

I became faint as the truth reached my benumbed mind and I struggled to keep upright. Dimly I perceived that I had shape-changed. The old truths were asserting themselves. I had been bewitched and my own body had been stolen away. Where were my brown eyes, and my yellow hair that

Leofgifu loved to comb? What thing had come in the night to suck the strength out of my body?

I groaned as the awful truth struck home like a murderer's heart-hungry knife.

I was being punished for my wrong doing. I had abandoned my gods and they had stolen my body in revenge. I had also fled unharmed from the field of battle. Cowards were hanged from a tree or pressed to death in a swamp, but none of my battle comrades was left alive to do what should be done.

I had no choice but to do it for them. In that way I might atone for my despicable behaviour.

I reached out and took up the knife that Wihtred had forgotten. The cool iron edge was sharper than any bronze razor. With its eager help I would reach the Otherworld, where, although I didn't deserve it, I might join Finn.

Even as I placed the edge against my throat something held me back. Although in deep despair I knew that to kill myself would be a mistake. Suicide to cheat an enemy of victory or revenge is noble, but the spirit of a person who commits cowardly suicide haunts the scene of that sad deed for eternity.

My limbs lost their strength. I fell sideways and my face went into the ground. I lay with grass and leaves in my open mouth. I was too weak to cry. I was too weak to groan. I lay on my lonely shelf in the fading light and waited to die.

Chapter 11

'Adhelm, Adhelm, wake up! Woden grant that we are not too late.' Hands were shaking me and Wihtred's voice penetrated my befogged mind.

'Here, roll him over. Help sit him up.'

I opened my eyes. A boy was helping the woodsman.

'It is not your fate to die just now,' said my friend. 'You'll be here on Middlearth for a long time yet.' His voice was cheerful but his eyes were anxious. 'What were you doing sleeping out in the open in your state? And look, here is my knife. Were you keeping it warm for me?'

Feeling came back to my bones in waves of pain.

'Fetch the warm ale, boy,' said Wihtred.

The lad went to a back-sack stuffed with straw and lifted out a clay pot. Wihtred removed the bung and held the pot to my lips. The ale must have been only blood warm but fire raced through my veins as I sipped it.

'Good, eh? Strong Welsh ale. Just what you need.'

'I must have slipped,' I croaked. 'Who is the lad?'

'This is my son. I am teaching him the woodsman's craeft. I sent him up here at first light to get my knife and he found you sprawled out. He was unable to rouse you, so he ran all the way back to fetch me.'

'Thank you,' I said to the boy. 'I hope one day to be able to repay you.'

'It weren't nothin',' he said, twisting a toe into the grass. 'Besides, I don't want anything from—'

Wihtred interrupted him, 'Now, unpack the things we've brought, there's a good lad. The food goes into the cave.'

The boy nodded and went over to a larger pack standing near the cave entrance. Out of it he took some bundles and went into my lair.

My woodsman friend gave me meat and bread then watched me eat.

'I am not going to be able to come and see you for some time now,' he said. 'I am wanted to fell trees and make more timbers for the new church. Wulfhere has given money so now the bishop can pay me for my work. The timber is to come from the oaks at Burrow Cop, a place on the other side of Lichfield, a long way from here.'

I noticed that he was explaining things to me as if I were a stranger to the area but I made no comment about it. 'Your boy doesn't like monks?' I said.

'With cause,' he said. 'When they were building their new house by Lichfield church they dug up some graves – Saxons and a few Britons. Because they weren't Christian remains, the monk in charge wanted to throw them on the midden. People got very upset about that.'

I desperately wanted to tell him that I was living at Hints when that happened, and had nothing to do with the incident, but I also felt I had to keep up the pretence that I was a hermit and out of touch with events.

'Pagan Saxon and Briton – were they forgotten burials?'

'Not by us. They were our people.' Seeing the look on my face, he explained, 'Grandfather's first wife was Saxon. They lived at Curborough. She died of the river sickness and he married again, this time a Briton – she was my grandmother. That's where they are buried.'

'That is truly dreadful,' I said. 'The bishop should always be told when graves are discovered.'

'If I lived in Lichfield village I would have seen the work start and told them. But I live at Alrewasse and only heard about it later.'

'Alrewasse! It is well named' – I laughed, trying to get off a subject causing him so much pain – 'for there never was such a marshy place to be, among those ancient alders.'

'How do you know that?' he shot at me.

'I . . . I came through it on the way here,' I hastily said. 'Down the Portway then across the river near Alrewasse.'

We sat in silence.

'What of you?' he said. 'I tell you of myself, but what of you?'

'We have things in common. My mother was a Briton. My father was Angle, from Northumberland.'

'I suppose that is so,' he said. 'But your appearance . . .'

'Truly, it is so,' I said excitedly. 'Look at me. Can't you tell from my brown eyes and yellow hair?'

He fell silent. I shut my eyes and leaned back, hoping against hope that he hadn't realised what I'd said. I half opened my eyes as he suddenly moved, but he only went over to the cave where he talked to the boy for a moment.

'The lad and me are going to forage around,' he said, coming back. 'We'll try to find some better bedding and some wood so you can make a fire. In the meantime, have a rest – you look tired out.'

I rested against the rock in the warmth of the sun. I felt guilty at being suspicious of Wihtred, and I did not like having to deceive him about my identity. Should the opportunity arise in the future, I would tell him the truth, but for now . . .

I awoke with a start. The sun was going off the shelf. The boy was stretched out on the grass, asleep with his head on his arms.

Wihtred was sitting by me, poking moodily at the ground with his knife.

When at last he spoke, he began slowly. 'Adhelm – if that is your name – there are more twists and turns in your tale than there are in a magic maze.'

Now he appeared to be scratching in the earth to some purpose.

'For a newcomer, you seem to know a lot about this part of Mercia. You were frightened of Aethelred; why should you as a monk have reason to be frightened of him? You went pale at the mention of Owini yet he is a fellow brother in the Church. You seem weak and exhausted yet there is fat on your flanks. You think you have yellow hair and brown eyes. I see white hair and watery bloodshot eyes. You are in this cave which is known only to a few of us and the wolves.'

He paused, and began to make a row of short lines in the earth with the knife.

'You also have a staff with secret marks upon it.' As he spoke my heart had grown heavier and heavier. I must have looked full dejected, for he when he spoke again, it was with a gentle voice.

'Can you not tell me what is in your mind?' he asked.

I was torn between telling him and trying to conceal what I had done. He had befriended and helped me. I tried one more time to fend off his probing, gentle though it was.

'It is not right that we should argue,' I began feebly, 'but you make a lot from a little. You have builded a house of straw upon a bed of sand.'

The old saying neither annoyed nor amused him. Instead he simply said, 'My boy showed me the carving on a square section of your staff. Without his sharp eyes I would not have seen it. It is in the Irish ogham writing and says, "Finn had me made". Because of the writing, my boy thinks you must really be of the British Church and so are to be trusted. What shall I tell him?'

The knife had been busy as he spoke the last words and now a full-sized face with strong features was looking up at me from the earth. The sad yet wise eyes reached into my heart and filled me with a great yearning to tell the truth. Unable to withhold my story, I poured it out to Wihtred, beginning from when I first arrived at Lichfield. He listened intently, nodding from time to time. When I came to where the wolf had guided me to the cave he looked at me with a strange expression on his face but said nothing.

'And now I am here,' I ended. 'I can run no longer. I must yield to my fate.'

'And what is your fate to be?'

'How can anyone know? But I am convinced that whatever is going to happen to me will happen in Lichfield. That may seem strange to you, perhaps?'

Wihtred shrugged but said nothing.

'There is little to be seen in the village,' I continued. 'The mere, houses . . . the mill. The church, of course, but there is something else which is pulling me there. Do you feel it? Did others feel it: the people who buried their treasure under the Elderford and Swinefen lows, for instance?'

Wihtred lifted a protesting hand to stop me. 'Of course we feel the power,' he said. 'It is a sacred place – a bottomless lake with rivers and forest all round it. The annual sacrifice to the water goddess makes the power even stronger. The British Christians were jealous so they stopped the Britons sacrificing to her. And now these Roman Christians want to stop our people sacrificing to her. If she gets angry she might summon the dragons from those lows, then there'll be trouble for us.' He shook his head, seemingly puzzled by such stupidity, then said, 'Do the Roman Christians feel the power?'

He went on, without waiting for an answer, 'I suppose they do, that's why they build here. It must give them some advantage, somehow.'

I noticed that his disparaging remark about 'these Roman Christians' didn't seem to include me. Clearly, he assumed I was of the British Church. I let it go. Besides, there was something I needed to confirm.

'What sort of sacrifice did they make?' I asked.

'Animals, mainly. Sometimes jewels or weapons. Now and then prisoners; but why are you asking me that? You ought to know.'

'It was talked of at Lastingham, and when I came down here Chad showed us places where it had been done, but I've never seen weapons sacrificed, or anything like that – especially not prisoners.'

'People round here are too poor to sacrifice weapons or jewellery now,' he said. 'Anyway, they need their scramasaxes to protect themselves against the Welsh and the Northumbrians – no offence to you, of course. These days, food does quite well for sacrifice. It has to be something that means a lot, you see?'

We sat in silence for a while, then Wihtred turned to me and said, 'My grandfather's spirit came to see me a few nights ago, while I was sleeping. He came with bad news about our religion. He seemed to be warning me of trouble ahead. These things make me uneasy, Edwin.'

He started to gather his things together.

'You and I will talk about this more,' he said. 'But first things first. You are nearly asleep, the light is going and I must be off. I will speak to my niece and she will bring food. Although she is sometimes erratic in her behaviour you can trust her. Farewell, and may the lord of the forest protect you.'

Picking up his belongings, he called to his son, and they went.

I sat unmoving for some hours after their going. I wanted to sleep but my mind was turning over and over.

What did it portend that Wihtred's grandfather had come with a warning? Wihtred was no unthinking pagan believer (he had been tutored: his ability to read Ogham showed that) yet the ghost brought bad news about his religion. Was it intended as a warning to me?

Finn and Madoc were fine examples of men strong in their British Christian belief, as were the Britons I worked among.

King Wulfhere's pagan father had slain the King of Northumberland – a Christian of the Church of Rome – yet now King Wulfhere himself encouraged the Roman Christians to build churches, instal bishops and oust the British Christians. Where did his loyalties lie?

Chad had appeared to slip from one Church to the other with little trouble; something I found impossible to emulate.

Where should I place my loyalty and faith?

'To that which is true, of course,' I answered myself, and I realised that I had spoken aloud. But what is it that is true?

I had no answer to my question and there seemed no way

to find out, either. I was being torn between three faiths, yet all had failed me – or I had failed them.

A thought came to me: is truth certainty? There had been certainty in my life – I would find the man who had killed my father and I would kill him. That was something I knew would happen and therefore it was a true thing. I drew comfort from that, but the comfort faded as I realised that my fate had taken away the chance to do that. The outcome of the battle meant I was further away than ever from avenging him.

Fate was truth! I seized hold of this new thought like a dog snapping on a rat. Whatever actually happened was true, and since one's fate determined what happened, fate was truth.

I had scarcely started to take pleasure in that thought when I began to lose confidence in it. The Church of Rome rejected belief in fate completely, saying that it flew in the face of belief in God. That was a hard thing to accept, for all Saxons knew that their fate governed their lives, so what was there for me to believe in?

As I sat alone and forsaken in my misery, a recollection came to me of how, as a boy, I had gone to the coast. The great waters had looked so calm that I had walked in their edge. Suddenly a vast wave had swept over me, knocking me down, filling my lungs with water, and nearly taking me back into the depths. My father had rushed to me and had pulled me out of the water.

In just such a way had the events of the past days all but engulfed me, but now I had no father to save me.

I was nearly overcome with despair and I felt tears well up in my eyes. My only wish then was to be with Leofgifu.

I decided to make a sacrifice to Freya to bring her to me. There would be risk for she sometimes took it amiss when cowardly people sacrificed to her but I felt I had nothing to lose.

Recalling Wihtred's words, I made sacrifice with the few drops of ale and crumbs of bread that were left.

I crawled into my cave. There I found that Wihtred and his lad had made me a fine bed of moss and ferns, and I gratefully laid myself upon it. His kind act raised my spirits a little, and my gloom began to lift. Then, at that very moment, Freya sent a dart of fear through my heart. Leofgifu could already be dead! The last time I'd seen her was at the fort. She could have been captured by the Mercian soldiers and hacked to death or hanged as a traitor. She might be brought to me, but in some terrible broken or bloodied form.

I had acted unthinkingly and now it was too late.

Chapter 12

'Edwin! . . . Edwin!' came Leofgifu's voice, calling.

She called again. Feeling excited yet fearful I rose and went to see what I might see.

She was standing just below me on the slope, looking about her. She was so beautiful to behold that tears started to my eyes. I called her name and she looked up. As she caught sight of me she could not conceal the gasp that sprang from her lips.

With some effort I went down the slope and embraced her, partly fearing that my arms would pass through her. She was, all praise to Freya, solid enough. I tried to help her up the slope with the large sack she was carrying but instead got in her way. Back on the ledge she took off her cape and scarf and laid them to one side.

'What's in the sack?' I asked.

'Food, clothes and other things for you, from Wihtred.'

'He's your uncle? Why didn't you tell me about him before?'

'You've never been interested in my family. The only time was when you asked me when and how my parents died,' she replied, and although she said it with a little smile, I felt annoyed that people were talking about me. I must have pulled a face for she added, 'And I didn't tell you about Wihtred and the others because all our family are what you call "pagans". You'd have only got upset about it, especially as the Church of Rome means us mischief. It might have caused trouble for you.'

She clasped me in her arms again.

'Hold me tight, Edwin. I was so happy when Uncle Wihtred told me to take these things to a hermit in the cave. I knew immediately that it must be you. I'd thought you were dead. I searched the bodies, but they were so badly . . . I couldn't find you.'

'I ran away,' I said. 'I ran from the battle, just as I ran from the ordeal.'

'You didn't "run away" from the battle; you couldn't since you weren't fighting, and you didn't have a thegn to be loyal to.'

'I left Finn on the field.'

Her face clouded when I said that, and she replied heatedly, 'Finn was a good friend to both of us, but you didn't owe him death loyalty. And you went through ordeal, didn't you? You could have run away from that, but you went through with it. What Finn did was to make you run away from the gaol. Without him you would not be in this mess. Now help me undo the sack.'

As we unpacked I came across a mysterious item wrapped in soft moss. I unwrapped it and found myself holding a small wooden figure about two hand-spans tall. He was boldly ithyphallic and two horns sprouted from his forehead. He was painted dark brown, and had yellow hooded eyes.

'Why give me this?' I asked her.

'Cernunnos? Wihtred made him for you to draw strength from. I like the name Cernunnos; it sounds nicer than Herne, but it means the same.' She smiled, running her finger over the figure. 'He's not only the forest god, you know, but also the god of malehood.'

'Wihtred carves pagan gods, yet he also cuts timber for the new church?'

'Yes. And when he shapes the timbers he carves magic signs on them. It brings good fortune to the church. As long as people continue to respect the gods of the forest, sky and water they will never let harm come to the churches even though they are built for the new gods. The old and new gods are the same, of course, just with different names.'

I looked at the figure in my hand.

'I don't know,' I said. 'It is made with great craeft but Rome says we are not supposed to have such things.'

'Who is "we"?' she said. 'Now, help me take these things into your hidey-hole.'

She was right, of course. I did not know what I was or who I belonged to. She took the sack with my new clothes and began to drag it with her into the cave entrance.

To avoid kneeling on the hem of her tunic she gathered up the loose material in her free hand. This action raised the hem. I knelt to follow her and was bewitched by the sight of the backs of her bare knees. Her hips widened when she knelt and they swayed as she pushed into the cave. Herne regarded me with knowing eyes; I seized him tightly and followed her into the seclusion of the cave.

'You can use this sack as bedding but it may be better used to fetch food when you go about. Here are a pair of shoes. Wihtred guessed the size but I think he had it aright. I will take these old ones of yours back with me, and I will grease them for you.'

As she spoke she arranged various things around my cave.

'Two pots. One for drink, the other for storage. Here's a small knife – it will go in your waist-purse. Don't lose it,' and she waved the knife at me. She carried on chattering. 'And a wooden platter. Here is fresh under-linen. I couldn't get a new monk's robe, of course. Not without stripping one of those do-gooders from the new church, I couldn't.' She laughed at her own joke.

I watched her hungrily, not really listening to her talk.

'Now then, Edwin, oops, I mean Adhelm, take off that under-tunic and put this on. I'll take it back and clean it for you.'

I knelt up and pulled off my robe. Then I slipped my under-tunic off. I made no move to put the new one on, but knelt, as I was.

Leofgifu looked at me and came close. In the dim light she examined the bruises on my body. She traced the small scar on my hip with her fingertip. She knelt up and pulled off her woollen tunic. Then she raised her arms and took off her own linen under-tunic. It was longer than mine and she struggled as her arms touched the low roof of the cave. I leaned forward and slipped off her remaining garment. She put it down carefully, and turned to face me.

We knelt in silence looking at each other. She had her back to the light from the cave entrance. It lit up the fine golden hair on her arms, her flanks and her thighs and made her outline glow as if she were made of gold. I looked at her full breasts, the rich globe of her belly, and the darker hair below. I had taken her before, but this time her female mystery filled me with awe and made me not a little afraid.

'You are beautiful,' I whispered, my voice hoarse with the beginnings of passion.

'Come to me, Edwin, don't be afraid,' she whispered softly and drew me to her. I seized her and pressed my lips to hers. Her smell filled my nostrils and I kissed on her neck and shoulders. As I kissed her breasts her nipples began to stand.

All the while she was running her hands round the nape of my neck, and up and down my back.

I bent and kissed her belly. I pushed my hand between her thighs. She opened them wider. I pressed my mouth more firmly against her mouth. I gently bit her nipples, now standing as large as the end joints of my fingers. She made small noises and I could feel that she was ready.

I took one of her hands and pressed it against me. She reached with both hands. Her small, strong fingers cupped, squeezed and pulled. A deep groan burst from my lips. I kissed her mouth and her rapid breathing filled me with her moist breath.

I fiercely bit and kissed her neck. I violently kissed and squeezed her breasts.

My body was not responding. I was limp and shrunken. There was no fire in me – nothing, nothing.

Now she was crushing her swollen breasts against my chest and raking my buttocks with her nails. I put my arms around her and pinned her arms to her side.

'I am no longer a man,' I said into the soft warmth of her body. 'My hair has gone white, I have no strength and now I can no longer mount you.'

Her rapid breathing slowed and she comforted me as her voice caught and wavered with subsiding passion. 'Poor, dear, Edwin,' she whispered, stroking me gently. 'This happens to men who've been in battle. Your white hair as well. My grandmother told me this might happen. Don't worry. It will get better, it will all come back again.'

She turned away from me and started to dress herself. I pulled on my clean under-tunic and my robe. I felt angry and sad at the same time. I picked Herne up. Now his eyes were mocking me so I threw him to the far end of the cave.

'I shall have to become a celibate,' I cried angrily. 'Herne has bewitched me. He has stolen my sap.'

Leofgifu turned and faced me. 'No, it was my fault, I was too eager. We must be patient. He helped you part of the way. Soon you will travel the whole path. And, the gods willing, it will be with me.'

How ashamed I felt. My anger was with myself, not her or Herne. I took both her hands and kissed her gently on the lips.

'Dear Leofgifu, you shall be my life companion. I vow it.'

I could say no more for I was filled with remorse.

We went out of the cave and sat on the grass. There was a faint smell of smoke on the air from the burning wood to the south. Leofgifu handed me bread and meat. I was not greatly hungry but I ate.

'Shall I tell you what's happening?' she said.

I nodded.

'The monks have caused a wooden cross to be set up in the street among the houses in the village till the new church is done,' she said, disapprovingly, 'and the bishop does his preaching to the people there.'

'Is the cathedral work going well?'

'While Wihtred is working he overhears the monks and Bishop Wynfrid. They talk of it finishing soon. Owini shouts a lot. People's houses near the church have been pulled down, though no one knows why. Oh, and what seem to be defences have been made along the edge of the mere, but I don't know why.'

'Wihtred overhears the monks, does he? Could he take them a message?'

'I am sure he could, but if he would is another matter.'

'Why do you say that?'

'There's hardly one of them he would trust. The monks

and the church militia took our figures of Woden away, and
they try to stop us worshipping him.'

'You worship Woden, yet you and Wihtred revere Cernunnos – a god of the Britons! Wihtred carves idols yet
fashions beams for the Church of Rome. What beliefs do you
have?'

'Well, what about you?' she retorted. 'First it's Woden and
then it's Jesus. I don't mind that, we all do it. But I get angry
when you laugh at our beliefs.'

'I don't.'

'Yes, you do! Up in the fort you laughed at my leechcraeft,
asking if it was good against shot of elves. And you said
unkind things about Cernunnos. But you didn't mind calling
on him just now when you . . . you wanted to fuck me!' She
shouted the last bit and tears welled up in her eyes.

'Don't be angry with me, Leofgifu,' I said. 'I've been
through great torments. I love you, you know that, but my
thoughts are . . . well, I don't know what I believe any more,
and it's getting worse.'

She came and sat next to me. She put her arm round my
waist and her head against mine.

'You say unkind things, but I know you love me, so I'll
help you,' she said. 'First you should respect all beliefs. If you
do, it will stop people using you to get what they want.'

I tried to nod, but her head was against mine so she nodded
with me and it made us laugh.

'Then you must find a belief that works.'

'Yes. But how do you find out if it works?'

'Well, I don't know what monks want,' she said. I
squeezed her and she gave a giggle. 'Apart from that,' she
said. 'But stop it, I'm trying to be serious. We want winter to
end and spring to start at the right time. We want rain and

sunshine for good crops. Those things, that's what we want, and our gods give it to us. That's why we believe in them.'

'But Jesus can do that. The story of the sower and the seeds – that's all about getting good harvests.'

'My grandmother says the stories of the Church of Rome are simply our own stories told in other ways.'

'Your grandmother seems to know a lot of things.'

'Yes. She is a Wise Woman. But your Church calls her a witch.' She snorted in disgust. 'A witch, indeed. The fact is, Edwin, your Church cannot accept that other people have their own beliefs. They call our gods "daemons". I think they're frightened of the power of the true faith.'

'Look, I can't explain it to you now,' I said. 'What I really want you to do is to ask Wihtred to give a message to Brother Trumhere. You can trust him. Will you do that for me?'

She nodded.

'Good,' I said firmly. 'Now, this is the message. Tell Trumhere that I am repentant and living the life of a hermit. Ask him if it is safe for me to return. That is the message. Do you think you can remember that?'

'I am not a child,' she said tartly. 'But how do you propose that the reply, if any there be, shall come back to you?'

'Why, I was hoping that you would . . .'

'I shall do it, Edwin, because I feel love for you, but sometimes the things that you say cause me great sorrow.'

'I'm sorry, Leofgifu, but I have to be master. That is the natural order of things.'

'The natural order of things?' she flared. 'What is that nowadays? Our kings are descendants of Woden, but now they turn to this new Church of Rome. If they think they can get more power, more advantage from these new ideas then they accept them without delay.' She was looking dismayed.

'Our kings, our thegns, the priests – they are all like . . . like children standing before a bush of ripe blackberries,' she said. 'They reach here, they reach there, not knowing where to start first. They stuff their mouths with whatever tastes nicest.'

She paused for a moment, then continued in a sad voice, 'They seem to think that being able to pick and choose will somehow make them wiser, but if they turn their backs on the true gods . . .'

'Yes, what will happen then?'

'Then we will live in never-ending winter if they stop sacrificing to Hreda. If they scorn Cernunnos then our forests will disappear. If they abandon Tiw our warriors will be crushed in battle. And when that happens Woden will let us be taken into slavery; all of us, for ever. And where will you be then, "master"?' She was silent for a moment then she added with an air of finality, 'That is the natural order of things.'

The daylight was fading.

'Well, Leofgifu, a gloomy prophecy indeed,' I said, 'and if you go now, perhaps tomorrow I shall know what my fate is to be.'

She drew in her breath sharply, then said through tight lips, 'I was going to tell you something, but now it will have to wait. Anyway, you won't be hearing from me or anyone else for a few days. We are making ready to celebrate the new life that is about to be brought forth by Eostre.' Then her mood changed, and she continued more cheerfully, 'Of course, your brethren also worship our spring goddess, but they call her by another name. They call her "Easter",' she added, looking pleased with herself.

She rose and put on her cape and scarf, wrapping the loose end over her head.

'Goodbye, Edwin,' she said, with a little smile. 'I'll come back as soon as I can.'

Trying to draw a response, I called out after her, 'What day is it?'

She would not stay but mockingly called back, 'Wodensday.'

What had she been about to tell me? Gossip about the battle, maybe. Then it came to me that she must have news of Finn, but had chosen to withhold it for some reason or other. How unkind she could be at times.

My mind leaped unbidden from unkindness to cruelty: Aethelred had discovered me or rather 'Adhelm'. I might be safe as long as that little deception held, but eventually it would be uncovered, and then what? Like a hare pursued by hounds, my mind jumped again, this time back to Leofgifu's parting words.

Easter! I would celebrate it and then await my fate.

Chapter 13

The next two days were a misery because I was unable to work out when Easter day should fall. I could not even recall the Roman way of calculating it. My mind was left bemused by the effort. I thought that the trials of the ordeal, the fighting and the horrors of the cave visions had addled my brain.

Another thing plagued me: Leofgifu seemed to have changed. She was challenging me in all ways. She argued where she had not before. Had her love for me been weakened by the dreadful sights of the battle?

What she had said about the old gods was interesting. However, sacrificing for rain and crops belonged to churls and others who worked on the land and so didn't concern me. I was also no warrior invoking Tiw in time of battle, hoping to be carried to the Otherworld. The Otherworld! I had forgotten – Finn had died as a warrior and had been taken there. I would never see him again. Could Jesus intercede with God to take Finn up to heaven where I, as a monk, was destined to go? To be certain of salvation, though, I had to celebrate Easter. This brought me back to my immediate problem: when was Easter?

In prayer to Columba it came to me that the British way of calculating Easter, being the older, was therefore the true way. But still I was unable to do it. I had always relied upon the elders in the Churches to work it out. I vowed there and then that if I were spared I would learn the tables and never forget them.

I spent what I hoped was Easter day on my knees in prayer. In humility I thought of Leu, the god of the British in ancient times, who perished in a tree stabbed by a spear. I recalled the fate of Woden. He, too, was sacrificed in a tree. He was gashed by a spear or scramasax. He sacrificed himself to himself so as to gain understanding. Here was a mystery. I shared the agony of our Lord who, as Jesus, sacrificed himself. He, too, was pierced by a spear.

Woden hung on the tree for nine days, but I fasted till the third day, as Colman taught we must, then I celebrated the renewal of Jesus. He rose again, as the new sun rises from the tomb of night, and as the new year rises from the grave of the old.

I heard, too, the call of a cuckoo, her voice ringing in the woods. She had risen from her winter spent in the earth, perhaps in the low at Elderford, bringing her message of reassurance from the Otherworld. 'Good news, good news,' she called, and then I knew that Finn was safe.

Fasting helped me in my search for direction, for after a few days a voice spoke to me. 'The cranes are mating on the Crane Brook. It is time to go, Edwin. Make your way to the Britons at Wall.'

The voice was not in my head but came from without. It was high and clear, like a woman's but not one of this earth. There was such beauty in it, such longing and sadness, that tears sprang to my eyes.

I had never heard the voice of my fate so clearly before.

Taking my staff I set off straightway for Wall, making my way along the paths that wound round the many small hills. I would see how the Britons there were faring. They could tell me what was being said about the battle and whether my name was being mentioned in connection with it or not.

I could also do some good with healing or prayer. After that I would go on to Weeford and Hints and see how my little flock of Britons there was progressing.

At each bend in the path and at each clearing in the trees I took great care. There could be bounty hunters out searching for outlaws or runaway slaves but I was in luck and there was nobody about. Birds chased each other and quarrelled noisily in the branches. At one place, two screaming wood elves leaped up in my face with raucous cries. With my heart pounding I watched them turn into magpies. At least that was a good omen which would bring me luck.

I had gone about a mile when I came to a ley. A good part of it was covered with docks and plantains, and where the heavy clay soil had been tilled, couch grass was springing up. A movement at the scrub at the ley's edge caught my eye and I was straightway wary. In springtime the wild boars can become very dangerous. I approached with caution, gripping my staff.

There at the very edge of the ley were a churl and his woman. They were both lumpish and no longer young. Their violent efforts were making them both grunt. The woman saw me. She tried first to cover her naked legs, then to bring her knees together, but she couldn't move her swain. Instead, she hid her face in the hood of his tunic. I turned my back.

'Hail, master!' the man called, showing his teeth in a wide grin.

In sober tones I returned his greeting.

'Have you come to speak to us of salvation?' he queried.

'No. I go to Wall, to visit the Britons.'

'Poor devils,' he said, 'they've got nothing, there. No land, nothing. Not like me, though God knows 'tis wretched soil hereabouts. That's what me and my woman were doing.'

'Doing?'

'It's our custom, see?' he explained. 'It's because we were late with everything – ploughing, sowing . . . and we're doing this so that Erce and Freya . . . no, I mean the Lord Jesus, begging your pardon, will make the crop good this year. If it isn't, then it's all up with us.'

He paused, then a thought seemed to strike him.

'Here,' he said, 'would you give the land your blessing as well? Shouldn't do no harm. Might do some good.' He turned to the woman. 'What do you think, wife?'

'Oh, yes, master,' she said to me. 'Please say a spell. Please. We can't afford no more taxes for the new church, not this year, not unless we get a good crop.'

I wanted to get on to Wall but what she said intrigued me.

'Taxes for the new church?' I asked. 'Why not for the king?'

'Well, it wasn't much, not at first,' he said.

This reply irritated me and I was about to berate him for obduracy when I realised that his grin was gone. Their grey faces showed strain and desperation. The churl seemed confused so I turned to the woman instead.

'Tell me about it,' I said to her. 'I might be able to help.'

'What he's trying to say is this. We used to live in the village with his dad,' she said, pointing over her shoulder with a jab of her thumb. 'Wulfhere let his dad clear this bit of forest on account of the fact that they went afighting together, up in Northumberland. It's poor land and so Wulfhere never asked for much.'

I wondered if I should tell them of my own father, killed by a Mercian brute led by Penda, accursed father of that same

Wulfhere. Bad blood to them all! But it would do no good with this man, so I kept my peace.

'Then half the village died of the plague, including his dad, and we came up here. We made a go of it and Wulfhere was pleased with what we sent him.'

'We brought up four children,' interrupted the man. 'Six of us in all, making a living on this clay.'

'The king's reeve come one day and said Wulfhere had given the land to Chad,' she continued, 'and we were to give the food rent to the church instead. That pleased us. It would bring good luck and we'd be all right in the Otherworld.'

'We were wrong. They deceived us,' said the man.

'They deceived us,' echoed the woman, becoming bitter. 'But barely one moon after Chad died, the new bishop, what's it . . . Wynfrid, sent word they wanted more. And in money, not in barley. How can we get money? And then they wanted more each year. We can't afford it no more.'

'Do they want much more?' I asked. Farmers always say they are poor but it might ease them to tell me their story.

'Last year, before Lughnasa, we were told that as pagans we would have have to pay up, or be put off the land. Our land.'

'Lughnasa?' I gently prompted her.

'Celebration of the harvest. Some call it Lammas.'

'Ah, yes. But who threatened you with this?' I asked, but I thought I already knew the answer. There was one person who would gladly take their money and even more gladly evict them.

'It was a monk they call Owini. He was very threatening.'

'But here you both are. Presumably there was a good harvest.' I stopped for now they were weeping.

The man said, 'She can't speak of it. We had to put our first son into bond-slavery. He was only twelve years old. Now he works with the building of the church at Lichfield. The money paid off last year's tax, but as for this year . . .'

'Will you pray with me?' I asked them and we knelt together on the stiff clay. I called upon God to make the land fertile and fruitful and I beseeched Him also to make the couple fruitful.

The prayers seemed to ease their pain, and I left them in that miserable place. As far as I knew it had no name, so thereafter I thought of it as Churl Ley.

My thoughts were still upon the injustice I had uncovered when I saw that I would be coming down to Cress Well. I could not bear to go near that dreadful valley of death so I went wide of it. Ashmore Brook was in spate and I got muddied because I forgot to say the charm to ward off the water elves before crossing.

A light wind blew from the west, bringing the smell of the burned wood. I began to fear that it would bring before me the evil spirits again. To keep them away I bethought me of the bravery of my companions and of the merry moments we had.

Then a dreadful sight drove out my grieving thoughts and brought me to a standstill.

My way was barred by a grey wall of giant corpses spread across the valley in front of me. They were wrapped in mouldering shrouds and as they stretched their bony arms and fingers to the sky they sighed sadly in faint voices.

I fell to my knees, aghast at the sight. It was some moments before my pounding heart slowed and my trembling stopped.

Then a lesson from Oak-man came to my aid. He had showed me how to look outwards as well as inwards. My thoughts had been with dead friends when I had come upon these trees, and I had seen them as I was looking in. Now I made myself look outwards to see them anew, to see them as trees.

Even so, walking towards the dreadful vision was not easy for me and I was thankful for the support of my staff.

The trees were alders shrouded with grey lichen. It formed grey crusts with rough warty surfaces. Close up, quite beautiful pink discs on it could be seen. Now I was seeing the lichen, not my mind.

With the change in my thoughts came a memory of Chad. With sudden clarity I remembered that he had once brought us near to this place. 'Over yonder is what the Britons call Leto Ceto, which in their tongue means "the grey wood",' he'd said, in his dry voice. 'It is their custom to make from the grey stuff a reddish-brown dye with which they colour their garments. I have seen such a thing among the Britons of the north as well.'

As I made my way through the forest of tall alders I had no fear at all. Now I felt that these gentle grey trees were my friends. I had learned a lesson.

It was typical of Chad, I reflected as I went, that he could speak several dialects of the Britons' tongue. None of the other churchmen at Lichfield could or would utter a single word unless they were in need, and then they might give a single command to some slave. Chad readily spoke to all Britons in their own tongue, save those few of higher degree who preferred to speak Englisc.

The yellow soil of Pipe Hill was still very wet from the winter run-off. I fell, and this made me take extra caution, for I was about to cross the way going from Lichfield down to the Street. This well-worn track was used by people coming and going from the west and often brought strangers.

Suddenly I heard the sound of hooves, and quickly hid myself.

A thegn whom I did not recognise rode past, followed by a band of armed and sweating men. Their faces were red with exertion and they were constantly moving their heads from side to side, as if searching the trees and brushwood for ambushers. They were heading in the Lichfield direction. The thegn held his long scramasax unsheathed and his men were clearly ready for war. I was greatly relieved that I had remained unseen.

When the track was clear I went across. The alder trees were not so plentiful at this height and I could see across the great clay valley to the Brown Hills in the south. I plunged down into thickets and swampy land and followed human and animal paths leading to Wall.

Some attempt had been made to garland the reed-roofed huts with spring flowers and blossom, but it was poor compared with earlier times. Clearly, the Britons had not much heart for Beltane this year.

There were very few people about. Usually the settlement in the ruins would be full of young and old. Dogs would be running and barking at any who ventured near the huts, and cattle would be wandering freely. Now, though, it was as if the plague had struck, as it had some years before.

Again, Chad came to mind. In my head I heard his quiet voice saying, 'Many are of the opinion that the Britons caught the plague from the other Celtic peoples who travelled freely between Britain, Brittany, and the Iberian Peninsula. There is merit in the idea, for the many battles and struggles now going on between our kings and others greatly restrict free movement for all people, with the result that the outbreaks have diminished.' Then he added something that had made me look at him anew. He said, 'Now they no longer die from the plague. Instead, they are persecuted to death.'

As I stood in the settlement I heard the sound of cries, shouts and the cracking of whips coming from beyond the huts.

Behind the great ruins the land rose up steeply. On top of the rise stood the former temple, now the small church of John the Blessed. I had put my ordeal there out of my mind but the sight of it brought back painful memories. Behind John's church, and stretching back to Lichfield, was the wide field which produced many fine harvests.

Up the steep slope inched a cart laden with two huge stones. It was being drawn by a yoke of six oxen. Men, roped together, were also heaving at the cart. It came to a halt. Men and beasts strained in unison to move the massive load. Whips slashed across the backs of the slaves while other men pulled at the noses and horns of the oxen. The cart inched upwards then stopped. Blood and sweat glistened on the naked bodies of the swarthy men roped together. Once more the whips cracked and slashed. The cart moved again.

In this way it reached the top of the slope and then went on, headed towards Lichfield. I climbed the steep slope that was by now a sea of churned-up mud. The slaves who had pulled the cart up the hill were being led away still roped together. They were reeling with fatigue and several collapsed. The Mercian guards whipped them till they were picked up by their fellows. The spent slaves were being replaced by fresh ones for the cart's journey. I recognised many of them as Britons from Wall and the area around Hints.

One of the guards saw me and came across, grinning. 'I bet these black devils think they're back in hell with their master, Satan,' he said.

'Is this the worst there is?' I asked him.

'I dunno. Come and see them taking their ease.'

He led me along the track and we came to a small hawe fenced around with tall alder stakes. 'Inspection,' he called out to the guard at the gate. 'Open up for a visit from Brother . . . er, sorry, what was your name?'

'Edwin,' I said unthinkingly.

'A visit from Brother Edwin.'

The armed guard opened a small picket gate for me, and I stepped into the enclosure.

Behind me the guard on the gate asked, 'Who's that?'

'I dunno. He's called Edwin. I suppose he's to do with the new church.'

'Better tell the boss, just in case,' said the other.

The horrific sight in the enclosure caused me to pay no heed to the import of their words. All around were gangs of slaves, still roped together. Some were trying to rest. One gang was squabbling furiously over food dropped in the mud and dung; clearly, the hawe had recently been used for cattle. As they pushed and struck at each other the food became trampled underfoot. One gang was waiting patiently for a water jug to be passed to them and the members of another were jostling to use a latrine pit. A few gangs huddled together in apathetic silence.

I saw faces I knew. Most were Britons but one or two were Mercian. In one group I saw a lad whose ugly features could only have belonged to the son of the couple at Churl Ley.

I heard my name being called and the guard beckoned to me.

'Who in the name of God has done this?' I said, as I came up to him. 'Enslavement, beatings – such mistreatment of Britons is an abomination and the perpetrator must be punished.'

'Er, yes, right, I'll pass that on,' he said, holding the gate for me as I stepped through.

Waiting for me were four armed men.

'Brother Edwin,' said one, 'you are under arrest. You will be confined here overnight. Tomorrow you will be taken to Lichfield.'

'By whose order?' I demanded of him, still seething with anger.

If I was to go to Lichfield I would report this disgraceful treatment of the Britons to Bishop Wynfrid.

They saw my anger and thinking it to be directed at them levelled their spears.

'By the order of Wynfrid, Bishop of Mercia,' the leader said.

Chapter 14

I completed a full circuit of the enclosure and found at least two places in the fence where a man might push through. I didn't get out, for I had given my word to the leader of the guard that I would not attempt to escape. In return I was allowed to roam freely in the enclosure instead of being roped up with one of the gangs. They had taken my staff, though, and I felt at a loss without it.

I was bitterly disappointed at myself and at the Britons. By my foolish action in coming here I had thrown away my chance of finding and killing the man Shitlegs. In my pouch I had the small knife given to me by Leofgifu and round my middle was a good strong leather belt. I had planned that I would partly strangle the wretch then saw away at his throat until he died. It was the traditional way of executing a coward, but now my plan was for naught.

As for the Britons, they made me angry. It would only take one man in one gang with a bit of common sense to unpick the ropes of another gang and they could have all freed themselves. There were few Mercian guards and now that evening was coming on most of them would be back in their huts starting to fight over the ale buckets. It would be easy.

I was beginning to feel faint from fatigue and hunger so I sat on the mound of the fence and watched the Britons prepare for the night. They seemed witless and inert and it grieved me to see them so.

Presently a roped-up gang came weaving in my direction. To my tired mind it looked like a monstrous hairy ten-legged centipede. It lurched drunkenly as it came and I saw that the legs were roped together by the ankle.

The ghastly creature came right up to me then stopped, swaying as it stood. Ten night-black eyes swivelled as one and regarded me levelly. Then, to my horror, a hole at its rear end opened and speech came forth.

'You are Brother Edwin?' enquired the fundament, in Englisc.

I threw off the blanket enveloping my mind and struggled to see the monster for what it was. The last man in the gang had asked me a question. He'd spoken politely, so I replied likewise.

'Welcome to our humble home,' he said, using the time-honoured greeting.

The other Britons smiled at this irony, then one said in an aside, 'He doesn't look like his description.' He spoke in Britisc, not knowing that I could understand it well enough. The others hushed him.

'I am sorry to see you all thus,' I said. 'At the moment I can do little, but tomorrow I am being taken to Lichfield and there perhaps I may see someone in authority who will put this disgraceful thing right.'

The Englisc speaker didn't reply to that but instead said, 'Forgive us, we are forgetting our manners. Are you hungry? Here is bread. You will have to go to the water trough yourself, I'm afraid, but you are in luck because it is not necessary to go far.'

He indicated the surrounding fence and again the other men smiled at the irony.

I took the bread. Then I realised that they must be

desperately short of food so I broke a portion off and returned the rest. He accepted it with dignity.

'Do I know any of you?' I asked, unable to see their features for the caked dirt and dried blood on their faces.

They seemed not to be offended by my thoughtlessness and merely shook their heads.

'We are not locals,' said the Englisc speaker. 'We come from the other side of Sarn Wydellin, from beyond the Brown Hills. Owini bought us from our mistress. But we know of you, Brother Edwin. Word of your ministry and skill at story-telling has spread far.'

'It is all God's work,' I said, absent-mindedly. 'But what did you just say . . . some place . . . Sarn . . . ?'

'Sarn Wydellin.'

I shook my head, so he added kindly, 'In Englisc it would be "the Irish Road", but your people twisted the name into Watling Street. Our ancestors built it and drove their chariots along it long before the Romans came.'

'Chariots?'

'War carts with two wheels.'

I must have frowned because he said, 'Yes, we could make war carts once. With respect, though, it's history now and best forgotten.'

'I'm sorry. I don't wish to cause you offence.'

As he talked I saw that the other men in his gang had carefully placed themselves so that they could see all around. They then made their separate reports: three guards near the gate idly talking and laughing as usual; no interest being taken in the holes in the fence; the stone cart with its guards gone on its way; the 'Traitor' is penned.

He began to ask them another question, but I interrupted.

'Forgive me,' I said in Britisc, 'but I can understand what you are saying.'

It was only politeness that stopped me from laughing aloud at the expressions on their faces, but they recovered themselves quickly.

'And we can understand what you are saying, as well,' said one with dancing eyes, and they smiled their ironical smiles.

'All right,' the Englisc speaker said to them firmly. 'It is enough that we can understand each other.'

'Are you their leader?' I asked. 'And how came you here?'

He turned to me and said, 'We know about you, Brother Edwin, and know we can trust you. I talk to them thus because we are all related – three are brothers and two are cousins.'

The others all shook their heads simultaneously and I could see that their faces bore the family likeness.

'I said that Owini bought us,' continued the Englisc speaker, 'but that is not quite true. When Owini's men came round looking for labourers, our mistress said that we could go if it meant working on the new cathedral. She said she ought to get something out of it, though, so she "rented" us to Owini. It cost him a lot, but not as much as it cost us. We did not know what it would be like here.'

I saw the sores from the ropes knotted savagely around their necks and the scars on their backs.

'We would have escaped at the first opportunity,' he went on, 'but we heard about the plan to take Lichfield back for our people, so we stayed. When the word came, we were to take the guards' weapons and meet up with the Welsh prince and his men.'

I looked round the enclosure. There were upwards of fifty men of fighting age, together with a few lads, and a couple of Mercians.

'All of these, marching on Lichfield!' I sighed. 'It would have been a grand sight.'

'Not all, I'm sorry to say. Many are dispirited or broken and no longer hold their heads up. There is one – we call him the Traitor – who would readily betray his own people to gain favour with the Saxons. We keep him surrounded at all times, though.' He grinned evilly as he added, 'He often tries to open his mouth but no sound comes out.'

'You know of what happened, then?' I said. 'The battle at Cress Well?'

'Alas, yes. We don't know everything, of course, but enough to know that our chance is lost.' He looked away, blinking his eyes to stop the tears.

We remained in silence for a while.

'What will you do now?' I said.

He lowered his voice even though the guards were some distance off. 'We are escaping from this place of sorrow tonight. It should be an easy matter to undo the ropes. I'll start on the knots that bind another gang. It shouldn't take long.'

As he spoke I began to see a way of achieving what my heart most desired. If the Britons were all like this man and his kin then they might come side by side with me to the settlement where my father's murderer lived. There would only be a few armed men; we would take them by surprise and I could kill the wretch. Then we could disperse, disappear into the woods and forests.

I gave thanks to my fate who had led me here to this place and at this time.

But first, I needed to know how warlike they were. I wanted no mass slaughter. The Britons in the whole of Mercia would suffer cruel retribution for that. I simply needed their numbers, more as a bodyguard, not as a raiding party.

'And the guards? How will you deal with them, after their treatment of you?' I asked.

'We'll leave them. They'll be punished by Owini when he finds we've gone.'

'But don't you want your revenge? Don't you want to kill Owini for what he has done to you?' I persisted.

He looked at me strangely. 'We belong to the British Church,' he said, 'and we try to follow Christ's precepts and his example.'

His reply showed him to be useless for my purpose. His rebuke, however, served to bring me back to my own situation. A great weight of despair pressed down on me and involuntarily I lowered my head and groaned.

'Bear up, Brother Edwin,' he said, and the other Britons reached out their hands and patted me on the shoulder. This tender gesture brought a tear to my eye.

'Why don't you escape with us tonight? At our house we will give you food and help you find your way,' said one, and the others nodded their heads and made encouraging noises.

'Come with you?' I said, already seeing in my mind the friendly forest beyond the Brown Hills, the sheltering forest that men said went on for ever until it reached the Southern Sea. 'Alas, no. I have given my word,' I said. 'Besides, I have a task I must perform in Lichfield. I must also help these other Britons, many of whom may be in my ministry.'

'You speak of a task in Lichfield . . . it concerns a man—' began the Englisc speaker.

'You know of him?' I interrupted, eager to hear of the wretch whom I would destroy.

'We thought you would know, having been there.'

'Would know what? I beg of you, tell me!' I urged him.

'He is dead. He was mortally wounded at Cress Well. By

the time he had been carried back to his hovel he had died.'

I was stunned. It could not be possible. They seemed reluctant to say more but I pressed them. 'Are you sure? What do you know about him?'

'His real name was Wulfstan. He was a pitiful drunkard and was barely accepted by his own people . . . because of something that had happened in the past.'

'How did he die? Not bravely, surely?'

'Some of our people were ordered to carry him from the battlefield. They said that in between his curses and groans he kept saying he'd seen a ghost. He seemed more terrified of that than of dying.'

'He said he'd seen a ghost!' I echoed.

An image came to me of the wide-eyed grizzled Mercian standing over me, his gory scramasax seemingly motionless for eternity. So that was Shitlegs – Wulfstan was too noble a name for him – and we had come face to face.

Now I understood. In my home country people had often remarked how like my father I was in appearance. The murderer must have thought he was reliving his foul deed all over again.

I shuddered. But for Finn, I realised, the creature who was lower than the foulest bemired worm would have claimed the last of our family.

'Finn, oh Finn,' I breathed in muted anguish.

The Britons looked on, dimly aware of my distress. I had lost Finn and now I was learning of how I had been cheated of justice. Visions of my mother's agony and her nights full of weeping, and of my uncle's set, deathly white face came before me.

At that moment I sorely missed my staff. The Britons put out their arms to support me.

'Is there a family?' I demanded.

'He has a worn-out wife and a witless daughter and they live in squalor. Now that he is dead they will probably starve . . . But surely you are not going to pursue them?'

The note of his voice made me look at their faces. They were staring at me aghast.

'I will take revenge for the death of my father killed by that worthless wretch,' I said, emphasising the word 'will'.

The Britons nodded dumbly.

I tore my gaze away from their accusing eyes and looked elsewhere. The path is easy for them, I thought. Not having sworn a binding oath of vengeance, they can be generous of spirit.

I wasn't going to become confused again over the issue of the blood feud; I was no weak-minded princeling like Aethelred who had come to my cave and showed himself to be irresolute.

Night was advancing. There was no cover anywhere in the hawe and I saw the gangs of the other Britons shuffling their way to a corner where they squatted in the lee of the wind. Huddled together with their heads down they would wait out the night with its cold and rain.

If I can't have my revenge on that rotted animal, I thought, then, by Woden, I'll wreak destruction on his diseased spawn.

I indicated the mass of the Britons. 'I will address them,' I said to the Englisc speaker. 'Perhaps a message of good cheer?' I tried to sound open and unstudied, but I couldn't throw off the feeling of foreboding.

'You will preach to them?' he said.

Catching the inner meaning of his question I said, 'I, a monk of the Church that will destroy their faith? No, I have another idea. I will tell them a story told by Chad, who as you know was trained in the British tradition, so it will appeal to them. A story I hope that will fill their minds.'

'Ah, yes. Edwin the story-teller,' said the Englisc speaker. 'Perhaps it is better to fill their minds than their bellies.'

The Britons smiled their ironical smile.

'Will you interpret for me?' I asked him. 'My version of Britisc seems to amuse people.'

He looked discomfited by my little barb, but he agreed to help.

I stood on the mound of the fence so that I was somewhat above the huddled Britons. My centipede went among them, cajoling and bullying until they were in some sort of order, but one which I could not discern.

The Englisc speaker then introduced me as 'Brother Edwin, a servant of God and a friend of the Britons who will tell us an uplifting tale as told by our beloved Chad'.

A few raised their heads and glanced at me then lowered their faces to the mud again.

The moon was growing stronger, preparing to claim the night for himself. I raised my clasped hands and prayed to him for Oak-man to be with me working his craeft.

'I will raise these people from the mud,' I vowed to him. 'I will turn them into fierce warriors with gore-stained teeth. This night these Britons and I will wreak bloody death on Owini and the pus-ridden Mercians.'

Chapter 15

A thrill of fear ran through me at the thought of the great forces I had invoked and at the response I would get from the people who, now roped and enslaved, crouched before me.

I lowered my arms and smiled.

'This is indeed Chad's story,' I said to the Britons, some of whom were beginning to shiver. 'Listen well, for it has a special meaning for all of us.'

'Many years ago,' Chad began, 'there were just Britons and Romans in this land. The thriving town called Letoceton by the Britons and Letocetum by the Romans had sprung up when the Romans built a staging post near the junction of the two great roads.

'My story is about two people of that town and so I shall introduce them to you. One is a young Romano-British man, Fabius Antoninus. The other is a beautiful young British woman, Mapona.

'Fabius and Mapona had first met in the animal market. She was selling a calf. Fabius had been drawn by her tawny hair but he feigned interest in the Celtic brooch fastening her cloak.'

'I'm glad you like it.' She smiled. 'One day I'll tell you what it means.'

'It has meaning? I thought it was just a pretty pattern.'

'I don't wear "just pretty patterns".'

'You are offended? Please accept my apology.'

She looked at him for signs of mockery but his concern seemed real enough.

'What do they call you?' she said.

'My name is Fabius Antoninus. And you?'

'Ah, the town diarist. As for me, I am Mapona. I am of the Cornovii tribe.'

'I see that I am known. Fame is such a burden.'

Mapona was annoyed by the attentions of what seemed to be yet another self-opinionated Roman youth. Yet she found herself attracted by his olive skin and curly black hair. There also seemed to be something more behind his dark almond-shaped eyes.

Fabius stood regarding her.

'Mapona? Mapona?' he teased. 'She's the goddess of horses, is she not, yet here you are selling a cow?'

'You are thinking of another goddess. And it's a calf, not a cow,' she corrected him, but she was not angry. The Romans knew about British religion and customs. Their own were similar, but she would have hardly expected Fabius to know of Mapona, a goddess of northern Britain.

'And you are Cornovii. Where does your territory end? Down at Manduessedon?' he said, naming a small settlement a few miles to the east.

'No, it ends here. I thought the Romans knew everything?'

'Well, they do, but this is border land and the politics are very fluid.'

'You said "they". Aren't you Roman, then?'

'Ah, yes. Father, a Roman general. Mother, of the Brigantii. I'm a true Romano-Briton.'

Mapona turned to a potential customer. She said over

her shoulder, 'I've got to sell this calf. If I don't it's likely that some soldier-cum-cook from the fort will requisition it for the troops. The Romans really ought to raise more cattle of their own. Look, I'll send word. Why don't you come to my house?' Before he could utter the words forming on his lips she added, 'And meet my mother and my brother.'

Fabius walked away. She was beautiful and his heart skipped a beat when he thought of what her fair skin might be like under her tunic. Yet she was disturbing in another way. Her mind was fast and sharp, and she had an air of authority unusual in the British women he met.

He went to the inn, a useful place for him to do some of his work.

Taking his spiced wine to a bench he wondered if he should put anything about the conversation in his report. Would they be interested in Viroconium to know that he had found the one Briton who believed that the Cornovii territory ended at Letocetum? The constant bickering between Cornovii and their Corieltauvi neighbours made the Roman governor nervous. Fabius's thoughts were interrupted by a bored drawling voice.

'Done your weekly report yet, Fabius? The courier goes this afternoon. Won't be another for four days.'

'It's all right for you, Maximus. You soldiers have got an easy life. A bit of drill and two meals a day, guaranteed.'

Captain Maximus stretched out his long legs. His studded sandals shone with polish. He looked at his drink. 'Things have been quiet lately, I must admit. Do you know, Fabius, this place is utterly boring. If Viroconium and Londinium could agree with each other, this collection of huts could become a civitas. But now that the Britons are doing the local administration it's just a glorified border post with a semi-decent bathhouse.'

Fabius knew all the complaints of the army off by heart. What Maximus really meant was that if Letocetum were to be recognised as an official town the status of the fort would go up and he'd get promotion.

Fabius sighed. 'If you got promoted you'd be posted away. But almost certainly to North Britain. The Scots and Picts could be on the rampage again. That's where you'd go, not to some comfortable white-uniform job in the capital.'

Maximus looked sharply at Fabius. This fellow was sometimes too clever for his own good. 'We keep the peace here,' he snapped. 'There is threat enough from the western tribes.'

'Six hairy savages stealing a couple of cows does not constitute a threat,' dismissed Fabius.

Maximus forced a grin. 'Maybe you are right, Fabius. But you must admit what with all these passing officials, untrustworthy petty British chiefs and other riff-raff, there's a lot to keep our eyes on.'

'They keep me busy,' agreed Fabius.

'Right, I'm off,' said Maximus, standing up. 'I have to be back to do yet another inspection of the troops.' He leaned down to Fabius. 'Speaking of which, and this is not to go in your report, we are going to take those moaning sons-of-bitches on a surprise forced march. Up to Deva, I expect. That will sort them out.'

'When will that be?'

'On Beltane eve. We'll be away for about four days. Best time to go, I reckon. This place will be full of drunken natives, loose women offering it around, bonfire smoke and cow dung. Might mess up our uniforms, eh, Fabius?'

He turned to go, then looked down at him. 'You didn't ask

me what Beltane is,' he sneered. 'But you wouldn't have to, being half native yourself.'

Fabius watched him clatter out into the street. The last remark had hurt. It wasn't so much what Maximus had actually said, for mixed marriages were now permitted and were becoming quite common. It was the fact that he had made a comment at all.

Many Roman officers still regarded Britain as just a colony and not part of the Empire proper. Their attitude was noticed by the Britons and it was resented. It could cause trouble.

Fabius brightened, and finished his drink. There would be something for the report after all.

Three days later Fabius was in his room in the mansio reading Caesar. A lad brought him an invitation to Mapona's house. He went to the early session in the bathhouse and came back to his room to change. He donned the tunic. The full toga was too formal and might be interpreted as a statement of some sort.

Mapona's house was on the east side of the town, down the hill from the mansio and near the cemetery.

He rapped on the door post and Mapona came out. She wore a long robe of bright colours down to her ankles. Her brushed hair shone like burnished copper.

'Welcome. Please enter our house.'

She was being quite formal. He was glad, for it helped him in his awkwardness. Stooping, he went inside and stood up.

'I dedicate this gift to the spirits of this house,' he said, in the Roman manner, and handed Mapona a small piece of Samian ware.

She introduced him to her mother and her brother. The old lady busied herself at the hearth while Mungo fetched a basketwork stool for him to sit on. He noticed that Mungo had a severe limp.

Mungo had the same tawny hair and the same green eyes as Mapona. There were scars on his face which a thick drooping moustache did little to hide. His torque was of dull metal and had conical terminals. Fabius politely indicated it with his hand.

'Your torque is most unusual. Has it a history to tell?'

'It should be gold,' replied Mungo, tersely.

Fabius nodded without comprehension.

Mapona fetched ale and wheat bread for him.

'Is there anything of news in the town, Fabius?' she prompted.

'The traders are bringing in their wares for Beltane,' he replied, grateful for the break in the tension. 'I have seen two stalls already. Pendants and amulets, mainly of Esus, Tarvos, and Cernunnos. They are poorly done this year, crudely made.'

'The gods are becoming less respected every year,' Mungo said.

The old lady suddenly spoke. 'The Romans pulled down our shrine.'

'When was that, Mother?' Fabius asked, puzzled.

'Over forty years ago,' broke in Mapona. 'She has never forgotten it. They say the Romans used the stones in the foundations of the mansio.'

Fabius felt embarrassed. His eyes fell upon Mapona's bracelet. Made of blue glass with white trails, it had raised bits on the surface.

'There's nothing like that bracelet on the market stalls,' he offered.

'I shouldn't wonder. It is from North Britain. Mungo gave

it to me,' she proudly said, holding out her hand for him to admire the bracelet. Fabius saw only her small fair hand with its golden hair and delicate freckles.

After a few more uncomfortable moments Mapona said, 'Come, Fabius, let us walk for a while. There is something you have to see.'

As he rose he gently indicated Mungo's scars. 'May one ask who gave you these?'

'Deceit posing as the truth,' Mungo replied.

People thronged the town in the early afternoon sunshine. A few Britons greeted Mapona. One Roman matron sniffed loudly as the couple passed her.

'Perhaps you should let me walk in front,' whispered Fabius.

They went past the mansio and the bathhouse, up the steep slope past the subterranean Temple of Mithras and then on through the woods past the freshly painted Temple of Minerva.

They talked as they walked along the track, Fabius becoming more voluble. Suddenly he interrupted himself. 'You know, I've never talked so much in the British tongue. At least, not since I was a child,' he remarked.

'How does it feel?'

'Natural,' he said, and was surprised at his own answer.

The track was narrowing as it started to slope down.

'We may be some time. Does that matter?' she asked.

'No. I've done my work for today, and no one cares where I go.'

She walked ahead of Fabius. He looked at her feet going in and out and an image came to him of her strong white legs under her robe.

Her voice broke into his thoughts. 'Did you understand what Mungo meant about the torque?' she called.

'No. He talks in riddles.'

'The sign of a true Celt. The torque is made of lead. He says he will wear it till we're free. Then he'll wear gold as we should as free Britons.'

'And what did he mean about "deceit posing as the truth"?'

'You speak the tongue of the Romans. Work it out for yourself.'

Fabius was silent for a while.

'I have it,' he exclaimed. 'It is a play on the Latin for truth, *verus*.'

'And do you know of anyone with that name?'

'Of course, the general, Julius Verus. They say he was a bit brutal with the Scots . . . Great Jupiter! You mean that Mungo . . . ?'

'Yes. He was there. Verus deceived them with talk of amnesty then cut them down. Mungo managed to escape but afterwards he nearly died of his wounds. He's very bitter.'

'I am ashamed to be a Roman.'

'It's not your fault,' she reassured him, but he wasn't sure which she meant, his being part Roman or the treachery of Verus.

They were crossing a newly cleared ley when Fabius idly said, 'I really ought to learn more of the ways of the British. I mean, us. The language as well.'

'Right. Let's start now.'

'Ah, all right,' he said, taken aback by her quick response.

She pointed to where bracken was sprouting. 'There, what's that for?'

'They'll cut that as bedding for the slaves.' He laughed, 'But some say they get pampered too much already.'

She ignored his attempt to be light-hearted. 'We extract the juices. British women take it to abort themselves when they've been raped by Roman soldiers.'

He felt chastened, and pointed to a dark-leaved tree growing by a small stream. 'I know that one,' he said. 'It is called taxus, and javelins are made from it. The roots go down into the infernal regions and because of that the berries are poisonous.'

'Good, that's better. But its real name is "yew", and we also use it to forecast the future.'

She showed him a smaller plant whose leaves were just breaking through. 'And this?'

He shook his head.

'It is called yarrow. In the weak form it wards off enchantment. We take it in stronger doses to change shape: a raven . . . a wolf. Then we can soar high above the trees and see an enemy coming, or go swiftly through the forest faster than any man can run. The Romans know nothing of it, and so they can't do these things.'

'I've heard of that. Shape-changing, I mean,' he said.

'There is so much for you to learn, but now I will show you the womb from whence our people came.'

He felt that he was becoming involved in something beyond his control, but as a diarist he felt he ought to know what was going on. Besides, here he was, alone with this wonderful tawny-haired woman, and no mothers or brothers to bother them.

She led him along a faint track running beside a small river where elm trees clustered, their shadows falling across the water.

Mapona stopped once, searching the ground.

'Few people come this way nowadays. The track is fading from lack of use.'

They followed the river and emerged from the trees into a broad marshy valley.

'Look,' she said, pointing. 'The river's quite shallow here and the bottom is sandy. We'll cross over.'

They waded easily through the water and on the other side followed the river on the northern bank. Mapona walked on steadily, and Fabius found it hard to keep up with her.

Then they were back in trees, on flat wooded land above the valley. The oaks here were a tangle of mossy, rotted fallen logs and crowded young trees. The going was heavy and Fabius was glad when they came out the other side.

'Behold,' said Mapona, 'the centre of our world and the origin of our people.'

Chapter 16

Before Fabius stretched a great lake, its surface sparkling in the sun. Water birds swam and flew in number.

'I never knew this was here,' cried Fabius in excitement and awe.

'It is called Lake Leaman,' declaimed Mapona. 'It is aligned with the highest part of the sun's path from the furthermost eastern shore of our land to the furthermost western shore. It also marks the line from north to south of our greatest hill-forts. From its depths have sprung our people and into its depths have been cast many votive offerings.'

She relaxed and smiled sadly. 'We don't make many offerings here any more. We don't work the land for ourselves, either.' She pointed up the other side of the lake where figures, tiny in the distance, were toiling in fields.

'How do you know all this?' he asked.

'We were taught it by our wise men.' She paused, then answered his unspoken question. 'The Romans slaughtered our teachers and so with each succeeding generation the understanding fades from our hearts.' She broke off.

'I am sorry, he said. 'I didn't know.'

'How can you know if no one tells you?'

'I do know one thing though, Mapona. I thought you were different to the other British women when I met you in the market, and I was right.'

'That's because you don't know them. Anyway, you asked

about the pattern on my brooch, remember? Here it is, before you.'

She pointed.

'This lake, the entrance to Brigantia's womb, is the centre. It is protected by the waters of Trent, Tame and Leaman on three sides, and by the Cannock Forest on the fourth side. Together, they make the first circle of strength.'

As she spoke she made the same patterns in the air with her hand.

Fabius thought that her white and shapely arm was the most wonderful thing he had ever seen.

'Round them are the shores of our land. That is the second circle. Beyond the shores, the land is surrounded by the force of the sea. That is the third circle of protection. Such powerful magic. Even the Romans felt it. They knew that if they built where the forces of nature came together nothing would stand. That's why they decided to avoid it and build where they did.'

Fabius had never heard of these things, and had never heard of Brigantia. He felt ignorant and didn't like the feeling. He became angry. 'The mansio was built next to the road, and the road itself built on the old trackway. Nothing to do with magic. Romans don't believe in Brigantia and mystic circles and all that kind of thing,' he cried.

'Of course they do!' she said, tartly. 'The Romans worship Brigantia, only they call her Minerva. And as for magic – you've just come through what's left of our ancestral sacred grove, so why did the soldiers cut it down if they didn't believe in its power?'

'The Druids were dangerous and their oak groves had to be destroyed.'

'The Oak-men were the wisest of all men, and did great

good. You shouldn't believe everything you read in those books of yours.'

In silence they retraced their steps, but instead of going back to the town, Mapona followed the river, going into ever deepening forest.

'Have you been along this river before?' she said.

'No. I hardly ever leave the town. There are enough important things there for me to do.'

They came into a clearing just above where the lake broadened out.

Mapona stopped. 'We are here,' she said.

He looked about him. 'I feel . . . something. This place, what is it?'

'Shut your eyes. Open your heart and your ears. Listen.'

Something he'd read came to him. ' "Ancient Celtic groves inhabited by the gods," ' he quoted. ' "The wind never blows on the trees. Birds are frightened to perch on their branches." '

'I don't like that. Where did it come from?' she asked.

'The words of an ancient scribe.'

'A Roman?'

'Yes. Or a Greek, I forget which.'

She stood and looked about her.

'Look, there,' she said, pointing. 'Three, no four, small blue and yellow birds. And listen – that's a linnet. Fabius, those words you recalled were said by someone who was no friend of ours.'

Her annoyance gave way to a more solemn mood.

'This is a sacred place and there is the River Leaman flowing from the body of the Great Mountain Mother.'

On one side of the clearing stood a carved and painted wooden female figure. Her breasts were clearly delineated and her face was serene. She gazed with understanding upon the pain and passions of the human world.

'What or who is that?' he exclaimed.

'Nemetona, the goddess of our grove. You are afraid?'

'Not with you here, no.'

'The voice of the raven and the crane have told me that you should be chosen,' she said.

'Chosen?' he exclaimed. 'Chosen! What for? I mean, to do what?'

'To help our people who have lost their way. The Roman army destroyed our warriors. The Roman towns seduced our leaders. And now the Romanised Britons have brought a curse upon the spirit of our people. We are withering away like grasses in the winter. We need a leader.'

'Your brother, Mungo. Could he not . . . ?'

'It is our custom that our leaders shall be perfect in mind and in body. His mind is sound. His body, alas, is no longer perfect.'

'But I am Romano-British. A fusion of two cultures. One of the very people you say are destroying you.'

'On our own we are unable to free ourselves. The Romans do not wish to free us, they want us to be mere pseudo-Romans.'

She stopped for a moment, consumed by her thoughts.

Fabius kept his silence.

She spoke again. The bitterness was gone; her manner was authoritative, knowledgeable. 'What you and I are about to do should properly be done at the time of leaf fall, when the forest king claims his own, but our people cannot wait till then. If the gods will it, you shall become the leader of our people and master of the wild beasts.

'If the gods do not will it, then I cannot say what may befall us, for we are invoking powerful forces. However, this I know: the thing must be done by someone who is from both worlds and has love for both.'

She took his hands in hers and looked full into his face.

'Will you offer yourself to Cernunnos, mighty horned god of the forest, and to the goddess of our tribe?'

All about him were the great trees. The alien goddess looked on with penetrating eyes. The woman standing before him had a female presence such as he had never experienced before.

What might have been fear sparked briefly, flickered and died.

Awe came over him as he realised the ground he stood on was so mystical, the spiritual forces of nature about him so powerful, that they exposed Minerva and Mithras for what they were; pale and feeble man-made conceits.

With a profound sense of relief he saw that some of the dilemmas in his life could be resolved.

'I will.'

'Brave Fabius,' she said quietly. Then her voice changed, taking on more force. 'Now, do as I say. Go to the edge of the clearing. Follow the path of the sun but do not look back. Go round three times, then stop.'

She turned towards the graven figure and raised her arms.

He did as he was bade. Three times he went round then he stopped.

There was silence.

'Turn around,' said Mapona. She stood before him, naked save for a necklace of many-coloured beads. Around her head was a garland of leaves. In one hand she held a short stick with a phallic end. In the other she held a small bag made of animal skin.

'Undress and kneel,' she commanded.

She touched the stick to her breasts, put it to his lips then back to her breasts again.

'Go on all fours; by your side there is a branch. Hold it to your head.'

He held it to his forehead and suddenly he had the antlers of a stag.

Mapona circled him stroking his flanks, arms and legs with the phallic stick.

'Do the noise of rut.'

He began to make the guttural roar of the challenging stag.

Mapona circled again. She chanted words and patterns of sounds.

The stick went across his back, under his belly, between his legs. His body began to respond.

She stopped at his head, right in front of his face.

The tawny triangle filled his vision.

'Go on to your back. Put your arms by your side.'

She opened the bag and strewed leaves and feathers over him. She stooped and smeared some wet substance across his face and over his lips.

'Lick,' she commanded, and he licked his smeared lips.

At first it stung, then the stinging went away, and as it did so all his anxiety left him.

He felt an exciting heat running along the veins in his arms and thighs.

His breathing became rapid and shallow and the centre of his chest tingled almost unbearably. Then the heat and the tingling moved down towards his lower belly. His awareness and almost every fibre of his body became concentrated on his erection which had never before been harder or longer.

He felt that it was a part of him, yet at the same time it was a separate being, with its own urgency, its own imperative.

She stood up again and with her legs parted one on either side of his body walked slowly down towards his feet. She turned and knelt. For a moment she regarded the dual entity before her: the man and the masculinity.

The balance between the two was not quite right but she knew what had to be done.

She was holding in her hand a few freshly picked leaves. She put them into her mouth and quickly chewed them, then leaned forward. Lowering her head, she let the juices dribble from between her lips.

The result was almost instantaneous. Every other part of him became drawn up into the phallus.

The man was translated into the primary force that brings new life from the earth every year, and with it, new hope.

Slowly, carefully and with veneration she bestrode him.

The daylight was beginning to fade as they made their way back through the trees to the town. Now it would be unsafe to be in the forest but Fabius was not afraid.

He was unable to explain to himself his experience in the sacred grove. At one point, the self that he called Fabius had become as nothing, yet at the same time he felt that he had become part of something that was both ageless and universal. In the same way as a droplet of water in the sea is both nothing yet part of the great ocean, he imagined.

It had brought about a change in the way he thought of himself. He felt more mature, more able to take a real part in the world of men.

'Is your ambition changed now, Fabius? Or do you still mean to be the town diarist for ever?'

He laughed, and would have kissed her but somehow it seemed inappropriate. 'You know the answer, don't you? But we shall have to discuss what I can do,' he replied.

He was excited, and began to talk about meeting with other Britons in the town. He said he needed to know how many men they could call on, what weapons there were, and he wondered if the men were all able to use sword and spear.

'There are women, too, you know,' she said, 'and other sorts of weapon besides iron ones.'

'Such as?'

'Such as luss–cre.'

He shook his head – the British word meant nothing to him.

'A potent herb some call speedwell. We take it before a battle and then even the weakest woman can kill a Roman soldier.'

She looked at him to see his reaction. His answer might show he realised that freedom for the Britons would inevitably mean death for many on both sides.

Instead, he nodded vaguely. In his mind he was doing what he'd seen Roman officers doing many times: drawing up lists of requirements such as food and transport.

Then, borne on the evening breeze, there came the sound of a military trumpet. Three plain notes, urgently uttered, repeated twice.

To Mapona the sound hung in the air like brass links in a chain that fettered the British people to Rome.

'Ah, they're changing the watch,' he murmured automatically, and before he could stop himself, said, 'I'd arranged to go with some of the officers to the Temple of Mithras. They're consecrating a newly imported bas–relief of Mithras slaying the bull, and I'm invited to observe the ceremony.'

Mapona stopped and turned towards him. Her eyes were hard. 'Fabius, you must find your values in us, with your own gods, and your own roots. This afternoon you have been given new strength. Use it.'

'I have never lost my values. Part of me has always been British,' he protested, caught unawares by the vehemence of her attack. 'I just don't know what I've got to do next, that's all.'

'I am beginning to feel that you want to go back to their ways. I cannot stop you. I have given you everything I had to give, as a priestess and as a woman. Now it is up to you: either you do nothing, and take the consequences, or you do something to save us . . . and yourself.'

She turned and went back to the town, leaving him staring after her.

In the failing light, alone and bereft of inspiration, he followed in her path. He was beginning to realise that he had taken part in something of the greatest significance yet his behaviour had been most insensitive. He knew he had refused to face the issue of responsibility and he felt sure he had belittled much of what Mapona had said.

It came to him that his first priority was to regain her respect. Never mind anything else; he had to do something that would restore the esteem she clearly had for him when they first set off together.

As he went he prayed to Fortuna to let the dice fall his way for once, just this once.

The idea burst upon him with such force that it halted him in his tracks. He had little influence, and no military skills. There was one advantage he had, however, that no one else had. He would have to exploit it to the full.

A sense of mission came over him, and he set off for the town, excitement growing at every step.

Chapter 17

Once in the town he forced himself to slow down to a casual walk.

He went searching in the taverns and brothels for a particular Ordovician, one of the few of that tribe in the town. They were regarded as wild and uncivilised by the Romans and there was an uneasy truce between the governor and the tribal leaders.

Fabius found his man and drew him to one side. He showed a purse of money to the Ordovician whose dark eyes narrowed with greed.

'Take a message to your father as quickly as you can. Tell him to intercept the courier to Viroconium. Oh, and tell him to make sure that he has someone on hand who can read Latin. Do this, and the purse will be yours. Now go.'

The Ordovician slipped away.

Good, thought Fabius. With any luck the first blow will soon be struck.

He went back to the mansio and started to compose his report. If questioned later he would say that he had misunderstood. He had thought that he was meant to show how alert he was by noting the forthcoming exercise on Beltane eve.

Fabius could hear the shouted commands and replies coming from the fort.

'Are you ready?'

'We are ready!'

Thrice went the question and thrice came the response.

The trumpets blared and the gates of the fort swung open.

The Roman troops marched out with their commanding officer mounted on a white horse at their head.

Behind the commander came two other mounted officers including Captain Maximus. After them came the standard bearers and then the infantry. The column wore light armour and marched six abreast. The centurions in their red-crested helmets went to and fro keeping the cohort in order with curses and blows from their heavy vine sticks.

The soldiers didn't get into their full stride till they reached the Street. There they struck the pace that would carry them twenty-five miles in a day.

The fort gates closed and all that could be seen were the helmet and pilum of the patrolling sentries.

Fabius watched the column go past. Maximus and he exchanged glances but Maximus was too professional a soldier to nod or wave. He had a look on his face which troubled Fabius but it was soon forgotten as he turned to go in search of Mapona.

Had Fabius been a more astute observer he might have realised that the cohort, which had already crunched its way out of sight, was unaccompanied. There were no heavy support waggons carrying the supplies that would be needed to sustain the soldiers in the field.

On the edge of town, the two big Beltane fires had been lit and the cattle were being marshalled into place. Soon they would be driven between the fires to ensure fertility, good luck and prosperity for the coming year.

The streets were full of Britons. People had come in from

all around for the brightest and most cheerful festival of the year. They pushed through the noisy market-place with its stalls, jugglers and musicians. They spilled out into the alley-ways between the mean houses, laughing, arguing, drinking.

There were no Romans to be seen. They knew they weren't welcome at this the most important event of the Britons' year. The single men kept to the bathhouse and mansio or the tavern in the quieter end of town and the families gathered in the villas in the countryside.

With the intended consequences of his plan in mind Fabius did not want to be recognised as a Roman so he disguised himself by wearing a cape with the hood pulled over his head. He slipped through the back alleyways to Mapona's house. He was disappointed to find it empty. Perhaps, he thought, they had gone to bring in their own cattle. With an un-accountable sense of fear he prayed that their fields were a long way from the fort. Uncertain of what to do he started towards the main street.

The raiders struck from the south-west. Their blue-patterned naked bodies glistened with oils and sweat. Brandishing swords, they yelled blood-chilling war cries as they invaded the town.

Fabius nearly ran into them. He quickly doubled back, then, with face averted, made for the east of the town, to the tanneries and workshops deserted for Beltane. As he went he tried to work out what had happened, for things were not proceeding as he had intended.

It was obvious what the Ordovicians should be doing. They should be skirting Letocetum to avoid the crowd, then going on to take the undefended fort. There they should kill the small duty detachment, fire the fort buildings then make off with the money chest from the treasury. That is what they should be doing.

When he came to the great road he scuttled across it as quickly as he could, for it would be too easy to be seen or even caught there. Once across he dodged down the little lanes between the buildings, consoling himself with the thought that perhaps he had only seen the diversionary party. Obviously, the main raiding party was already making its way past the town and was even now forming up to take the fort.

Fabius was wrong. Certainly the Ordovicians were taking advantage of the army's absence, but they were not on their way to attack the fort. Instead, they had come to steal cattle. Their reasoning was simple. Killing Roman soldiers and stealing the Legion's money would lead to reprisals on a scale not seen for a generation. Stealing cattle from the Cornovii, on the other hand, would damage the Romans indirectly, since in effect they owned everything, but they would be most unlikely to do anything more than just send out a retaliatory patrol or two. Besides, as the Ordovicians saw it, cattle were of more practical value.

The main body of the raiders charged their way through the terror-stricken crowds to where the cattle were milling around. A handful of raiders, though, hotly declaring it would be impossible to drive cattle through the streets, decided instead to go looting. They burst into the bathhouse. There, two fat and naked bathers, faced with the ghastly apparition of the blue-painted Ordovicians, were only too glad to hand over their finger-rings in return for being spared.

It wasn't much, and the raiders were becoming despondent at the lack of riches when their eyes fell upon the glittering gold taps of the baths. Forgetting the orders of their leader, they wrenched them from the wall. Three Romans rushed forward and tried to stop them. Angry but fearful, the Ordovicians slaughtered them and pushed their bodies into the water.

The other Romans there took up swords and swiftly organised themselves. They drove the raiders into the mansio where they were trapped in the small colonnaded garden and cut down.

In the confusion, one wounded Ordovician, leaving a bloody trail, crawled from a store-room into a corner of the mansio and hid his loot. He died for the sake of a spearhead and an axe.

In the streets outside, one angry Briton turned upon a raider. Soon Britons were fighting Britons. The cattle panicked and many people were badly trampled.

In the turmoil the raiders became separated. Shouting war cries above the screaming and shouting of the crowd, they managed to re-form into three groups.

One group fled to the north, past the main fort and into the safety of the forest.

Another smaller group ran into the mansio. There they came across the bodies of their fallen comrades. The Romans, gory swords at the ready, tried to defend themselves but were hacked down as if their blades were straw. The raiders put torches to the mansio and the bathhouse, then, seizing the taps, came out and joined up with the third group of raiders who were frenziedly driving their stolen cattle through the town.

As they went the raiders shouted and argued about the best way to get back to their own territory. They were slowed by the cattle and burdened by the heavy gold taps, so instead of going cross-country they decided to take the Street, the risky but most direct route to the west.

They came out on to the great open road and ran straight into the Roman cohort returning at the double.

The raiders fought bravely but they were driven back to the town.

There, trapped between the Roman swords and the inferno of the blazing buildings, they died.

Fabius wandered about the devastated town. He had come back from hiding in the tanneries to the east. He was appalled at what he had brought about. He had been unable to find Mapona and he sank to his knees by the smouldering ruins of her house.

He did not struggle when seized by strong arms from behind. Two soldiers forced him to his feet.

'So, you've come back?' a cutting voice said.

He was wrenched around. Staring at him with bloodshot eyes was Captain Maximus.

'Satisfied with the results of your work?' he asked bitterly.

Soldiers and townspeople were trying to identify the less badly charred bodies. Slaves were digging graves and burying the dead. On a cart were the naked blue-stained corpses of the slain raiders.

Maximus continued as if reporting to his commander. 'Roman bodies in the cemetery. Trusted Britons or those of high rank also in the cemetery. Children with their parents. That British woman you were friends with and her brother, put together in the same grave. Unknowns, itinerants and raiders – into the communal cremation fire.'

Maximus was still talking but Fabius no longer heard.

Mapona! Dead! A great cry of agony burst from him. He screamed and howled at the sky like a dog. Finally he broke down in tears. 'Help me,' he sobbed in anguish. 'Help me, it's all gone wrong.'

Maximus – calm, urbane Maximus. He would help a fellow Roman in trouble, but to his horror the officer said bleakly, 'You are under arrest.'

The soldiers tightened their grip. Fabius seemed unable to believe what he was hearing.

'It's all wrong. I'm a Roman citizen. It's against the law for you to detain me.'

Maximus spoke swiftly and concisely. 'You are charged with treason. The departure of the cohort was a deception. Only the fort commander and I knew that. I was ordered to tell you, and only you, that the cohort was leaving. You put this information in your report even though military matters are expressly forbidden. You purposely told an Ordovician spy about the content of your report. The courier was intercepted and the rest you know. You set it up. You are a traitor. You have no defence or redress.'

Fabius struggled and his mind whirled. He sought for something to say, something to break the spell. He wanted to scream out.

The captain's eyes that had seen death in every form in every province of the Empire stared into his, draining his willpower. He whispered, 'Say a prayer to whatever god you think you have.'

The soldiers knew and admired the technique. Just as the awful truth is sensed, the advice to pray is whispered, causing the victim to search his mind for the most supreme power he can appeal to.

It inevitably pacifies the victim, and Fabius was no exception.

Almost imperceptibly he relaxed. His mind tried to ignore

the sharp-clawed terror that was beginning to scrabble in his guts and he gratefully took up the task of choosing: Mithras? Cernunnos? Teutates?

As if by magic the much-feared Roman short sword leaped from its well-greased scabbard into the officer's hand. With practised ease the glittering blade came into Fabius just three times – two inches deep, no more and no less.

The first stab cut his larynx and severed a throat artery: he could no longer cry out.

The second stab sliced into his right armpit severing the tendons: he could no longer use his arm.

The third stab slid into his groin severing muscles and the great artery. His left leg folded itself up and he fell to the ground powerless to move.

The blood pumped out from the three gaping mouth-like wounds. A roaring darkness engulfed him and the golden Land of Promise welcomed his eager spirit.

'To the cemetery with him, sir? He was half Roman, wasn't he?'

'He betrayed Rome and he betrayed the Britons. Put him on the fire,' ordered the captain.

And so perished Fabius Antoninus.

Chapter 18

I had come to the end of Chad's story. My listeners remained in silence: enslaved Britons, men who had just been told of the humiliation and slaughter of their ancestors.

I waited for an outburst of anger, but none came.

'Rise up,' I shouted. 'Free yourselves and—'

The Englisc speaker interrupted me. 'They are going to talk about the story,' he said, 'and I will tell you what they say.'

I felt a flash of anger but then thought of the way the monks trained the boys in the monastery. A little patience and a lot of thrashing. I would be patient . . . for the moment.

Some of my 'warriors' spoke at length, and in spite of my anger I found myself drawn into their words.

They drew lessons from the story which I had not appreciated before and I began to feel ashamed at my misjudgement of the depth of their understanding.

They had little sympathy for the raiders, whom they saw as mere cattle thieves. They admired Maximus, who had acted as a soldier should. One Briton had been impressed by the way Maximus had told Fabius what he was guilty of before executing him.

There was a stifled ripple of laughter when another asked where he could find a woman who'd do with him what Mapona did with Fabius. Most of the other Britons scowled at this, though. They had immediately recognised her as a priestess and a leader. They admired her for giving herself for the sake of her people.

There was widespread dislike of Fabius. They saw him as a traitor and unmanly. He had used Mapona, although they conceded he may have loved her. To them, he was 'bookish' but not very clever.

The Englisc speaker, who was clearly a leader, then gave his view. He said the story was a riddle in that one could read many things into it but some things were clear: Fabius was a symbol of our times where confusion about identity was commonplace; the Romans appeared to have acted correctly – unlike the Saxons of today – but it was they who had created the problem in the first place. Most important of all: Mapona was the spirit of the Britons that would rise again from the ashes.

His final words gave me an opportunity, and I turned to address the slaves, once more to gain support for my mission.

I was astounded to see that many of them were now free of their ropes. I realised that while I was telling them Chad's story they must have been busy undoing the knots.

I looked for the guards but there were none in sight. A few short steps to the gaps in the fence and the Britons would be gone, leaving me on my own. 'Listen,' I called. 'We must strike a blow . . . a blood feud . . . to avenge my father . . .'

My voice tailed off.

The mocking moon was shining his light down to show me that many of the Britons had curled up where they were, having made themselves comfortable, so they could sleep all the better for being free of the ropes.

I saw the Englisc speaker and his kin making for the other side of the enclosure.

'Wait,' I called and ran after them.

They stopped and the Englisc speaker said, 'You have given a lot up for us, and you look like losing even more if you stay. Won't you come with us?'

'No,' I said. 'It is as I say: I have given my word.'

'I see: a man who rides two horses,' he said enigmatically. 'But we salute you.' He hugged me and kissed my cheek and his kin did likewise.

Then they started to squeeze through a gap. The Englisc speaker was the last to go.

'I can give you nothing,' he said, 'but you respect our history and beliefs so I feel I can tell you something: the wise Briton called Morien said that a man comes to God through his own deeds, regardless of what others may try to make him do. God demands that men choose between good or evil through their own free will. It is a matter of personal responsibility, Edwin, not fate.'

He held my arm for a moment. 'I understand why you told us Chad's story,' he said, 'but for your sake I am glad you didn't succeed. You must find peace of mind by yourself. Think about what Morien said, but be careful who you tell about it. God be with you.'

Then he squeezed through the hole.

'Where can I find this Morien?' I called after him.

'He went to Rome to teach Christianity and never returned,' he called back and was swallowed by the night.

The moon had let a thin wind draw clouds across the sky and before I could appeal to him, he turned his face from me. Why had he done this? He was the master of the night, and my intentions were surely as dark as his domain.

Shivering, I stumbled back across the enclosure to the black huddled mass of the Britons. I should have to sleep up against them for warmth's sake or I might not survive the night.

As I bedded down with them in the dung and mud I hurriedly pulled a door flap of thought across the door of my mind. Why should I be careful about telling people of Morien's ideas? And who were they, that I should be careful of them?

Outside the flimsy flap stood the great Beast of Despair. I had failed utterly in every single one of my plans – every single one. I had lost my family, my friends, Finn.

If, during the night, I as much as lifted the door flap the beast would seize me in his fangs and destroy me.

He roamed around the door of my mind for the greater part of the night. At one time, when I was half asleep, he pushed his huge shaggy head in and his warm, stinking breath erupted over me. I screamed and came fully awake, only to find that a sleeping Briton was responsible for my fright.

I shifted away from him and tried to sleep, but I could not. Images came and went. Pages of the scripture turned before me and whole sections of text stood out in letters of fire. Leofgifu came and stood silent before me, holding her stomach with both hands. The faces of other people appeared and spoke. Some were full of praise, but most rebuked me.

Ideas twisted and turned upon each other like slimy eels caught in a woven withy trap.

Then the pale and ghostly faces of Chad and the Englisc speaker came. They appeared behind and before me until they blurred into one and flowed over me like a river of watery milk. I became so vexed that I sat bolt upright and shouted at them in the name of God to let me sleep.

I found that I was sitting in the early morning light with my head and shoulders protruding from the ground mist. All about me I could hear the Britons stirring, disturbed by my shouting, but I could hardly see them through the grey sheet that stretched across the enclosure.

I started to shiver and my stomach was a clammy clenched fist in the middle of my body, but my heart! At first I thought that I must be ill again but then I realised that the serenity I felt was beyond illness. My spirit floated over this sorry mess of mud, dung, stink and pain like a white bird gliding above a slaughter pit.

I knew that there would be difficulties ahead, but I felt that I could face Bishop Wynfrid and King Wulfhere with full confidence. I had made mistakes but I had paid a heavy price for them. They might seek to punish me – well, so be it – but somehow I knew that they would be inclined to forgive. Wulfhere especially: Chad had told me that the king had a soft place in his heart for spirited and enquiring young men. If so, I would be successful when I came before him to plead my case.

A great feeling of contentment came over me, and as the first rays of the morning sun lit up the sharp points of the alder palisade, turning their tips into gold, I turned my face to heaven and cried, 'I thank thee, O Lord, for at last I have found peace.'

A short distance from me the black matted hair and swarthy face of a Briton popped up through the mist. He sat and blinked in the light. Then, a little beyond him, another popped up, and then another, until thirty or so pairs of shoulders were protruding through the mist, supporting heads that blinked and coughed and spat. One or two looked in my direction but most were looking across the hawe to the gate. We sat like that until the clanking of weapons beyond heralded the arrival of the guards.

A party of four heavily armed Mercians marched towards

us. One carried a few loaves of bread, and as they came near he tore them in halves and threw them among the Britons. Once again I saw them scrabbling in the mud for food, and the early anger began to return.

The guards seemed not to notice that the Britons were no longer roped together. Instead they came up to me and halted.

'Brother Edwin, are you unharmed?' one asked, but he seemed too preoccupied with some weighty matter to wait for a reply. He thrust bread into my hand. 'Come with us, if you please,' he said, and the civility took me by surprise.

I could not walk fast, so we moved slowly towards the gate.

Shouting broke out behind us and we turned to see what was happening. One slave had leaped up and was running towards us.

The cry went up, 'Stop the Traitor', but he nimbly dodged the outstretched hands.

As he came he shouted, 'Edwin has betrayed you. He persuaded many to leave in the night. He preached sedition.'

'Hullo, here's trouble,' said one guard laconically, and they formed a shield wall.

'Halt,' he warned, but the Briton came on.

'Arrest Edwin. He prayed to the moon,' he shouted.

In a practised movement, one guard braced his right leg and levelled his spear. The charging Briton, unable to stop, impaled himself on its point. The spearman skilfully rode with the impact and the slave stood for a moment, rolling his eyes in a foolish way. With blood foaming out of his nose and mouth, he fell to the ground.

The pursuing men came to a halt and stood watching as the spearman put one foot on the fallen Briton to remove his spear. The point appeared to have lodged in the slave's backbone, so two other guards put their weight on the victim while the grunting spearman pulled and twisted the shaft until it finally tore free. While this was happening the dying man arched his back in agony and drummed his heels on the ground.

'You killed that man,' I protested.

'He killed himself,' said the spearman, wiping the blade on the grass.

A younger guard said, 'They sometimes do that. We call it an "outburst". They just suddenly charge at us . . . by the way, anyone know what was he saying?'

'Not an inkling,' said the spearman in a voice that ended the matter and we continued on our way to the gate.

'What are we going to do now?' said the young guard as we went, and I knew that he wasn't talking about me or the casual killing of the Briton.

The guard who had carried the loaves said, 'Should we wait here or report back to Tamworth?'

They were talking as if something serious had happened, but I was unconcerned. I found myself smiling as I saw with my mind's eye how it would be when I came before my thegn, the Bishop Wynfrid, and my lord, the great King Wulfhere. What a tale I would tell them, what discoveries of Morien and of how I had found that the Britons had a history as rich as our own.

'We stay here until word arrives,' said the dogmatic spearman.

At the gate they gave me my staff back and handed me over to the armed group who arrested me the night before. It amused me that they seemed to be glad to get rid of me, and I was still smiling as I left the alder hawe.

Chapter 19

As the guards marched me off, I stumbled on a rock in the track. On the instant, one man drew his scramasax.

'Escaping already?' he sneered. 'Just try, that's all. You'll be sorry you even thought of it.'

As I retaliated I felt there was something familiar about his hostile voice and manner of speaking but I couldn't place it.

'How dare you threaten a member of the Church in this manner,' I said, as loftily as I could. 'King Wulfhere shall hear of your disgraceful behaviour and then it is you who will be sorry.'

'Hear that, mates? This holy man is going to tell tales to Wulfhere,' he guffawed. 'He might get the chance sooner than he thinks, eh?'

The other guards laughed at his wit. This pleased him, and he sheathed his scramasax.

'Here's something for you, your omniscience,' he said. 'Wulfhere is dead, God rest his soul. Aethelred is now king, and he hates troublesome monks of the British Church even more than he hates pagans. Wynfrid backs him up in that. So watch it, right?'

My heart grew cold at his doom-laden words.

'Come on, come on,' the leader said. 'We haven't got time to stand around.'

'And Owini? What of my brother monk?' I said, trying to make my legs move again.

The unpleasant guard snorted. 'Your brother, Brother? He's thrown all the nuns out of the Church. Can't think why, can you? Anyway, I hear tell that it pleased Aethelred.'

What a fool I had been not to have foreseen Wulfhere's death. Aethelred had even warned me of it at the cave.

If the guard was speaking the truth then I was in a worse position than ever before. Ranged against me now were the dangerous and unstable Aethelred; Wynfrid, become turn-coat; and the villainous intriguer Owini.

How worthless those three men are compared with my own dear Finn, I thought. God grant it that he will come to magic me away, as he once did before. My spirits rose for a moment as my thoughts dwelled on such a wondrous possibility. I had heard of mortals being saved by those from the Otherworld, but cold reality seeped back into my bones. There would be no miraculous rescue. Mutilation, outlawry or death awaited me.

We moved on but my guards seemed in no hurry to get to Lichfield. We'd gone by the ruin of a building being used as a smithy and had just passed the potters' claypits when a strong image came to me.

'Stop!' I cried. 'I have had a vision.'

The guards halted. Now they seemed nervous.

'Tell us what you see,' demanded their leader.

'I see drinking vessels and water jars being smashed by unknown men, by outsiders . . . there is danger.'

Their reaction was stronger than I would have thought. With exclamations of alarm, they drew their scramasaxes and started looking about them with anxious eyes.

'Can you see who these men are?'

I shut my eyes. 'One is called King of the Wicce . . .'

Before I could finish, the guard who had threatened me

with his scramasax blurted out, 'Those traitors from the Severn valley? You can't trust any of 'em! And all that Aethelred did for them, as well.'

The leader of the guard stood looking at me thoughtfully. 'It's true that Aethelred has let some of the Wicce settle to the north – they are already calling it Wiccenor – but I don't see how that makes them any danger to us.' He paused, then said, 'I'd like to know if our all-seeing friend can tell us any more.'

I seized the chance. 'Yesterday, on my way to Wall, I was nearly attacked by a thegn and twenty or so armed men going along the Pipe Hill track towards Lichfield. They were strangers and in a hurry. What is happening?'

The leader looked troubled. 'Aethelred has proclaimed himself High King,' he said. 'Many other kings and lords are displeased with this. Some openly dispute his claim. They may seek to overthrow him. Perhaps you are loyal to one of these?'

Before I could answer, the guard who disliked me spoke. 'There's trouble brewing. I don't trust this monk.'

The others said nothing, but stood looking along the track and into the woodland bordering the fields. I saw that their minds were going ahead to where there might be fighting.

He persisted, 'What say we run him through and then get on back to Lichfield?'

I quickly glanced at his feet to see if he was preparing to strike at me. Their shape caught my attention. They were almost as broad as they were long. A man with feet like this could never sink in the mud of winter. Then it came to me: he was the warrior who had nearly caught me in the reed beds.

I looked him straight in the eye and in my best preaching voice said, 'I can see into you, my son. I see doubt and uncertainty. I see one who professes to love the Lord but who is perhaps a pagan in his heart. I see one who professes loyalty to Aethelred but who perhaps reserves his love for the king who has gone on the long voyage into the sinking sun. I see a man whose loyalty hides a greed for shining weapons and shirts of link-mail.'

His mouth fell open. Fear replaced the hate-light in his eyes and he licked his lips nervously. If I got the next words wrong his keen blade would wreak its wicked work.

'Come, let us kneel in prayer,' I said, and before he could move I knelt before him with my neck bared and vulnerable. I was still holding my staff but instead of being a potential weapon it was now just a support for an elderly man.

He stood for a long second. He was either raising his heavy scramasax aloft or he was looking from my defenceless form to his comrades.

He knelt.

I began to pray. 'O Lord, forgive us our doubts. Make our minds clear and let us open our hearts to thy truth. Give us the gift of understanding and the wisdom to receive thy message of hope. Give us the strength to reject the ways of the old and to embrace the ways of the new.'

I sensed that I was losing his attention so I said, 'Amen.'

He muttered something, and started to get up. I put my hand upon his shoulder and stopped him rising. I needed to say something else. I prayed again, but in a quieter voice, so that only he should hear.

'I call upon thee, O Lord, to give this loyal servant the great gift of invisibility in battle, so that his undoubted courage shall be doubly rewarded. I know that this is a rare gift, O Lord, but grant it just so long as he cherishes me. Amen.'

This time he added a full amen and we rose together. He embraced me and called out to his companions, 'Shall we go?'

'Go where?' said the leader, taken aback by this sudden change of heart.

'Why, to the bishop, I suppose,' said my new-found friend and protector. 'We shall have to look after our brother and keep him safe from the Wicce or rebellious Britons.'

'Why yes, you have it aright,' said the leader, still looking bemused, 'but I suspect that certain of the people at Lichfield will be more of a threat to him than any Wicce or Briton we may meet.'

We resumed our progression towards the village and it became easier for me to walk as the track changed from clay to sandy soil.

Suddenly we were halted. Something had alerted the leader. He ran to a clump of trees ahead. Beyond it, a thin line of smoke was rising. I sat on the side of the track. The guards drew their scramasaxes and looked warily about them.

Soon he came back.

'There's been fighting,' he said.

'Good,' said one guard, edging in the direction of the smoke which had now become a marker of death.

No one else moved and he looked in surprise at his companions.

'Aren't we going to join in, then?' he said.

'Our task is to deliver Edwin up to Bishop Wynfrid, and we shall not fail in that, I assure you,' said the leader. 'But I promise that if we are attacked you shall bear the brunt.'

The guard looked mollified by that. He sheathed his scramasax and waited for further orders.

'We'll stay here until it is clear,' said the leader. 'Let us get off the track. Then we'll eat our food.'

We made our way to a small stand of trees and sat in their cover. I had no food, but the warriors each gave me some of theirs without question or prompting. My protector seemed a little reluctant to hand his contribution over, though, and one of the other guards soon discovered the reason: he had white bread.

They mocked him for it. 'Where did you get that?' they said. 'Do you now eat at the king's table?'

He was unrepentant. 'It was thrown out by the church,' he said. 'I saved it from going to waste.'

The other guards seemed unsurprised at his reply, but I was greatly intrigued.

'Has Owini taken to eating white bread, then?' I said.

'Oh no, not him. 'Tis the bishop. I hear that him and Owini don't see eye to eye on that, and other things besides.'

Water bottles were passed round and I was offered more to eat but my stomach was already beginning to protest at so much food after my recent involuntary fasting.

While we were eating, two Britons appeared on the track, going in the Lichfield direction. They halted when they caught sight of us, but when the warriors with me took no notice they went on, although with frequent glances in our direction. From their condition and their frightened manner I took them to be escapees from the alder hawe.

I asked my guards if they knew what was happening in that dreadful place but they shook their heads.

I told them a little of it, and they seemed disgusted. When I pressed them for their reasons, though, it became clear that they were divided. My protector and a tall thin fellow, taking the Britons' side, protested against their inhuman treatment. The leader and the other guard were more concerned about the waste of labour.

'It has become more and more difficult to get workers,' he said. 'My father tells me that there are far fewer Britons than there used to be. They are not breeding so readily now, and those that do come along are weak and workshy.'

He spoke of them as one speaks of livestock, and I noticed that my new-found friend was biting his lip. I, too, held my peace: after all the leader was a Mercian and therefore totally lacking in feeling for his fellows. Nevertheless, it was an interesting observation. The Britons were confined to their owners' lands and were, in consequence, like to suffer from inbreeding.

Then, as we talked, someone noticed that workers were coming back to their tasks in the hitherto deserted fields. They took no notice of us but bent their faces to the ground and started work again.

Watching them prompted my memory and I decided to pass on what I had recalled to my guards.

'Here is something Chad told us. There is a legend, he said, that in the days when the Britons were the owners of these fields they supplied the entire Roman army with grain and leather. Of course, the monks laughed at that, but he reproved us, saying there may be an element of truth in the legend. He said the Mercian people could not have made these fields so fruitful in the short time they have been here.'

No one spoke when I finished the tale but I wondered if the seeds I had sown would bear fruit later on.

The leader of the guard said, 'These people coming back to work suggest that the way is clear. I'll take a look.' Then he added pointedly, 'Stay here and keep good care of our prisoner.'

Yes. I smiled to myself. I think I pricked his heart and he didn't like it.

Soon he was back, saying, 'It looks all clear now, but keep a sharp look out. Come on.'

We moved cautiously along the track with scramasaxes drawn.

My new friend seemed unready as yet to test his newly gained powers. 'I'll look after you,' he muttered, and came so close by my side that he kept knocking me with his shield edge, but I supposed he was unaware of this.

Soon we came to a farmstead. The bellowing of cattle rose up from behind a thick hedge set with sharpened stakes. It made a fearsome barricade against wolves and thieves.

'This place is called Maccstoc. My family knows Macca the cattle-man well,' said the leader quietly. 'He has one of the finest herds in the region. Perhaps there's been a cattle raid. We must help. Come on, but be careful.'

I had heard of Macca. He was of Irish origin and Chad had managed to persuade him to donate generously to the Church.

A hawthorn tree at the entrance to his land stood garlanded with flowers of yellow and blue, ribbons and bows of cloth. It drew no comment from my companions. Perhaps they were so used to seeing signs of Beltane or May Day about them that they gave no special thought to it.

Through a little gap in the hedge I could see many fine-looking cows in the compound. They needed to be milked. The leader called us on and we went softly to the farm buildings.

Two of the outhouses were smouldering and here and there were bodies. Men and women were running hither and yon at the direction of a large red-haired man. He was still holding his scramasax even though the immediate danger seemed to be past.

'Stay here,' ordered the leader and we stood in a huddle while he went towards the scene of slaughter. He stopped some fifty paces from the big man and, unslinging his horn, sounded two blasts.

He then called Macca's name and identified himself saying that he came in peace.

At the sound of the horn the red-haired man swung round, his bloodstained scramasax raised ready for action again. He paused for a moment then lowered his scramasax. Only then did the leader approach him. They talked, with Macca pointing to the corpses, then he went back to his sorrow-laden task.

'Come,' said the leader. 'There is nothing we can do here. He has it all in hand.'

My impression of Macca had been one of great strength and authority. Heaviness lay in my heart, for he would surely have been an ally had Madoc and Finn taken Lichfield. With the support of powerful men like him a Celtic brotherhood of Britons, Welsh and Irish could have easily regained and held their ancient lands.

My armed escort and I took to the track again and the leader began to tell us of what had happened.

'It was not cattle thieves or outlaws,' he said, 'but it was as we thought. A party of about twelve men led by a wounded thegn, perhaps the group seen by Edwin, came past here in a hurry. It seems they'd been to Wiccenor to rouse up the people against Aethelred but had been repulsed. They'd set fire to houses there then fled. They came through Lichfield and were attacked. They stopped here just long enough to set fire to two buildings. Macca's sons and some of his men set upon them and captured three or four. Before they died they told Macca all they knew. The rest had run away.'

As he was speaking we came upon the stone cart from Wall. A wheel had gone into the ditch, and the cart was on its side. The two enormous stones had tumbled into the field and lay half buried in the soft soil. Of the oxen there was no sign.

The British slaves were there, though. They were still in their bonds and roped together. Some had broken necks and others had been killed by the blade. The fleeing thegn and his cowardly men had done this to spite Aethelred.

As we passed the cart my friend with the frog's feet snorted. 'Owini won't like that,' he said nastily.

'What won't he like?'

'Why, the fact that he's lost those stones, a cart and maybe the oxen. Oh, and some slaves, of course.'

'But it will all be made good, surely?'

'Ah, that's where you're wrong, see. We heard that when Chad died, Owini went to King Wulfhere and boasted that he could build the new church himself. It wouldn't cost the king a penny but it would be well made, he says, certainly good enough for a new bishop. And then, folk say, he winked at the king.'

I was stunned by the crudity of the thing.

Frogfoot took my silence for lack of understanding, for he continued. 'Don't you get it? Owini wants to get Wynfrid out and get the bishopric for himself.' Then he added, as an afterthought, 'Why am I telling you this? You ought to know more about it than me.'

I sensed danger. 'I have been in retreat. Living in a cave. Ever since Chad died I've been trying to get nearer to God. 'I've had no news of the church. Is it done yet?'

'No, of course not. Owini couldn't really do it for nothing, could he? The news going round is that Wulfhere was secretly giving him money to do the work. Aethelred didn't know about it. If he finds out, though, Owini will be in the shit, I reckon.'

'Enough, Britaelis,' the leader of the guard said. Then he gave the guards an order: 'Sheath your scramasaxes! Spears at the trail!'

We walked in silence, for we were coming to the reed-thatched roofs of Lichfield village.

We stopped at the boundary of the common land and the settlement. I felt strange, disembodied even. I had been away for a little time yet Lichfield had changed greatly. More huts had been built here on the south side of the pool where the ground was marshy and unhealthy.

The leader unslung his horn and blew two blasts. He was taking no chances.

Neither were the inhabitants of Lichfield.

Before the blast of the horn had died away, armed men came out from between the huts.

'Who goes there?' one called.

'Leader of the guard, with two men from the royal household. And Britaelis from the church militia and Brother Edwin, who is to attend a hearing with the bishop tomorrow,' he answered.

At these words, one of the armed men turned and ran off. He was going to check the story.

For my part I could have held the leader in my arms and kissed him as a brother. He had identified me as a monk and had worded the reason for my presence in such a way that I could get a reasonable lodging. Had he said that I was a prisoner then I would have been chained up in a pigsty for the night.

We waited in the silence. The light was fading and a chill mist was rising. My guards were becoming uneasy at the delay. They glanced back up the track from time to time, shifting the grip on their spears.

On one side of the track were the stream and the reed beds, and on the other were herb gardens belonging to the huts. Women called the children in, for night was coming.

'Which of you is the armed member of the church?' I said, to ease the tension.

'Him,' said one, cocking a thumb at my protector, who smirked.

His slight build and swarthy face stood in contrast with the height and ruddy faces of the others.

'An honour for you, Britaelis, I'm sure. Do you share your military duties to the church with many others?' I quietly asked him.

'We be a dozen in number,' he announced proudly.

'I expect that Bishop Wynfrid is an easier master to serve than King Wulfhere?'

'I don't serve him,' he said scornfully. 'I serve Owini. He's hard he is. Mind you, Wulfhere was stern, but he knew how to do things properly. Owini's a rough sod.'

'Like master, like servant,' said one of the guards, and they laughed.

Instantly came the order, 'Be quiet. Keep alert.'

They fell silent.

There was a soft chinking of iron on iron and an armed man came out from the shadows of the huts. He called the leader over. They talked for a moment then he came back to us.

'Things have changed,' he said. 'Edwin is to be closely guarded. Aethelred is coming to Lichfield to deal with him in person.'

The words were like a slap on my face.

Aethelred to deal with me . . . in person!

The leader was talking to the other guards. Their attention was on him. I quickly looked at the tall clumps of reeds running along the stream. Once among them it would be hard to spot me, especially in this poor light. I would go back to the cave. After that . . . into the forest, deep, where no man could find me.

I edged towards the reeds.

Chapter 20

Britaelis materialised at my side, his spear pointing in my direction, or so it seemed.

'What have you found, master?'

He startled me but I swiftly covered my intentions.

'Look,' I said, indicating a herb growing on the grassy path. 'Here's plenty of speedwell – useful for my leechcraeft . . . but is there news?'

He grinned up at me. 'I have been given the honour of guarding you, master,' he said. 'Me and my mate here. And because you are accounted to be a man of honour, you shall sleep on clean straw. I know the place where we'll stay. Come with me.'

He led the way to one of the huts. The guard leader and the other warrior left but we were not permitted to cross the sandy ford to the settlement on the north side. We had to stay on the southern side of the pool and not on the church side. That worried me.

Although I had been prepared to make my own way into the darkness, I did not like the idea of passing the night in one of these flimsy huts. We would be an easy target should the band of armed men make a dawn reprisal raid.

The hut was reasonably dry and the floor had been freshly strewn with hay. It smelled musty. This should have been fodder for cattle lucky enough to have survived the winter. In the middle of the floor was the hearth. The flickering fire lit up our faces and that of an old woman. Britaelis asked her to get food and ale.

'Yes, I'll go,' she said. 'But who is to pay?'

'Owini,' he said.

At that, she made no movement but spat in the fire instead. With a sigh he opened the purse at his belt and gave her a coin. She looked closely at the coin then went out into the dusk.

Britaelis and the other warrior squatted on their haunches in front of the fire. I was too tired and stiff to do likewise so I sat with my back against the wattle and daub wall. Britaelis tried to get the other man to talk but he was a laconic type who said little. We sat in silence. My eyelids started to droop. The warmth came into me as from Leofgifu when we lay together.

A log shifted in the fire.

'I'm as hungry as a wolf,' Britaelis said. 'Where's that woman got to? I'll see if I can hurry her along.' He rose wearily and took up his spear and shield. 'Keep an eye on my master here,' he instructed. 'I don't want to lose him before I must,' and he went out, chuckling.

Britaelis's words had brought me back to reality. I sought for something to say to take my mind off what was to come. Then, as if I had said something, the silent warrior spoke.

'We killed a wolf the other day. Great big thing with yellow eyes.'

Hearing about this man's hunting and success at killing wasn't what I needed but at least he was talking. He spoke again, as if I had said something to him.

'Yes, up by Long Don. To the south of Briar Don on the edge of Cannock Wood.'

For no real reason I grew cold at his words. There were

many wolves in the region. Men killed them all the time. Yet I feared what he might say next. I bit my lip and kept my silence.

His face was expressionless as he gazed into the fire. He nodded, as if there were a conversation going on inside his head.

'Yes, Owini sent us. He said there was a daemon living in a cave. Sometimes it took the form of a wolf and sometimes the form of a man. We were to kill it.'

The blood pounded in my ears. I forced myself to listen

'That's right. I've never seen anything like it. I'll swear the wolf was leading us away from somewhere or someone. He led us on and then . . . he seemed to let us kill him.'

My body was rigid. I wanted him to shut up, but I needed him to continue.

'When the spears went in he screamed just like a human.'

The warrior turned his face to me. He must have seen the tears running down my face for he spoke softly.

'That wolf, if wolf it was, showed great loyalty to someone. I'd be for ever proud to have been loved like that.'

He turned his face to the fire and lapsed into silence. My spirit was in turmoil and anguish. How bitter was this life. Oak-man, the wisest holy man I had ever met, or was ever likely to meet, was dead, slain at the behest of the ignorant Owini.

I no longer cared what happened to me, for my fate was ordaining that I should be drained of love. I saw that I was to be emptied out of every emotion save fear before being put to death.

Britaelis and the old woman came back. He held the door flap and she came in with a hempen sack over her back. She carried a wooden bucket in one hand.

Britaelis swaggered about, bursting to impart some great bit of gossip he had gleaned while eavesdropping. He propped his shield and spear against the wall. I didn't want to hear his tales, so just as he was about to speak I got up and took the bucket from the old woman. It contained ale. I lifted the sack from her shoulders and she straightened a little with a grateful sigh. 'Thank you, thank you,' she said, and started to take food out from the sack.

Britaelis seemed unabashed by my rudeness.

'I see we are all too hungry to hear my news,' he said, 'so I'll tell you later, when our bellies are full,' and he squatted down by the fire in eager expectation.

The old woman poured ale then cut ham and barley bread. The two warriors started eating. They put pieces of ham into their mouths and cut off what protruded with small knives. Now and again bits of bread went the same way. When the whole process looked like coming to a halt, ale was poured in and the mills started grinding again.

I became angry with myself. Once again in the face of great threat I had become fascinated by some trivial item.

The old woman motioned at my food. I remembered the knife in my purse, took it out and started to eat. She refilled our horns then took some food herself.

She tended the fire which from time to time billowed smoke. One cloud seemed particularly acrid and I looked across the hearth. Although she was trying to hide her actions I could see that she was burning small scatterings of grain.

She looked up and our eyes met. She said nothing but her pale blue eyes were defiant. Clearly, she thought that I might protest at this pagan custom.

I nodded at the fire. 'Someone has died?'

Her lined face relaxed then took on an expression of

resigned sadness. 'Yes. One of our young men, wounded in the raid earlier. We couldn't save him. It was his fate to die on the very last day of Eostremonath.'

To die in the month of rebirth was a cruel irony, I thought, sharing her sorrow, but I also reflected on the contrast about me. This community was clearly following the old ways, yet scarcely a sling-shot's distance away across the pool a new church was being raised. That church represented the new way of religion. It wanted to crush the old ways and perhaps even the people who practised them.

We finished our meal. The old woman offered me more ale but I refused it. She set the wooden bucket down between the two warriors. They would see to what was left. She offered to clean my knife. I noticed her examining it closely in the light of the fire. She cleaned it well with sand and dried grass, making the blade shine.

She handed it back, saying, 'A nice knife.'

'Yes, a good friend gave it to me.'

'And would this friend's name be Leofgifu?'

As the old woman said these words something caused the flame of the lamp to flicker suddenly. I felt uncomfortable. I had never fully understood the power of the old way and things happened that I couldn't explain.

'And if that were so?' I said.

The old woman was smiling to herself. She rocked back and forth. 'She is my granddaughter. She got our blacksmith to make the knife but she put the handle on it herself. This knife has been dedicated to Weyland and so has special properties. If you look you may understand.'

Mention of the god of ironworking surprised me. I examined the knife but could see nothing.

'You are a good man, Edwin, even though you do not always see the wondrous things before you.'

Puzzlement must have showed on my face.

'Give me the knife. Now, look at this sharp shining metal,' she said, and she turned and twisted the knife so that the blade caught the light of the fire and instantly became a dragon's fiery tongue. 'It has such power, such life, yet it was created from nothing more than a few handfuls of dull stone. Is that not magical?' she whispered. 'And it was made for you, especially for you, only for you. Look at it again and you will see it differently.'

She gave the knife back to me and I sat motionless staring at the blade.

She chuckled and, gently taking my hand in hers, turned the knife so that the end of the handle was uppermost. She pointed to where the tang was hammered over. 'Look closely. What do you see? Here, Edwin, here.'

I struggled to look where she was pointing. 'It is the letter X,' I finally said.

'No. It is the rune "g". It stands for "a gift", and the knife is a special gift to you from Leofgifu.'

I felt uneasy at her linking me with this magic knife and Leofgifu in the hearing of the two guards but she seemed unworried.

She reached out her hand and gently closed it over mine. 'Put the knife away, Edwin,' she commanded, and I obeyed.

We sat in silence and my own mind, which had gone to I know not where, slipped back into my head, like a dog returning to its kennel.

This woman crouching by the fire was the Wise Woman whom the Church of Rome called a witch and I had just experienced her power.

'What of Wihtred?' I asked, in as firm a voice as I could command.

'He married one of my daughters. He is a good man. He comes to see me when he does work on the new church.'

The warriors were intent on finishing the ale. They had exchanged a few words, mainly about the shortage of lime wood for making shields. They had also touched upon the merits of Frankish spears but neither topic was contentious and so now they were drinking in companionable silence.

Soon I would be on trial for my life. To keep my mind off the unthinkable near future I took refuge in the past.

'May I ask if you were born here? What was it like here when you were young?'

'Born here? No.' She paused, as if reluctant to say more. The fire shifted and she put a log on it, but old people like to tell their stories so I waited.

'My mother was pregnant before she left North Germany to come here. I was born somewhere near Repton. By then there was no one to help her except for my brother. He was just three winters old. Aiyai.'

The sound conveyed the intense feeling she had for that young woman giving birth alone in an unknown and hostile land. She fell silent, and stared back through time.

'When our people came here they found the Britons ill. There were many warriors but they stayed in their huts. They had the plague.' She made a little sign with her hand to ward off the evil spirits then continued, 'Their fields were neglected and their cattle were dying for want of food, water and milking. Our men had come prepared to fight if they must but instead they helped those whom they could. The monks from their monastery weren't much better off.'

She paused, staring into the fire.

203

'Some of the Britons recovered and they and our men burned the dead. We built our own houses and worked the abandoned fields. Some of our men took their women as wives and soon there were babies. Many of their descendants are still among us.' She nodded in the direction of Britaelis and said quietly behind her hand, 'Like him, for example. He's a Briton, apart from his feet. They're Saxon.'

Foolishly, I nearly laughed out loud at that.

She frowned at me and hissed, 'Still your tongue and sharpen your eyes. The Britons have slim feet and we Saxons have broad feet. Yours are mid-size which tells me something about you. Now, am I to continue?'

I was rebuked, and felt as though Chad himself had spoken. I lowered my head and nodded.

'In those early days most of the Britons had become Christians of the British Church but some were still pagan. We Saxons, though, were all pagan. Of course, we were their enemy, but in truth the pagan Britons and ourselves found that we had a great deal in common.'

Britaelis upended the bucket, trying to get out the last drop and the old woman spoke to the warriors. 'The fat in the lamp is almost done. There is no more, so it will go out soon.'

I noticed that when she addressed the warriors she gave only the facts. She expressed no opinion nor did she make any suggestions about what to do. They in turn did not question what she said. They seemed to respect each other's positions.

Outside, the wind was getting up. Britaelis spoke to the woman. 'There will be no feast fires tonight, then.'

'No,' she replied. 'People have died today. We must all stay in our huts for fear of another attack. It won't be the first eve of Beltane we've spent in darkness and fear, and likely it won't be the last.'

'That's the problem with living in a border region like this,' said Britaelis. 'We just exist from one day to the next.'

Then the laconic warrior spoke. 'It's lucky for you that we do,' he said. 'If you lived in East Anglia there'd be no Chad to pluck you from the dung and dress you in finery.'

'Why do you say that? I am a loyal and brave warrior,' flashed Britaelis.

'Exactly so,' said the other man. 'Here in Mercia it's what you do that matters. Further east they judge you by how much money you've got. All the Britons there are slaves. They live with the pigs.'

'And so do I!' retorted Britaelis.

There was a silence then the two warriors burst out laughing and they rocked to and fro. Then the lamp began to sputter and the sound brought them to their senses.

Britaelis tapped his forehead. 'That reminds me: there was something I was going to tell you . . . Ah, yes. Owini has been taken by the king's men, by order of the High Reeve!'

The old woman and the other warrior looked up sharply at that.

Britaelis continued, 'Oh, and Aethelred has taken counsel, and he will be making a declaration about the future of Lichfield.'

'What do you mean, "the future of Lichfield"?' I asked him. What he'd said didn't make sense.

'Well, I don't know the details, but they say that Aethelred is only interested in the great cathedral at Peterborough so he's undecided about having a cathedral here as well. And it's easier to defend Tamworth than this place. They reckon he's spent enough money on the new defences here already and doesn't want to spend any more. Mind you, that raid by the Welshmen might have changed his mind.'

We all sat in silence at that news. Was Aethelred going to throw us to the dogs? The implications of what could happen made me forget my own dilemma for a moment.

The old woman leaned across to me. 'I've still got my late husband's razor, so tomorrow I'll give you a shave and attend to your hair. You'll want to be presentable, won't you? Especially now that Aethelred has taken up with the fashionable idea that long hair on a man means he is a lover of men.'

'But I'm not . . .' I started to say, then shut up. How could anyone else understand how I felt about Finn when I couldn't explain it to myself?

'Right then, prisoner and escort,' Britaelis said cheerfully. 'Time to piss before we bed down.'

On our return from the midden Britaelis laced the door flap to the upright then dropped a stout timber across the doorway into its brackets.

'I'll sleep here,' he said to the other warrior. He settled down near the door. He put his spear so that his right hand was touching it and he pulled his shield over himself.

The warriors carefully spaced themselves so that if trouble came they could defend themselves without stabbing each other with their scramasaxes.

The old woman and I took places on the far side of the hearth at the guests' end of the hut. She put out the smoking lamp.

In the darkness the laconic warrior said, 'When they come in they'll get you first.'

Britaelis replied, 'Oh no, they won't. They won't see me for I shall be invisible.'

Then silence folded round us like like a soft cobweb. Outside, the frogs croaked without stop.

Restless thoughts kept me awake. I felt guilty at telling

Britaelis that he would be invisible if he protected me, and I resolved to clear myself with him. Then great sadness came upon me thinking of Oak-man. He was gone, and Ardal, and Madoc too, that fine prince. The Britons of Wales would never get their spiritual homeland back and I had lost Finn. By some great irony I was in Lichfield for Beltane but not with my companions and not in celebration. My thoughts turned to Owini. Was he in trouble or was that simply a rumour? Why would Aethelred have him arrested?

Then it came to me. Aethelred was doing what Chad had done. Bit by bit he was bringing together all the different factions around him. Threats from the Wicce kings had been weakened by letting some of their people settle at Wiccenor. No doubt Aethelred would do the same with other Saxon folk.

This devious king would surely be angered by Owini thwarting his plans.

The image of a wrathful Aethelred came unbidden to mind and I hastily turned my thoughts to Leofgifu. She had made that knife for me. A gift. Her smiling face came before me. Her eyes shone. Her breasts, whiter than swan's down, smelled sweet. My body experienced another more pleasurable sensation. The devotions I had made for Easter were being rewarded. The celebration of the cycle of death and renewal had succeeded. The force for new life was returning to me.

Then came yet another cheering thought. Things may not turn out so badly after all. I smiled in the dark at the realisation: the few Mercians who had seen me during and after the battle had mistaken me for another person. In truth, there was no one who knew what had happened after my flight from the pit. For that matter there was also no one who knew what work I had really been doing before the ordeal.

No one, that is, except Leofgifu.

Then, with a shock like falling into an icy stream, I came fully awake. Leofgifu might not be at the hearing! The blood tie outweighed all else and some of Aethelred's warriors were her kinfolk. Because of me some had been killed. I had taken her love for granted but if her loyalty to her kin were greater . . .

Without her there would be no one to speak for me tomorrow, no one to stand between me and Aethelred.

God have mercy on my soul!

Chapter 21

The blaring of trumpets jerked us awake, hearts pounding in fear of a dawn attack.

Then a sharp rapping on the door frame made my bowels turn over.

'Open in the name of the king,' shouted a harsh voice.

I seized my staff ready to defend myself.

In the gloom of the hut Britaelis motioned for us to be quiet. He was already on his feet and crouching by the door.

'Who goes there?' he called.

'A soldier of the king's household. Now open up, I say,' came the impatient reply.

'Is that old Badger-arse out there?' said Britaelis, gripping his scramasax more tightly. He was being careful; this could be a ruse by an enemy.

'If that's Britaelis, he'll learn about arses and this blade if he doesn't get the door open.'

'All right, all right, my bold friend. No sooner said than done,' called Britaelis, and he removed the cross-timber and unlaced the door. The flap was roughly thrown back and the pale light of early day came into the hut.

A large warrior with a scramasax stood outside. He looked disciplined, alert and well fed. He had a white streak in his dark hair.

'You took your time,' he grumbled. 'Now, who is in here?'

'Me, my mate Hant and Brother Edwin.'

I had wondered if Britaelis would dare to call him 'Badger-arse' to his face but he didn't.

'Who's that in the corner?'

'Elfrida. This is her hut.'

The warrior called over Britaelis's shoulder, 'I hope this toad hasn't frightened you, good mother,' and without waiting for a reply carried on talking to him. 'Right. Until the king arrives you stay here with Edwin. You'll be summoned. If he escapes then it'll be you sitting on the sharp stake instead. Hant, you are to come with me. We have to search the area thrice before Aethelred arrives.'

Hant stepped towards the door then stopped and turned to me. He spoke quietly, almost sadly. 'We all agreed with what you said about the alder hawe – about slavery. May your fate be kind to you on this day,' he said, and stepped into the light.

'Wait. What day is it?' I said.

'Beltane,' Britaelis said.

'Tiw's Day, the first day of Thrimilki,' called Elfrida from the back of the hut.

Hant looked at me. 'What say you?'

'I think it's the first day of May,' I replied.

Smiling wryly at the confusion of so many calendars, he strode off with the other warrior.

After a moment, Elfrida also went out of the hut. 'I'll call you when I'm ready, Edwin.'

'A kind woman. Hant, too, seems to be good and kind,' I said to Britaelis.

He nodded. 'Don't you ever cross her, that's all I'll say. As for Hant . . . a sad story, his. He was coming up important what with his sheep and fields and all. Tuppenhurst was his, lots of sheep there all right. And most people round here know Hant's Acre even if they don't know the man. Then his wife died when the Trent flooded and things went wrong for him. Lost it all. That's farming for you. He had to borrow money to keep his children. Wulfhere took him into bondage. Saved his bacon that did. The bond now goes to Aethelred. Hant's got about a year to go then he'll have worked the debt off. That's why he is sensitive about slaves and bondsmen.'

This story moved me and, with Elfrida out of earshot, I made to tell Britaelis about the invisibility deception.

'Britaelis—' I began, but Elfrida's voice broke in.

'Come, Edwin.'

Britaelis nudged me. 'Look sharp, then.'

She had a three-legged milking stool ready, water in a bowl and a bronze razor. The curved edge caught the sun and I prayed that it was sharp. She stropped it a few times on the sole of her shoe, and said, 'Sit.' She made up lather from a piece of rancid pig-fat soap and spread it over my face.

Britaelis tittered at the sight but Elfrida quietened him with a look.

'Let it soften your beard, while I do your hair,' she said, and set to with a coarse comb.

Britaelis sat on the grass. He chewed barley bread, and watched my agony. The painful tugging on my scalp brought to mind an image of my person in intimate connection with a sharpened stake.

I hurriedly started to speak to Britaelis. 'Did you serve Chad in the church militia?'

'No. He would have none of it,' he replied. 'He said he'd seen enough violence in his life. My job was to look after the temples in this district.'

I was surprised by that reply. 'But I didn't see you going about when I was here.'

'Well, I saw you,' he said, 'especially when you underwent ordeal in Wall temple.'

'The church of John the Blessed?'

'Ah, yes. Chad did tell us to call it that but I keep forgetting. Well, after the goddess was taken away, Chad consecrated the temple and made it a church. Then we could still worship there, see? He was very wise. We miss him.'

It was coming to me that Chad had indeed been wise. Had I listened to him in the first place I would not be so deeply bemired.

I held my hand up and looked at it. The skin was clean and wholesome but it was still claw-like. I supposed that it would stay so to the end of my days. Which might not be very long now.

While I was looking at my hand Elfrida was speaking to Britaelis. I didn't take much notice, but I caught the words 'people he knew at Wall'.

Britaelis laid his hand on my shoulder. 'I've got to see somebody, urgent like,' he said. 'Er, you won't run away, will you?' He said this so plaintively that I almost smiled.

'No. I pledge my word.'

'Thank you, Brother Edwin. I'll not be long.' He went off among the huts and reeds.

By this time there was a ring of children gathered about us. They were very noisy, laughing and pointing. Elfrida told them that it was rude to point, and they laughed the more but they immediately stopped pointing.

I sat in silence while she tugged and unknotted my hair.

'Not too many lice, and a few nits,' she said, half to herself. 'Not bad for one who has lived as a hermit. And the golden colour is coming back.'

Across the pool I saw that our church had been enlarged but was clearly unfinished. Great ladders leaned against one end and the roof was yet to be laid, but even so the church was not as it should have been. Chad's cathedral was to have been like the very ancient one he said once stood at a place in Wessex called Cadbury. In plan it was to take the form of a Greek cross. A slightly tapered central four-sided tower would have small naves coming from each face.

Inside there would be no obstruction from one end of a nave clear across to the far end of its neighbour opposite. The corners of the tower at its foot were to be cunningly thickened to take its weight, and so there were no walls inside the naves. Chad knew that there was just enough solid rock under the soil in this one place at Lichfield that could take the weight of the tower.

The altar was to be placed on a dais at the very centre of the tower. Its walls were to have piercings to allow shafts of sunlight to fall upon the altar at solstice. Chad knew the magical power of this arrangement.

Instead, Owini had merely added a large hall to the eastern end of Mary the Blessed's church. Its walls were of the most part wood resting on a low base of stone. Although it was unfinished I could see that it would look most ungainly when completed.

Great sadness filled my heart at the way in which Chad's wishes had been cast aside. The new cathedral had been built very quickly, perhaps too quickly. I wondered if it would stand.

Then I noticed that where there had been houses between the church and Chad's oratory there was now open land. Leofgifu had mentioned house clearances; was this the place?

'Do you want this balding bit combed over or shall I leave

it?' asked Elfrida. 'The more monk-like you look, the more lenient he might be.'

I realised that choosing wrongly from Roman, British or no tonsure at all could well hasten my departure from this world.

'Thank you. Please shave just the top.'

'Very well. But I'll do your face first,' she said. Then she chuckled. 'You people. You lot shave just the top. The old lot shaved the sides as well. Only Woden knows what the next lot will shave.'

'Who did you mean, "the old lot"?'

She didn't answer, but instead whipped up more lather and started to shave my face.

'Look up,' she commanded, 'and keep still, if you value your nose.'

There was movement behind me. Door flaps were opened and let fall. Spears rattled against shields.

'The soldiers are searching again,' Elfrida said.

I watched her as she scraped at my face. Her eyes held a fierce determination. Her lips worked as she concentrated on the task but her hands were steady. She was very old, about sixty winters or so, I supposed. She was strong now so she must have been formidable when she was younger.

Round her lined neck she wore a silver chain. Suspended from it was a pendant in the form of a boar. As she raised and lowered her head, the better to see her handiwork, I noticed a blue mark under the chain. I managed to look closer and saw that it was a band of body-marking going full round her neck. I had seen such as this on some of the older Britons who, it was said, were versed in the ancient religion.

Then she turned the razor to my tonsure.

Her robe had a high neck with a short slit down the front

which fell open from time to time as she moved. I could see that she had blue circles on one shoulder. The marks were faded and I supposed that they were made by Britons a long time ago. I had heard that for a Saxon to be initiated into their religion was a high honour and one reserved for people for whom they had the greatest respect. I wanted to ask her of it but dared not.

She washed the soap off my head and stood back. She nodded. 'Leofgifu will find you much changed,' she said while she wiped the razor clean.

The shaving was done and the children had gone to their work in the fields. A cheerful voice called out, 'Ho there, good mother. Don't cut his throat just now, will you. Wait till Aethelred gives you the word.' It was the king's man again.

Elfrida snorted in disgust. 'Where is that Britaelis? He ought to be back soon,' she said under her breath, but then we both saw him between the huts. He was too cunning to be absent while the third search was in progress.

She took up one of my hands.

'I will cut your nails,' she said. She sat on her heels and began to trim them with her scissors. She carefully collected the clippings into a small leather pouch, together with the hair she'd cut off. 'For your protection,' she explained.

Her words and actions brought me comfort, for she would work some magic with those parts of me, but I felt uneasy none the less.

The thought went out of my head, for I had seen three armed men go to the edge of the water and stand guard over a low wooden causeway built across the marshes and the pool. It was so narrow that only one person could go across at a time. Women were bringing water or milk in buckets on yokes. The guards let the women pass but stopped every man and questioned him.

I said, 'That causeway is new, Elfrida. When was it made?'

She looked at me so sharply that I felt constrained to add, 'I speak honestly, I do not know about it.'

'My house was there between the new church and the monks' house. Then Wulfhere gave the land to the church. When he died Owini ordered us out. He had our houses pulled down. We had to come over here in the swamp and marshes. That's why we have only these huts to live in.'

'Cathedrals need more land than churches,' I said, 'yet this is a most dreadful thing. But what of the causeway?'

'Owini is the type of man who boasts before the battle but then is nowhere to be seen when the blood flows. We threatened to burn the church down and Owini with it. The king's reeve ordered the causeway to be built so that we may fetch water and take our grain to Chad's mill. It is made narrow so that the church militia can better defend that slug Owini.'

She was becoming tired. The third search would soon be done and then Aethelred would be here. I offered her the stool to sit on, but she shook her head, indicating that she preferred to continue squatting. I silently called on Woden to give her the strength to continue talking.

'Do many people go to the church?'

'That depends on who the bishop is and who is king.'

'I don't understand,' I said.

'When Chad was the bishop and Wulfhere the king, people of many faiths went, but now it's weak Wynfrid and Aethelred and things have changed. The Christians round here are mostly of the British faith and don't hold with Rome. But there is always a stream of pilgrims coming to touch the bones of Chad.'

She grimaced at something as she spoke but I didn't know what.

What she said was good news. While in the cave I had worked out a way of healing my hand: I would have to outwit Owini's church militia but the real problem would be getting to Chad's bones. From what she said, that sounded possible. On the other hand, her grimace made me feel that somehow she didn't quite approve of me. I wanted to show her that although a monk of the Church of Rome I was also one of the ordinary people.

I said, 'Chad was raised in the British faith, you know – as I was.'

'Yes, I know that, but some of the British Christians have gone over to the Church of Rome,' she said. 'They are no longer to be trusted; most of them would denounce anybody of another faith, given half a chance.'

She shook her head sorrowfully.

'It wasn't always like that,' she continued. 'Before we Saxons came here, the Christian Britons had many churches and the pagan Britons had their temples, although fewer in number. When the people of my faith came, the pagan Britons gave them buildings to use.

'There was one on Greenhill, which they let us make a temple to Thunor. There was another at Long Don. We dedicated it to our god of fertility. When I was a hot young woman I myself made many offerings to him . . .'

She smiled to herself, then continued, 'Yes, the British priests were good men and women. They commanded great power and it still worked for us in the temples they handed over. Of course, we had to build our own as well, like the one at Weeford.'

'At home it was different,' I said. 'My grandfather had been

217

a life-long pagan, but my father told me that the pagan Angles had a hard time of it and he himself had become a Christian for a quiet life. My mother was a Christian Briton, though, so perhaps he changed for her sake.'

Elfrida nodded slowly. 'I don't wish to sound harsh, Edwin,' she said, 'but you, Chad and the others are being used as pieces in a game. Mercia still keeps its ancient British Christianity and you were sent here to persuade it to change to the new Roman way. You might have succeeded, given time, but it isn't happening fast enough. We pagans are also in the way. I fear that other means will be used.'

Her words were uttered quietly but were all the more chilling for being so.

To get off the subject I told her about the carved stone I found in the pit.

'In length it was about the span of a man's arms, and an arm in depth. It was so cunningly made that the man and the bull seemed to be alive,' I finished.

She shook her head. 'The bull meant a lot to the Britons a long time ago. But now it is just a servant to Herne, lord of the forest. There are figures of our gods, of course, but I have never seen anything as you have described.'

The stone didn't mean anything to her. I half expected that. I was already surprised that a poor old woman like her could know so much. I asked if the British priests in Lichfield had been similar to those in Northumberland.

'I wouldn't know about that,' she said. 'I have never been to Northumberland. I was only a little girl when they were here. They were kind enough to us, but our people were frightened of them because they used to beat themselves and sometimes go without food for days.'

She nodded in the direction of the church over the pool. 'I

expect you know that there was a British church and monastery there long before yours – Holy Brigid's or Brigant's they called it. A goddess of water and of childbirth, as I recall.'

That caught me by surprise. 'Where is it . . . was it? I've never seen any ruins or anything like that.'

'Gone,' she said. 'It stood where your church now stands. It was pulled down by one of the most wicked of your bishops. The one who was here before Chad.'

'But that was Jaruman,' I said.

I must have sounded surprised because she looked hard at me, then smiled a little. 'I will tell you something because I know you to be a scholar trying to understand these things. Leofgifu and Wihtred told me so, otherwise these words would never cross my lips. Do you understand?'

I didn't want to tell her I was hoping to impress Aethelred with my learning so that he might be more lenient. Instead I simply nodded.

'We called him Jaruman the Destroyer,' she went on, scowling at the memory of him. 'He desecrated our temples. He pulled down or took over the British churches. He even destroyed holy things built by the giants down at Wall.'

'But why?' I asked. This was not the story told to us in the Church of Rome.

'He felt the force of this place and was frightened because it was stronger than the force he worshipped. So he tried to destroy everything that wasn't of his Church. King Wulfhere became afraid of retribution and ordered Jaruman away – perhaps in an attempt to make amends. He was sent to East Anglia, but even there he did the same things. Of course, upon his return, he died.'

'He died?'

'We pushed pins into his effigy. We made sacrifice to Woden. So he died,' she said in a matter-of-fact way.

'I would that I had such power . . . at my cave I made sacrifice to Freya and she brought Leofgifu to me,' I boasted.

Elfrida looked at me with blue eyes suddenly gone hard. 'Great God, Edwin, you are such a fool!' she said, and her voice was that of Leofgifu, but with an edge of authority that made me jump. 'You must never do these things lightly!'

'I needed to know who would answer my prayers, that was all,' I explained. 'As a scholar I—'

She stopped me with an imperious gesture of her hand.

'Now I see it,' she said. 'You want someone to tell you which is the way to God.'

I opened my mouth to deny what she was saying, but she ignored me and continued speaking. 'You are like someone who runs between thegns while the enemy advances,' she said. 'If you are not with one, then you are with none.'

She reached out and put a hand on my shoulder. 'Before you appear in front of Aethelred, you must make up your mind as to who and what you are, Edwin,' she said in a more kindly tone.

'One thing I do know,' I said miserably. 'I have failed to avenge my father.'

'Blood feud and vengeance – these are for warriors, not for such as you,' she said.

Her words stung me and without thinking I blurted out, 'I fought alongside great warriors at Cress Well . . .'

Instantly her fingers came over my mouth. 'Be silent!' she hissed. 'Never speak of that again. Ever! Do you understand?'

I stared at her, feeling very frightened at what I had done.

'Time is running out for you, Edwin,' she said, taking her

hand away, 'but I give you my word that I will try to help you. First, though, hear what I say.

'The warrior does what is right for his lord and he receives iron rings for his fingers and gold bands for his arms. The warrior does what is right for his thegn in the fighting and the battle is won. The warrior does what is right for a maid and he gets his reward.

'In the same way, Edwin, you must do what is right for your God. You must do what is right for your thegn, and you must do what is right for Leofgifu if you truly have regard for her.

'You must decide. Indeed, it is only you who can decide. It is your responsibility.' She fell silent.

I sat looking at the ground as thoughts whirled round in my mind like a flock of startled birds. Being a monk, my thegn was my priest, but I had no priest at the moment. It could not be the weak Wynfrid. It must then be Chad! And did I truly have regard for Leofgifu? Of course I did – I had made a pledge to her.

Questions started to form on my lips and I turned to Elfrida but she said, 'Look, here comes Britaelis. And for once he's moving quickly.'

Britaelis stood by us breathing heavily after his strenuous activity.

'They've closed the causeway,' he said. 'Now we're hemmed in.'

The guards stood with their shields held up. They were arguing with a man who wanted to go over. After a moment the man gave up and walked angrily back to his hut.

'Owini's men,' sneered Britaelis. 'Unloved by man, woman or goat.'

I was about to ask him a question, when he said, 'Listen, what's that?'

We fell silent, for the sound of voices raised in song was coming to us across the water. My brothers in the cathedral had been assiduous in their learning of the Roman chant.

'*Te aeturnum Patrem omnis terra veneratur . . .*' I sang with them.

Britaelis sighed. 'That is beautiful, yet sad as well. Like music from the Otherworld might be,' he said. 'You could do great magic with such as that, I reckon. What is the spell called?'

'It is called the Te Deum. It is new and has only just been brought here from Rome.'

Elfrida said, 'It makes me think of a song I heard sung here in our temples when I was young. Tell me, when do you sing it?'

'It is usually sung early in Matins in the morning, but they seem late today.'

'It seems familiar,' she said thoughtfully. 'Oh, now I remember. Our song to Matuta, the dawn goddess.' Then she chuckled. 'The Christians, always pretending that their tales are new. Of course "Mat . . . ins" is not new, it is very old.'

There was nothing I could reply to that.

She stood up slowly with stiff joints. 'I am going in now,' she said. 'There are things to be done.'

She took my hands in hers. 'Remember, Edwin, many people love you and are loyal to you. That will give you strength. I will also make an offering to Freya: I will ask that she does not take you from us just yet. May your fate be kind to you.' She kissed me on the cheek and I felt greatly comforted.

Britaelis, looking across the pool, said, 'I don't know how

old that spell of yours is, but I do know why your brothers are late with it this morning.'

'Oh, why?'

'It's because they waited for Aethelred. Look, there he is.'

Chapter 22

Glints of metal from the throng at the western end of the cathedral showed they were armed, but the day was now bright and the building cast a shadow. I had to doubt that Britaelis could see the king from where we were.

'How can you see him, my friend?' I asked.

'Look, there, the royal standard,' he replied. 'No one who wishes to keep their ears on their head would dare raise the standard without the king being present. So, where the standard goes, there is the king. Simple.'

He stood there nodding at his own logic.

Now a procession was going along the side of the cathedral. It seemed as if a whole army were there.

Britaelis held my shoulder and, pointing, tried to direct my gaze to the head of the procession. 'Look, there, at the front,' he prompted. 'What do you see?'

A childhood memory of the Northmen and their pirate ships came to my mind. Fear stabbed at my heart. 'It looks like a small sail.'

'That's it,' he said. 'That's the royal standard. Aethelred has ordered that it shall be carried in front of him wherever he goes.'

'But what for? Doesn't everybody know he's the king?'

'Not just king, he's the High King now. Here, hold up,' said Britaelis. 'What's the matter? It only shows that he is the King of Kings, that's all.'

My mouth filled with my own spit. I felt sick and dizzy.

'That's it,' he said. 'Sit down. You look very pale.'

He took my arm and helped me.

'Here, you aren't going to die, are you?' he anxiously asked.

Possibly this very day, I thought. Aethelred had gone the way of the caesars, the emperors, the despots and tyrants. My thoughts ran twisted together like the threads in a broken loom. A personal 'royal standard', carried for all to see, proclaiming 'here come I, lord of all'. The standard is the man, taller than everybody else, above everybody else. All others are trivial and of no matter.

The King of Kings would crush me like a beetle.

Britaelis's voice broke in. 'Here, put your head between your knees. It can't be that bad whatever it is.' His voice changed to pleading. 'Oh, Edwin, don't die now. I need you. I . . . we depend on you.'

I looked up and he wiped the sweat off my face. The privations of the past few days were having their effect on me. Now even a small exertion caused me difficulty and I wondered if I could stand up to a prolonged questioning.

A man dressed in finery had come across the causeway. He was coming towards me with the three church militia.

'They come for me, Britaelis,' I whispered and he turned to look.

'Shit!' he exclaimed. 'Wait here, I'll get your staff.' He ran back to the hut.

'Brother Edwin?' daintily enquired the man clad in rich cloth.

'Yes, that is me,' I replied, as calmly as I could.

'Come with me now. You are shortly to appear before the

High King,' he oiled, in the smooth manner of one who doesn't do the dirty work.

Britaelis came back carrying my staff which he thrust into my hand. With him was the soldier he called Badger-arse.

'May I bring my . . . my—' I started to say to the official.

'Attendant,' broke in Britaelis.

'Yes, my attendant,' I finished.

One of the church militia started to object, saying that Britaelis was not fit to appear before the king. It began to look as if the oily official would agree but then Badger-arse acted. In one stride he put himself right in front of the protesting militia man. Towering over him he said, 'Britaelis was a loyal and faithful servant to King Wulfhere and serves Aethelred equally well. I'll kill anybody who gainsays him.' So saying, he half drew his scramasax. The hapless militia man went pale and stepped back, lowering his head.

The oily man looked relieved. 'Of course. Anyone who might help, I imagine,' he agreed and walked off without looking to see if we would follow.

We squelched down the slope to the water's edge, where the rushes were almost as tall as a man. Marsh birds fluttered and sang. Insects flew on shimmering wings. The wooden causeway swayed as we walked out over the water. I clutched Finn's staff for comfort and Britaelis, close behind me, held my elbow. I was grateful for his support, for without it I would surely have fallen into the pool.

'Look at these new defences,' said Britaelis.

I could see an earthwork running along the cathedral bank of the pool and going along to the mere. I had to admire the cunning of the plan. In one simple move, the pool, the earthwork and the mere had been formed into a great defensive work, fully a half-mile long.

It came to me that Chad's mill house, being of stout wood and stone, would also form part of the defences since it was on the cathedral side of Curborough Brook. The mighty works protected the cathedral and its buildings, not the people of the huts. If attacked from the south they would have their backs to these defences with no means of escape.

'Do come along,' called the man in the fine garb. 'We mustn't keep anybody waiting, must we?'

I slowed, looking at the newly flung-up earthworks. My guards had also slowed but they were staring at the sight ahead of them. Up on the cleared ground between the cathedral and Chad's mill was a tent large enough to take twenty or so men. In front of the tent stood a throne, and along the grassy upper banks of the pool a murmuring crowd had gathered.

They tried to press forward to gawp at this symbol of power but the splendidly clothed and armed soldiers from the royal household kept them at a respectful distance from the throne.

I was taken near to the line of soldiers. While we waited I searched the sea of faces but they seemed to be strangers to me. My spirits dropped even more.

A slim young man came from the tent. His hair shone. He was dressed all in green and he wore a short cape over his tunic. He was carrying a bronze trumpet. The crowd gasped at his appearance.

'It's the king,' said one of the church militia with awe in his voice.

'No it's not, Oxhead,' sneered Britaelis. ' 'Tis just a lad in fancy clothes.'

His comment made me realise that possibly very few people in the crowd knew Aethelred's face. I knew him, but it was not from my choice.

The young man raised the trumpet to his lips and blew a long note to the west. From the distance there came an answering horn. He blew notes to south, east, and north. Each time there came the reassuring answer.

'Good,' smiled Britaelis. 'All is safe. Badger-arse has done a good job. Now the king comes, surely?'

Instead, Aethelred's thegns came out from the tent. They wore beautiful clothes, furs and gilded weapons that caught the sun. A murmuring noise broke out among the people. For a moment I felt as though I were in a bee swarm but then the noise subsided. Perhaps they were thrilled at the presence of such noble men but more likely they realised that it was their toil and taxes that paid for such finery.

Bishop Wynfrid was among the thegns. He looked shrunken with the conflict of different religions, and his grey face told of battles lost with Owini and Aethelred. Bishop of Lichfield he might be, but I envied him not in having to dance to Aethelred's tune. He meekly took his place by the side of the throne.

'The thegns are all wearing scramasaxes. Is that not a threat to the king?' I whispered to Britaelis.

'No,' he answered. 'Aethelred knows that their magic is not very effective if used against him outdoors. If the hearing were indoors he'd be vulnerable. Indoors, they'd have to go unarmed. Out here, it's all right.'

'I must tell you something,' I said. 'In case I don't . . . If there's no chance later. That prayer of invisibility. It's not quite what you may have thought.'

'Oh, that.' He smiled. 'I know. Don't worry about it. I knew you would tell me eventually. Certainly before I had to rely upon it.'

'Yet you still help me?'

'I trust you. But look now, something's happening.'

The trumpet was being raised again. This time it was sounded directly at us. The effect was astonishing. The hair stood up on the back of my neck. For a moment I was quite unable to move. Britaelis shook his head like a dog trying to get water out of its ears.

The royal standard rose up from a group of four mighty men in link-mail shirts.

'The king's hearth-companions,' said Britaelis. The lad carrying the standard was dwarfed by the men in their glittering armour but they in turn were small in comparison to the figure in their midst.

The group came between the thegns and went to the throne, then the companions stepped aside.

There before us was Aethelred, High King of Mercia, the most powerful man in the whole island of Britain. He stood motionless as if to let the crowd wonder at him and his sun-blazing glory.

In total silence they stared at him. He appeared to ignore them, and gazed over their heads into the far distance as if there were something of interest over the tree-shrouded Brown Hills.

All the time the soldiers were watching the crowd.

Aethelred wore armour such as I had never seen before. The link-mail shirt covered him down to his thighs. It had a tight-fitting hood and full-length sleeves. The over-tunic of brilliant blue bore a golden intricately patterned border. They were surely foreign-made.

A magnificent brooch of silver, garnet and amber fastened his cape, and glittering iron rings encircled his fingers. From his belt hung a small scramasax with a decorated scabbard and a fine whetstone with a silver capping.

On his thigh was a great sword fully a yard long. The figure of an eagle crouched on its gold pommel and its scabbard was set with precious gems. Such was its weight that it was supported not only by the belt but also by a strap over his shoulder.

The very sight of this fearsome sword sent a thrill of apprehension down my spine. It was the sword owned by Wulfhere who received it from his father, Penda, who in turn received it from the mighty Pybba, the first King of Mercia.

Men spoke of the sword in tones of awe, for it had sent untold numbers of brave warriors to the Otherworld. It had a name but try as I might I could not recall it.

I tore my eyes away from the sword as one of the companions took his place by the throne. He carried the burnished helmet that I had seen before. It had the same boar on top but now it also had a silver Christian cross fixed on the rim above the brow.

The last of the companions came to the throne carrying the king's shield. It was not flat as were all others but was was slightly curved and had a smaller boss. A blue boar was painted on the shield.

Aethelred sat down and started to look at the crowd. His gaze swept slowly over their faces. Then his keen blue eyes fell upon me. His chin jerked up and his hands tightened on the arms of the throne. He held me transfixed with his piercing look.

'Hold up,' whispered Britaelis and he took hold of my elbow.

Aethelred said something to one of the companions. This man snapped his fingers at my smooth-speaking summoner who went forward. His answer went back up to the throne.

Aethelred, whose gaze had not left my face, nodded and

then spoke. 'Welcome, Brother Edwin. Or should it be Adhelm? No matter, for we shall shortly discover which it is.'

In speaking he broke the spell and there was an outbreak of talking, commenting and marvelling from the crowd.

The soldiers took a firmer grip on their spears.

The king's High Reeve came before the throne. He was a haughty man, tall and thin with grey hair. His short cape of black bearskin was secured round his shoulders by a thick silver chain. This was Sigeberht, known to all.

'Silence!' he loftily commanded. 'This is a hearing commanded by, and in the presence of, the High King Aethelred, servant of God, son of Penda son of Pybba, Lord of Princes.'

There was a muted muttering in the crowd. Some had noticed the omission of the traditional title 'son of Woden', from whom all our kings are descended.

Sigeberht turned to the king. 'May I proceed?'

Aethelred briefly inclined his head.

The High Reeve called for Owini, and four soldiers ran to the cathedral. They came back marching in pairs with Owini stumbling along between them. They came before the throne and I saw that Owini's hands were tied behind him.

'Unfasten him,' ordered Sigeberht. 'Owini,' he continued, 'you stand charged with disloyalty and misuse of the High King's funds. How say you?'

Owini glanced about him. I knew from old that in one look he would have seen and noted most of the people present. His balding head glistened with sweat. He bowed towards the throne.

'O Great King, it is not so,' he said.

It did not escape the crowd that he had addressed the king directly. He was raising the stakes in this deadly game.

Sigeberht waited to see how the king would respond.

Aethelred's hands were resting on the arms of the throne. He raised one forefinger and an iron ring glittered. The finger pointed at Owini for a moment then flicked towards the reeve.

What influence Owini may have had with the king was reduced to naught by that single gesture. The king was now sitting in judgement on him. And now Owini could only speak to Sigeberht unless Aethelred addressed him directly.

Sigeberht continued. 'There are further charges,' he said, and recited at least a dozen. As Britaelis had rightly foretold they included the loss of the cart and its cargo of stones, and the death of the slaves.

Owini fought well. He made good reply to some charges saying, for instance, that the loss of a waggon was grievous but it was caused by the attack of the Wicce thegn and his gang of thieves.

Aethelred nodded once and so that charge was not talked of again.

As for the altar stones, why, they were free, from the city of the giants. They were not lost but could be recovered.

Again Aethelred nodded.

Owini grew bold. Had he not single-handedly all but completed the cathedral and at no cost to the king?

Aethelred remained unmoving.

Owini tried again. Had he not kept his word in accordance with the bond made between him and King Wulfhere? A bond that had died with the late king?

At that, Aethelred and the High Reeve stiffened, and there was an intake of breath from some of the quicker ones in the crowd.

Owini had overstepped the mark.

Perhaps he meant only to introduce an unassailable defence

by mention of a bond. Sadly for him his words carried the carrion whiff of blackmail.

The High Reeve called for Wulfhere's former reeve. A very old man was carried down from the tent. He sat between two soldiers who made him a cradle by gripping each other's arms. They bore him as lightly as a child. The High Reeve asked him to identify himself but I could barely make out his reply, made in a high, piping voice.

With a start I recognised the elder who had acted as go-between for Wulfhere and myself when I underwent ordeal. The cares of his office and the death of Wulfhere had worn him down like corn ground in a quern.

Aethelred, the old man and the High Reeve put their heads together for a long moment. At one point the High Reeve turned and looked at me.

Finally, Aethelred put out a massive hand and gently patted the frail old man on the arm. He was borne away back to the tent.

My heart leaped like a silver fish in the River Tame at that simple gesture. Aethelred was capable of tenderness. Would that he might extend it to me.

The High Reeve was speaking to the assembly. 'King Wulfhere, the great and blessed brother of the High King, did in his life make a bond with Brother Owini. The terms of the bond were that Owini was to build the cathedral at no cost to the king. In return the king would express his wish to Archbishop Theodore of Canterbury that, if it were possible in God's eyes, Brother Owini should be considered for the bishopric of Mercia as and when it fell vacant.'

There were exclamations of dismay and disbelief from the crowd.

'Do any here gainsay the bond?' Sigeberht challenged.

Silence fell as Aethelred looked directly at the crowd. Were there any among us who would dare to speak? I thought.

The High Reeve continued. 'Owini, the law is that the bond did not die with Wulfhere but continues with Aethelred in the person of the king.'

Owini's face went pale and his eyes darted this way and that as if he were looking to flee.

The High Reeve continued, relentlessly. 'Without permission, you increased taxes from the lands belonging to the cathedral, in some cases threefold. Not only that, you also spent all the money on yourself. None of it, not a penny, went to meet the needs of the king.'

At those words I wanted to speak out. The lands had been given to the Church by Wulfhere and so he had disclaimed all taxes from them. There was no need to give money to the king. The High Reeve must surely know this. But then I recalled Britaelis's words: Aethelred would be making a declaration about the future of Lichfield. A gulf opened before me. The pagan Wulfhere never actually gave the land to the Church and now Aethelred was going to throw us all out; Owini's crimes were to be the excuse.

The High Reeve's voice broke into my feverish thoughts: '. . . taken freemen and freewomen loyal to the king thus depriving him, and you have taken bondsmen and bondswomen who are his property. The cathedral is not yet finished but there has already been great cost to the High King. Answer!'

Because of the continuing bond, Owini dared not tell of the money secretly given to him by Wulfhere. That money would now be a debt owed to Aethelred. Perhaps Aethelred already knew. Either way, Owini was trapped and there was no escape.

Falling to his knees he held up his hands in supplication and started to plead: 'O great and merciful King . . .' Then he checked himself and a wild look came into his eyes. In a stronger voice he cried, 'I was bewitched! I had spells put upon me. I name the warlock who is among us even now.'

He jumped to his feet and pointed at me. 'I accuse Brother Edwin of witchcraeft and spell-making!'

The fickle herd starting shouting for my death. 'Burn him, burn him.'

The High Reeve called for silence and the soldiers levelled their spears at the crowd. After a moment or two there was calm.

'Keep hold of thyself,' ordered Britaelis, shaking me.

I wished he would stop, for at my feet was a pool of my own vomit.

The High Reeve levelled his finger at me. 'How say you, Brother Edwin?'

Unable to speak, I shook my head.

'We take it that you deny the charges.'

Through my befouled mouth I choked out a 'Yes.'

'Are there any who will speak for you?'

The worst of my fears had been realised. I was facing death and there was no one to gainsay it.

Aethelred the man might be harsh and inconsistent but Aethelred the king was judge and upholder of the law. He could see the unjustness of the accusation. I turned to him for help.

He sat unmoving, looking at me with expressionless eyes. Then a mocking smile began to play round his lips.

The chanting of the crowd grew louder. 'Burn him, burn him.'

Chapter 23

Cold water splashed into my face, went into my half-open mouth and down my neck. The calm voice that commanded me to drink was Leofgifu's and I thanked God for that.

Britaelis and she held me steady.

'I will speak for this man,' she cried.

The High Reeve barely heard her above the hubbub, but he made a signal to the men behind him.

One scramasax was slid from its sheath. It was enough: the uproar died away and the reeve indicated she should speak.

She took a deep breath then spoke directly to Aethelred. 'This man is a good man, O King. He was true to Wulfhere and will be true to you, as well. He has studied leechcraeft and has healed many people. He works hard for the Church and tries to bring everyone to the Lord Jesus, without favour.'

At this point she faltered and stopped. I could feel her trembling. What she had said was entirely true but equally it would not stand closer examination.

Aethelred gestured to her as if to ask, 'Is there more?'

She drew another deep breath then hurriedly said, 'Look at his old man's hair, look at his old man's face, yet he is but young. Owini has done this. I don't know why. Perhaps Owini was envious because Chad had chosen Edwin to be the next priest. Perhaps it was because Owini wanted my body but I refused him. Whatever the reason, Edwin is innocent and Owini is the guilty one.'

Her fading voice was drowned by the shouts and jeers against Owini from the crowd.

Aethelred beckoned the High Reeve and they exchanged a few words. Then the crowd immediately fell silent as Aethelred began to speak.

'This is the woman Leofgifu. She was charged with witchcraft and accomplice to witchcraft but somehow she escaped from gaol,' he declared. 'Some time after that, she tended to my warriors wounded in my battle with the Welsh invaders.'

He stopped, as if something had just occurred to him, then began to speak again but this time with great care.

'Among the dead was an Irish prince, one Ardal, brought to rebellion by being imprisoned by Owini,' he said. 'I am desirous of making peace with the Irish kings, and so Owini's act may be seen by this assembly as treason.' He nodded at the High Reeve, then turned back to Leofgifu. 'And as for this woman, I reward her for her loyalty by dismissing all charges against her. No man shall make this charge again.'

My heart filled with joy at these words but then my thoughts went back to Owini. I had no inkling that he had treated Leofgifu so shamefully. Had I known, I would have killed him with my bare hands.

I looked at her. Her face was full and I had never before seen her hair shine so. She whispered, 'You don't really look old, Edwin. I can see that your golden hair is returning and your brown eyes are so beautiful.' She was smiling up at me in a mysterious way and I thanked God that she had been spared.

The High Reeve ordered silence then addressed the assembly. 'With the permission of Bishop Wynfrid, I call the High Priestess of the royal household of Mercia.'

At these words my tiredness fell away. This would be the

very woman I had been hoping to meet when Lichfield was taken, the wise pagan who had so impressed Chad at their meeting. I leaned forward to see as the crowd parted with great deference to let her through.

Her tall, upright figure was clothed in a robe of magical purple, girt about with a belt of silver strands. Her thick silvery grey hair hung like a cloak down her back and her silver headband flashed in the sun as she graciously turned her head this way and that.

The soldiers hastened to stand aside and let her approach the throne and for the first time I could see her clearly.

It was Elfrida!

Leofgifu's grandmother, the woman who had shaved my chin and combed the lice out of my hair, was the highest-ranking pagan priestess in the land.

Chad had surely misled us by calling her a 'misguided but honourable' woman. Never mind; now I understood completely why Wulfhere had taken her into his household.

Bishop Wynfrid's rigid posture and stony face betrayed his great discomfort at being in the presence of this powerful spiritual leader, but my spirits soared as she placed herself before Aethelred. She inclined her head in a slight nod then began speaking to him. Her manner was more one of respect, not deference, and although he seemed to be in awe of her I could also sense tension between them.

As she spoke the glittering pendant at her neck caught my attention. In that instant I understood the connection between the boar at her neck and the same animal on his helmet and shield. Aethelred had taken as his personal emblem the boar, symbol of Frey and the pagan Church, and Elfrida was the High Priestess of that same Church.

She turned and called me forward. I did not respond fast

enough for Britaelis, who gave me a shove in the small of my back. She took my hand and held it up for the king and the crowd to see.

'Look at this hand. It is healed. All men may thus see that Edwin is not guilty of witchcraeft. Is that not so, O High King?'

Aethelred nodded.

A great surge of joy went through my heart, but I knew I could not be freed of all charges in such a simple manner. Elfrida must know that too; more had to be said in my favour, but perhaps the most dangerous point had passed. Surely I was not important to Aethelred: after all, it was Owini he wanted. I was uncomfortable at being so close to Aethelred and did not want to catch his eye but I felt forced to glance at him. He seemed not to be interested in the proceedings and was gazing ahead and upwards a little, his lips pursed. Then he shut his eyes, and I took the opportunity to ease discreetly away from the throne, back to Britaelis.

Elfrida called on people to speak for me. There was a pause, then out of the crowd came Wihtred. I had confided a great many things to this kind man and now he knew more about me than any living person, save Leofgifu. He, above all people, could swing the mood of the crowd. But then I realised he could only speak about two visits he'd made to the cave: the first time when he'd found me and the second time with Aethelred. To reveal that he'd helped me at a time when I was an outlaw and he was under a cloud of disobedience would place us both in great peril.

He didn't wilt under Aethelred's eye but declared in a respectful manner that I had made and placed a cross outside my cave and that he had seen and heard me praying to the true God.

Aethelred nodded.

Then, to my great joy, I heard Trumhere's voice. Leofgifu had, after all, taken my message to Wihtred who in turn had gone to him. Trumhere said that I had studied the scriptures and not only knew them well but respected and loved them. As a scholar I was without equal. 'Bearing in mind his age,' he added, in his pedantic way.

Aethelred nodded, perhaps remembering our conversation at the cave.

Then three Britons were brought forward. They were from near Wall and I realised that these were the people that Britaelis, at Elfrida's bidding, had run and fetched that morning.

Why had he brought them? In their ignorance of the nature of the assembly they would surely blurt out what had happened and thereby condemn me. My fearful anticipation made me weak and I had to shut my eyes and lean on Britaelis, forcing myself to listen as Wihtred started to interpret.

To my great relief they confirmed that I had healed them with proper leechcraeft. I had not used spells, they said, but while I worked I had spoken to them of salvation and forgiveness.

I gave silent thanks to Woden that the three appeared to have misunderstood what had been going on at the time. My herbal remedies had certainly worked, but they were taken from the forbidden books at Breedon. I had also chanted while I worked, but necessary and powerful spells, not some homily from Rome. In my relief I smiled inwardly at their mistake.

Still, it was odd that for some reason or other they seemed to need Wihtred to interpret for them, since I was sure they could speak Englisc well enough.

'They have said all they know, O King,' finished Wihtred. Aethelred nodded.

I raised my head and looked at the Britons' impassive faces but before I could read their eyes they were dismissed.

'That was nicely done,' whispered Britaelis in my ear.

Aethelred brooded for a moment then, half-twisting on his throne, he suddenly shot a question at me. 'The guilt that men carry is often greater than that which other men can accuse them of,' he said. 'Is there aught like that with you?'

He wanted me to accuse myself. 'I fled from King Wulfhere's gaol while under ordeal.'

He lifted a hand in a gesture of dismissal. 'Wulfhere on his deathbed forgave you all your transgressions against him. The High Reeve tells me that the forgiveness cannot be revoked. Is there anything else?'

Aethelred was being cunning. He was letting me go free but by placing the responsibility for decisions with the High Reeve or with Wulfhere he was leaving the door open for himself so he could act against me later.

'Only those sins which God alone can forgive,' I blurted.

Aethelred nodded but he seemed reluctant to do so.

He turned and gestured at the High Reeve who returned to the main object of Aethelred's wrath. 'Owini, you have heard all that has been said, including the response to your false accusations against Brother Edwin. What do you say?'

'I have nothing to say,' snarled Owini. He was glaring at me as if he would tear me in twain. He was at risk of losing everything yet still he was defiant.

The High Reeve turned to the crowd. 'Who of you will speak for Owini?' he called.

Owini's hot-eyed look went from face to face. But there were many there with memories of his harsh words and furious beatings. One or two had suffered broken bones from his inhuman strength. Now Leofgifu had accused him of even worse. How many other women had he used shamefully? Whatever the reasons, no one would come forward for him.

'Bishop Wynfrid! Owini is one of yours, is he not?' said the reeve.

'Owini was, er, is the deacon. It is he who is responsible for all the money matters, er, spending, paying bills and, and—',

The High Reeve cut the bishop short in a way that he would never have dared to with Chad: he turned his back on him then addressed the crowd. 'Is there no man here who will speak for him?'

He shrugged and turned to Aethelred. 'O King, do you find him to be guilty? If "yeah" then what is your pleasure with this wretch?'

This was the part that the crowd enjoyed. They delighted in hearing the dreadful punishment being described and then they shared a mutual thrill when it was carried out.

Aethelred looked at them, his eyes glittering. 'How say you, good people?' he hissed.

They were quick to take up the offer. 'Guilty, guilty, guilty,' they bayed.

'Hear them, Owini,' shouted Aethelred above the noise. 'You are guilty beyond any doubt.' And he smirked at Owini, who groaned.

Aethelred raised his hand for silence.

'Owini has offended me beyond measure. However, he has made the most terrible of accusations against Brother Edwin. Had he succeeded in his deception then Edwin would have suffered the very torments of hell. The punishment I therefore leave to him, for he has experience of the suffering of men's bodies and their souls.'

He turned to me. 'Give thought to this now, Edwin. Shall you merely pay him back with equal pain? Or should he get extra torment by way of interest on his investment? And shall you add even more to his agony for the hurt that he has done to Leofgifu and to your king? Think, then speak.'

There was something in his voice that should have warned me, but it was burned away by the revenge heat surging through me.

The crowd, the soldiers, the thegns – all were still and silent, awaiting my words.

The faint breeze brought with it the sound of Chad's mill. It made a harsh grating noise like a caged giant grinding his teeth in frustrated rage.

In my mind's eye I saw Owini being forced in between the great stones. I saw him being crushed and minced and ground into a red paste speckled with white splinters of shattered bone. Such agony, such exquisite drawn-out pain. Yes, yes, that would be it!

Half turning, my gaze fell upon Leofgifu.

She stood as if frozen, both hands to her mouth wide open in a silent scream. She was staring at me with terror-filled eyes. Her face showed she knew what was in my mind.

The sudden realisation that I was but one step away from destroying myself by offering an act of incredible cruelty sent a bolt of lightning through my whole frame.

I reached out and briefly touched her beloved face and as I did so I saw that my hands were shaking.

Aethelred shifted on his throne and I turned to face him.

With a movement like that of a woman offering her breast to her lover he leaned forward a little and offered me the pommel of his great sword. As he did so he gave me what he may have thought to be an encouraging smile. It disgusted me: I saw it as a smirk, a twisted grin of complicity, and in that moment I knew that he and I would for evermore travel on separate roads.

The darkness in my mind lifted and I saw him for what he was: a man utterly mean of spirit and corrupted by power. King he may be, but he was also a man whose heart was already made rotten by duplicity and dreadful deeds.

He raised his eyebrows in unspoken question.

My stomach churned but my head was clear as I began to speak. 'It is true that I have suffered pain to both body and mind but I bear no grudge against those who sought to destroy me,' I said. 'I would emulate the kindness and love of Chad who looked for the best in everybody. Owini is as we are: ignorant but well-meaning, a man who tries to do what he thinks is right in his and God's eyes.'

Aethelred's face was beginning to darken, but I continued, 'My punishment is that he be banished to Lastingham, there to spend his days doing penance and fasting, working and praying for forgiveness from God.'

Aethelred started half out of his throne, his hands white with the force with which he gripped its arms. 'How dare you go against me?' he shouted. 'I demand revenge on this traitor, this thief. Am I to crush him with my own hands?'

I tried to make an answer but I was mouth-dried and could not speak.

The crowd, which moments before had formed a groundswell of chatter, exclamations and booing, fell quiet.

Into this void of silence came the shaky voice of Wynfrid, once Chad's forceful deacon but now a spent bishop. 'It is a great and unforgivable sin in God's law to take the life of a holy man.'

Aethelred looked taken aback by this and he paused, his nostrils flaring like those of a maddened bull.

By speaking so, Wynfrid had embarked on a perilous journey which could end in disaster for him, but he bravely pressed on. 'If you kill him, Christ will no longer protect you in battle. The spear of the lowliest churl will shatter your shield. The dagger of the lowliest Welshman will pierce your entrails and then your blackened soul will be sent straightway to eternal torment.'

Aethelred half closed his eyes and Wynfrid's voice became firm and authoritative. 'I demand, O King,' he said, 'that you put your seal on this punishment. Banish Owini.'

Aethelred had no choice but to agree: killing Owini would risk losing the protection of Christ. 'So be it!' he snarled. 'But, Wynfrid, you shall write to Lastingham. Tell them it is your fault that the High King was caused great offence. Tell them about Owini. Tell them that all his possessions are forfeit to the High King and apologise for sending them such a worthless mouth to feed. Make it clear how they are to punish Owini when he is there . . . if he gets there.'

Then, in a gesture so imperious that it made the crowd growl, Aethelred stabbed a finger at Owini then stabbed to the north. Owini bowed his head and started towards the cathedral, there to collect perhaps his staff and hooded cape.

The High Reeve, shaking his head, stopped him. He was being expelled here and now.

Two soldiers took Owini up the sloping ground behind the tent and marched him on. They were to take him as far as Elm Hurst, where the woods thickened. There they were to leave him.

Owini was being forced to make his way, alone, through a wolf-dark forest stretching northwards for a hundred miles or more.

Thus Owini faded from the minds of men.

Aethelred didn't watch him go but again sat with pursed lips. What wickedness was going through his mind? I wondered.

He half turned and said something to one of his companions and they both laughed.

He faced the crowd again and began speaking in a calm voice. 'Now, hear what is in your king's mind,' he said. 'God has entrusted me with great tasks. I am to chastise the unruly and unholy people of Kent and I leave shortly to do this. God also told me, unworthy as I am, that the people of East Anglia need guidance and spiritual help. When I prayed and asked him how this should be done he told me that the bones of holy Chad must be translated to Peterborough. He also said it must be done now – today!'

At these words, a pain worse than the bite of a horse-leech struck into my heart. I had planned that as soon as I was set free I would go to Chad's shrine and there I would let my hand sink into the bone dust of his body. If my soul were pure then God would work a miracle and I would be cured. Now this was taken from me!

I was not the only person at that assembly with tears on my face. Some were wailing and some fell to their knees and started praying. Others looked at Wynfrid to see what he would do about this calamity. Wynfrid, however, made no objection; he was already busy sending two monks scurrying off to make the preparations. People cursed the bishop under their breath, but I could not condemn him.

I was certain that the thing would be done with no delay, since he had already come close to personal disaster by crossing Aethelred and would not take any more risks.

Aethelred seemed unmoved by the upset his words had caused. He waited till the subdued Wynfrid had resumed his place before continuing, 'Lichfield has caused me distress so I am minded to leave it to its own fate. Some here nearly brought about disaffection among the people. I am also burdened with a weak bishop who lacks missionary zeal for the Church of Rome but he will stay for now till I talk with the Archbishop of Canterbury about a replacement.'

He paused, frowning. Then he levelled a finger at the crowd and in a tone of warning said, 'The new church is not yet consecrated so let no man dare to call it a cathedral, but I command that work on it shall continue. When it is completed it shall be known as the church of the Blessed Chad and Mary.'

He paused to seek me out, then, staring at me with hard eyes, continued, 'I have no money for this work, though. That went with the rogue whom you spared, so the people shall have to pay for it.'

A groan went up from the crowd. He heard it and, spreading his hands in a cynical gesture of sorrow, said, 'I would have wiped out the debt with Owini's death, but some here pleaded for his life. It is to them you must turn after I leave here today.'

Again his hard blue eyes stabbed at me.

'The church must manage on the offerings from whatever pilgrims come here. It shall also have the mill on Curborough Brook and the fish market at Fisher Wic. Of course, the people must pay for their use and upkeep.'

The crowd was becoming restless and as Aethelred loaded the burden of taxes so their voices became the louder.

The soldiers guarding him levelled their spears, and his hearth-companions laid their hands on their swords in an unmistakable gesture.

'Hear me,' he said. 'I don't like having to burden you so.

I'd much rather find whoever was responsible and punish him. As it is, you will all have to suffer on account of just one person.'

By now, some in the crowd were openly complaining.

Aethelred clearly thought the time was right, for he suddenly shouted, 'Listen, my good and loyal people. I have a question that must be answered.'

Having captured their attention he stood up and in the manner of an accuser pointed directly at me. 'You claim that your name is Edwin. Why then did you say you were called Adhelm when I came upon you hiding in the Cannock Forest?' he demanded, and then sat down again, looking triumphant.

My brain froze and I couldn't answer.

The crowd broke into frenzied shouting. Out of the shifting mass came ugly shouts of 'troublemaker!' and 'interferer!' but worst of all came the accusation, 'Northumbrian spy!'

'See!' hissed Aethelred, leaning forward. 'They were thirsting for Owini's blood. Now you will have to suffer in his place instead.'

He sat back in his throne and lifted a hand for silence.

'Well,' he said. 'What is your answer?'

Chapter 24

Cunning Aethelred! It was such a simple question but it marked me out. Of course, it meant nothing to the crowd, but it had an unsettling feel of duplicity about it. I was now someone who used two names, and was 'come across hiding' in that dark forest which many of them feared. It all sounded so sinister and it gave them a target for their hate and anger, bad feelings which he could shift from him onto me.

The High Reeve demanded silence and the shouting from the crowd subsided.

I had to be careful not to be pushed into a self-incriminating answer.

'I could not use my own name of Edwin till I was sure that I was cleansed of my spiritual guilt,' I said. 'Adhelm is my hermit name which I used in my hermit's cave at the edge of the forest. If I am restored to my church I shall, with your permission, O King, use my given name again.'

Elfrida and Bishop Wynfrid began nodding in understanding.

People in the crowd saw that and, turning to their neighbours, appeared to discuss my reply. Then, perhaps having had enough of being played or perhaps being ashamed of their earlier behaviour, they fell silent.

My answer had not served Aethelred's purpose. His face darkened and his pressed lips went as white as curd cheese. At another time his appearance might have made me laugh but not now.

'I try again,' he said, seemingly to himself. 'You are a true Angle from an honourable family are you not?' he said, in a louder voice.

'I am, O King.'

'Yes, I am sure you are,' he said. He looked at the faces about him, then turned to me and shouted, 'Yet you failed to take your revenge. Why is this?'

I saw that he was playing a game with me, leading me on until I revealed my quest for revenge.

I wanted to cry out that I had relinquished my blood feud, that Wulfstan's family had suffered enough.

My eyes sought Elfrida. Almost imperceptibly she shook her head. Praise God, no one had betrayed me.

'I do not understand the question, O King,' I said.

'You are not so clever, then,' he said, and his shoulders unhunched a little. In that unconscious action I began to see the way it was. He could not, dare not, be bested in argument. Did he want me to show humility?

'Alas, no,' I said, shaking my head, 'but I—'

'Why is it, I want to know,' he interrupted, 'why is it that a person as devout as you seeks to punish these good folk? Owini deserved much, much worse than he got, did he not?'

In my relief that he was not talking about my father I made a mistake. I could see no sense in this endless wrangling and I wanted an end to this ordeal which was wearing me away as water wears the stone. I had tried argument and it had failed. I had tried humility and it hadn't had much effect, so I tried another approach.

I decided to appeal to that inner part of him which earlier at the cave had shown a glimmering of conscience.

I smiled and said, 'Our Lord said, "Forgive thy enemies. If thy enemy smite thee, then turn the other cheek." '

At my words he sat up, eyes narrowed.

'There may seem to be conflict between that Christian precept and the ways of our people,' I continued, 'but I want us to forgive our enemies, as Jesus said we must.'

He sat tensed and silent, his left hand fidgeting with the eagle-crowned pommel of his sword.

'We can still be true warriors even if we do not for ever seek revenge from our enemies,' I said, smiling at him. 'What is more, as I myself have heard from your very own lips, the blood feud must be abolished.'

There was a gasp from the crowd and someone, a huge warrior wearing a war-battered scramasax, laughed in open disbelief. I turned to him and nodded that it was so.

A sudden movement caught my eye and I whirled round.

Aethelred, eyes bulging and face red with rage, had burst from his throne. He was bellowing, almost incoherent with wrath. He said I was a traitor and that I was trying to bring down the Mercian people.

The blood ran chill in my veins.

Moving swiftly and lightly he closed on me, shouting that I was an Angle spy for the King of Northumberland and must die. His hand flew to the sword and the snake-patterned blade leaped out of the scabbard and began its glittering upward journey.

The crowd gasped and as men recognised the sword, cries of 'Brain-biter!' went up, some in admiration, some in fear. A woman began to weep.

Brain-biter! I thought. Of course. The name I'd forgotten.

At the top of its swing the blood-edge hovered for a moment, bright in the sun, then swooped down.

How it came about I do not know but Finn's staff seemed to move of its own accord. Even as I grasped at it for support it sprang up and took the blood-hungry blade.

The sword's edge bit deep into the wood and the blow sent me to my knees. Britaelis was flung backwards into the crowd behind us.

Stunned, I was powerless to move.

Aethelred wrenched his sword free and hewed at me again, even more mightily than before.

Again the staff stood proud but this time Aethelred had got the measure of it, for the whistling edge cut it clean through.

I stared dazedly at the stump of my staff as the ever-eager Brain-biter began his final upward journey.

I would not beg nor plead but I closed my eyes so that Aethelred might read nothing in them that was not contempt.

The final blow did not come. Instead, soft cloth brushed my face and I smelled woman-scent.

Before me was the purple of Elfrida's robe. 'In the name of Woden I command you to halt this wickedness,' she cried.

The blade came slowly down.

She pulled me to my feet. I still clutched the stump of Finn's staff.

Aethelred's mood suddenly changed. 'You interfering old fool, how dare you do this?' he hissed at her and went back to the throne.

Elfrida, undaunted, advanced on him, dragging me with her. She released me and, going up to Aethelred, talked swiftly to him.

He sat in silence until his chest stopped heaving, then he spoke. 'It has been pointed out that Brother Edwin is a monk of the rightful Church and has in the past helped me when I most needed guidance,' he said tonelessly. Looking about him he continued with growing strength, 'The High Priestess Elfrida seeks my patronage for him and of course I hereby agree to consider this.'

Dazed as I was, I scented wickedness on the air as he made show of pondering the issue.

'Edwin, I agree to give you my patronage,' he said, 'but there are three conditions. The first is that all pagan Mercians and all Britons in this diocese shall be made to swear an oath of loyalty to the true Church of Rome.' The crowd gasped, but he smiled at them benignly, saying, 'It is said that Edwin sometimes appears not to be sure whether he favours Woden or Christ. This will help him to decide.'

To me he said, 'You shall have pastoral responsibility in this matter. They shall attend prayer and preaching in church and in open air. Those that do not shall be fined and half of the money shall be gifted to you and half to the church of the Blessed Chad and Mary. That shall be your living. You need not seek permission from Bishop Wynfrid – he won't object.'

'My second condition,' he continued, in a voice smooth with mockery, 'acknowledges that you condemn the use of slaves. How you intend that the fields shall be worked I know not. And how you intend that the good people of Lichfield won't become poverty-stricken for lack of labour, well, who can tell.'

He smiled at me as he continued. 'None the less, Edwin, you shall have your way. My second condition, then, is that you shall be responsible for buying the freedom of the slaves. Naturally you will decide who is to be freed and when, and you yourself shall see that the money is raised.'

The crowd stood with mouths agape in disbelief. My heart felt like a stone in my chest.

'My third condition is modest, but it pleases me. You shall set up and work in the new scriptorum. How say you to these conditions? Take your time.'

Here was cruelty incarnate. To fine the Britons for not

attending the Church of Rome would drive them into the debt beyond the grave, for they had no money at all. To force them to worship there would be a monstrous affront to their beliefs and to the oldest Christian Church in the land. Converting the pagan Mercians would be difficult but not impossible: all I had to do was to accept that the values of Elfrida and Leofgifu and Wihtred were in some way inferior to mine and those of the Church of Rome.

The outcome of the second condition would be exactly as Aethelred had intended. Making me responsible for freeing the slaves would at one move put the slaves and the Mercians against me, for even if I could find money to buy freedom who should I choose over anyone else? For among the slaves there were young and old, Britons, Angles, Frisians and even foreigners from across the seas. What's more, much of the land hereabout was so poor that many homesteads would not survive without the labour of slaves. I would be lucky not to get stabbed or poisoned before the year was up.

And as for me working in the scriptorum – Aethelred had observed that my writing hand was but a claw and it was unlikely that I could ever again hold a pen.

I looked with despair at his sly eyes and at his mocking mouth. Somehow he had uncovered my deepest secrets. Somehow he knew about the uncertainty of my beliefs and the confusion of my loyalties. Like a cunning angler he had embedded his hook in the soft part of my mouth: if I struggled the agony got worse; if I yielded he would draw me in. I was a fool ever to have imagined that I could outwit a son of Penda, that most cunning of kings.

Frustration and rage welled up in me, and tears sprang to my eyes. I wanted to shout, 'May the black hounds take you to hell,' but all I could do was to grind my teeth as Aethelred grinned and grinned.

Then, in that darkest of moments, I felt Chad standing there, just behind me and to my left. His presence, so strong, brought clarity to my mind and calm to my heart.

He himself had freed many slaves and now would free me – but from the chains of fear. He had led many people of different beliefs to the Church and, Elfrida having saved me, he would lead me back to the new Church.

While alive he had achieved much with only his persistence and determination, despite his infirmities. Now in death he would, through me with my modest affliction, achieve more.

In honour of Chad and the good that he stood for, I would strive to keep his name for ever in the hearts of men. His strength flowed into me and I knew what to do.

I sank to my knees and spread wide my arms. 'I thank you, O King, and I pray that the Lord rewards you in your battle for righteousness.'

He regarded me for a long moment, narrowing his eyes and nodding slowly as if he had just made a shrewd bargain. Perhaps he had, I thought – though not with me but with the devil.

My ready acceptance of his punitive conditions and his humiliation of me seemed victory enough and he turned his attention to the crowd.

He stood and said in a loud voice, 'Hear me. There is one more thing. The woman Elfrida must pay a price for her reckless deed.'

He suddenly reached out towards her and for one terrible moment I thought that he was going to strangle her. Instead, he seized hold of the boar pendant at her neck and gave it a pull that made her stagger. The chain broke and he held the sacred image aloft for all to see.

'Look, and mark!' he cried. 'Gaze upon this for the last time.' He shook his fist at the heavens, shouting, 'Frey, I renounce thee. Tiw, I renounce thee. Woden, I renounce thee,' and so saying, dashed the emblem of god to the ground.

There was screaming and angry shouts from the crowd. One woman fainted and a man with her shook his fist at Aethelred. A few soldiers raised their spears and had to be restrained from running at the people. Two thegns drew their scramasaxes and stood back to back as if afraid of sudden attack, but from man or gods I knew not.

Aethelred held up his arms and shouted for silence, then pointed at Elfrida. 'From now on, she shall be simply known as Elfrida, a woman of my late brother's household,' he declared.

In this way did Aethelred, King of Mercia, break the bond between himself and the religion of his forefathers.

Leofgifu's prophetic words at the cave came back to me: 'If they stop sacrificing to Hreda we shall live in a never-ending winter. If they scorn Herne then our forests will disappear. If they abandon Tiw our warriors will be crushed in battle. And when that happens Woden will let us be taken into slavery; all of us, for ever.'

Full of foreboding I began to look for Leofgifu, to give her comfort. After a moment I saw her: she was clinging to Elfrida, who was stroking her hair and whispering to her. Even in this darkest moment Elfrida looked strong and I wondered why she did not curse Aethelred then and there even though she would probably pay with her life. But there was something in the way she stood, in the way she held her head and the look in her eyes that made me understand:

Aethelred was going to pay a most terrible price for his deed this day, no matter what our fates would determine for the rest of us.

While the crowd stood looking on in stunned silence, he strode about giving orders. The High Reeve fetched men to carry the throne away. More people came and the king's helmet and shield were borne back into the tent. Grooms were sent to fetch the horses up. In all this activity Aethelred alone looked cheerful – his was the expression of a man who had resolved a great dilemma.

Britaelis was sitting near me on the ground so I went and sat with him. 'Here,' he quietly said. 'You might want to keep this.' It was all that remained of Finn's staff: the square section with the Ogham writing.

Looking at it brought back memories of the events of the past few weeks. Images of the prison pit, the battle, the wolf, the cave, Oak-man, Finn: all came crowding into my mind. Voices, laughter, screams . . . The stump possessed magical powers. It spoke to me of love and bravery and it reminded me that I had come through as many ordeals as any man could hope to survive.

My fate had brought me back to Lichfield at Beltane, not for vengeance but for reconciliation with Chad and Leofgifu. In my heart I felt stronger than ever before, even though my body was damaged and weak.

I saw Aethelred coming in our direction. Britaelis and I scrambled to our feet. He stopped a short distance away and addressed Britaelis.

'You, there. Britaelis is your name, is it not?'

'Yes, O King. Britaelis is my name, yes.'

'You're one of Owini's men, eh? And you've also been helping Edwin, have you not?'

'Yes, sir, I have, I have. I'm his attendant.'

'His attendant, eh? But, Britaelis, here's the question. Are you also loyal to your king?'

'First and foremost. Loyal and true,' he stammered.

'That's good, because you're mine now and you're coming to Kent with me. Adventure, eh? How say you? Don't worry about Edwin; my High Reeve will be keeping an eye on him while I'm away.'

'No need to ask, O King. I'm a warrior, and my place is beside you, just as it was beside Wulfhere.'

Brave Britaelis, he would not be browbeaten.

'Right, off you go,' said Aethelred. Britaelis embraced me and ran to join the men of the royal household.

Just for a moment Aethelred's eyes met mine. There was neither recognition nor spark of hatred. Instead, I thought I saw a flicker of unease, a premonition of what might lie ahead for him.

He turned away, put his hands on his hips and looked about him – at the bustle of activity, at the soldiers, at the frightened faces of the onlookers.

'It is good,' he said, to no one in particular. He called to the men, 'Look lively, my lads. I must be about God's business. And for those that join me I promise there'll be gold, slaves and even horses.'

The mood of the warriors changed and they formed up behind the soldiers of the royal household. For the first time in their lives they would be going into battle led by a king who had Christ and no other to protect him. They managed some nervous banter between themselves, albeit very different from their usual mead-soaked boasting the night before a raid.

They were beginning to look more cheerful and I supposed it was because they were thinking of the riches of Kent.

Aethelred and his companions strode to their horses. The companions mounted up and their attendants ran to stand with them. Aethelred swung himself up on to his black stallion which was now bedecked with silver trappings.

As he turned its head away he raised one arm in salute.